THE LAS

MW01484334

"Sara Blaydes's novel is a wonderfully satisfying mix of mystery, romance, and family drama, alternating between the present day and the Golden Age of Hollywood . . . This is a perfect read for film buffs who enjoy uncovering secrets."

—*Historical Novels Review*

The

RESTORATION
GARDEN

ALSO BY SARA BLAYDES

The Last Secret of Lily Adams

The

RESTORATION GARDEN

A NOVEL

SARA BLAYDES

LAKE UNION
PUBLISHING

Published by Lake Union Publishing, Seattle
www.apub.com

Amazon, the Amazon logo, and Lake Union Publishing are trademarks of Amazon. com, Inc., or its affiliates.

EU product safety contact:
Amazon Media EU S. à r.l.
38, avenue John F. Kennedy, L-1855 Luxembourg
amazonpublishing-gpsr@amazon.com

ISBN-13: 9781662533198 (paperback)
ISBN-13: 9781662533204 (digital)

Cover design by Mumtaz Mustafa
Cover images: © Viverra27 / Shutterstock; Les Archives Digitales / Alamy Stock Photo

Printed in the United States of America

The

RESTORATION GARDEN

Chapter One

JULIA

Present Day

We were three hours late by the time the taxi turned onto the gravel drive leading to Havenworth Manor. I had no excuse. My plane had landed on time, and the instructions my new employer provided for the rest of the journey were impeccable. But none of my careful preparation had accounted for Sam's meltdown the moment he realized we weren't going home.

He hadn't slept well on the flight over. My iPad and a carefully rationed supply of M&M's kept him calm enough for most of it, but eight hours across the Atlantic was too long to be confined to a cramped space. By the time we reached the baggage carousel, he refused to take another step.

I ignored the dirty looks from other travelers as I carried Sam and our suitcases to the taxi stand. I was used to the judgment of strangers, but I wished I knew how to spare Sam from it. He was too young to understand that all of this was for him. There was nothing left for us back in Chicago. We needed a fresh start, a chance for him to be a kid again away from the shadows of grief.

At least he was sleeping now. The rhythmic patter of rain against the windshield had lulled him to sleep, giving me a moment to take in the surroundings.

The gnarled branches of a wych elm scraped the top of the taxi like hungry fingers as we pulled through the front gate, no leaf buds or bright-purple flowers that should have been abundant on a healthy tree by now. I'd been anticipating disrepair—after all, that was the reason I was here—but not like this. The only sign of life was the sprawling English ivy creeping over the stone wall. The rest of the lawn was nothing more than barren patches of mud. Even the weeds had decided this was no place to set down their roots.

I wasn't sure this could be called a garden at all.

I pushed that thought aside. Everything could be fixed with a little hard work and determination. I'd staked my entire career on that belief. Historic-garden restoration was a rare specialization. Few professional landscape architects had the desire or patience for this kind of painstaking work, but for me there was nothing more rewarding than unearthing the richness of history lying dormant beneath the soil and breathing it back to life. When I saw the job advertisement looking for an expert gardener to restore the once-famed gardens of Havenworth Manor, I thought it was fate's way of giving me a lifeline after everything that had gone horribly wrong last year. A chance for Sam and me to start over.

In one of her rare moments of honesty, my sister, Rebecca, had told me her dream was to raise Sam in a big house with a huge yard, instead of jumping from one seedy motel to another. The kind of place where he could have a childhood full of nature and freedom. Havenworth wasn't ours, but maybe it could be our home for the next six months.

I winced at the memory of my sister, still unable to separate my anger from the overwhelming grief.

The house, at least, matched the romantic image I'd constructed in my mind: steeply pitched roof, wide staircase at the entry, and even a parapet. The warm stone facade fit perfectly into the lush fields and trees of the expansive countryside around it. The only part that wasn't beautiful was the garden itself.

"This is the place," the taxi driver said with a paternal wariness, as though carving out a chance for me to change my mind and admit this had been a terrible mistake.

"Thank you." I cast him a grateful smile. For better or worse, this was exactly where I needed to be.

The rearview mirror reflected the dismay in his eyes. "That'll be thirty-two quid."

I fumbled with the bills in my wallet, mentally calculating the meager balance of my bank account as I handed them over. But money wasn't the only worry sinking into my chest as the driver popped the trunk and unloaded our bags. Everything about this job had seemed too good to be true. What if that was because it was?

After Hartwell & Sons fired me, no one was willing to give me a contract. I had the skill but no portfolio of my own to prove I could handle the work without a big firm behind me. I had been almost ready to give up when I was offered the job at Havenworth. A successful restoration of a garden of this importance would prove I was still the best.

As long as I was successful.

I managed to extricate Sam still asleep, but his weight was too heavy for my tired arms. He startled awake as soon as I shifted him to my hip.

"We're here," I whispered as the taxi drove off behind us. "Our new adventure."

Rain landed in thick droplets that clung to his eyelashes as he stared at me in that unsettling way—hopeful yet wary, as though trying to see through the distortion of all the lies I'd told him until now. Before I could reassure him, he wrestled out from my arms and raced up the steps toward the entrance, oblivious to the fears that had rooted my feet to the ground.

"Hang on there." I gathered our bags and lumbered after him, mud splashing against my shoes. It felt silly to knock at a house this grand and imposing, but there was no doorbell in sight. I picked Sam up and let him bang on the iron knocker. Long seconds passed with no answer. "Maybe they stepped out for a minute."

We knocked again. This time I had no choice but to concede no one was here. I checked my phone once more. No missed calls or messages. Not even a response to the one I'd sent letting them know I'd be arriving late.

The rain was coming down harder now, and the stone entrance offered no shelter. I fixed an enthusiastic smile to my face to mask my growing panic. "Do you want to run through the hedge maze with me while we wait?"

The barren remains of what must have once been two rather majestic hedge mazes flanked the driveway. I chased Sam through the narrow rows of dying boxwoods, where the rain had turned the gravel paths into murky puddles beneath our feet, wishing I'd had the sense to wear practical shoes instead of dressing to impress my new employers.

Despite the dour weather, it felt good to be outside again. The sound of Sam's sweet giggles cut through the grayness, casting a light on what these gardens might have been. What they could be with a little care and attention.

This was a garden where children had once belonged. I could feel it in my soul.

Most people assumed my work was entirely scientific and rational. But gardens were more than proper drainage and balanced pH levels. Reviving a derelict garden required just as much magic as bringing any once-living thing back from the dead.

The faint sound of a car motor peeling up the drive pulled me from my roaming thoughts.

I let out a relieved sigh. Finally. Someone was here.

We followed the maze's twists and turns until we found the opening. Sam bolted ahead, too fast for me to keep up.

As I emerged from the maze, I saw a man step out of a dark-gray Audi. Sam didn't see him, though. "Sam! Slow down!"

My warning came too late. He collided with the man, letting out a terrible cry as he fell back onto the ground.

I ran to him, searching for signs of an injury. "Are you okay?"

"My arm hurts," he said through his tears.

"Let me see," the man said, crouching down next to Sam.

Without waiting for an answer, he took Sam's skinny arm in his hands, gently rotating it and pressing on his wrist. "Does it hurt when I do that?"

Sam shook his head.

"That's good. It means it's not broken. But you must be more careful and pay attention when you're running about."

"I'm so sorry about that," I said hurriedly.

"It's quite all right," the man responded, with a terseness I wasn't expecting after the warmth he'd shown toward Sam. He was slim and tall, with a sharply handsome face and perfectly tailored, expensive gray suit that looked out of place in the wildness of the gardens.

"Julia Esdaile," I said, trying to undo the terrible first impression we'd just made. "No one was here when we arrived, so we decided to explore the grounds while we waited."

"Andrew Morrison," he said, brow furrowing as he shook my hand. I couldn't tell whether there was a hint of contriteness in his annoyed expression. "I apologize for that. I was called into the emergency department at the last minute. I asked my sister, Helen, to stay and greet you, but it appears she had somewhere else to be."

Andrew Morrison, the man who had arranged for me to come here on behalf of his godmother. The woman who owned Havenworth. Andrew and I had spoken only once by phone, then done the rest of our correspondence by email. For some reason I hadn't anticipated him to be so young. His questions had been sharp and direct, but there had been a weariness in his voice. Seeing him now, I thought he couldn't have been much older than me—somewhere in his late thirties.

"We arrived a bit late," I said.

"We might as well get you out of this rain."

To my surprise, he collected my bags for me and carried them inside. I followed behind, clinging to Sam with a viselike hold so he wouldn't get into any more trouble.

"I've arranged a room for you on the east wing of the second floor," Andrew said as he approached the stairs. "I should warn you, Havenworth Manor is a four-hundred-year-old estate with invaluable history and crumbling walls. It's not a particularly child-friendly place. It's important that you watch Sam closely while you are here."

I held Sam tighter to me, embarrassment flushing my cheeks.

A heavy thump sounded on the stairs above. An elderly woman in a long brown dress and a mass of gray hair coiled in a bun descended the steps, one bony hand gripping the handrail and the other an intricately carved wooden cane. "Nonsense. Havenworth has survived rebellions, plagues, and more than its share of bombs during the Blitz. It can certainly handle a five-year-old child."

Andrew climbed the stairs to assist her, but she batted his arm away. She continued down the steps slowly, tipping forward precariously each time she set down her cane.

Finally, she reached the relative safety of the wide landing at the bottom of the stairs. Only then did she accept Andrew's arm, though her attention was squarely on me. "You must be the new landscape architect. I'm Margaret Clarke. It's lovely to meet you."

I shook her outstretched hand. Her grip was shockingly strong and sure, despite her tiny stature. "Lovely to meet you, too. I'm Julia and this is Sam."

She smiled down at him. "Welcome, Sam. We're delighted to have you at Havenworth. It's been far too long since there have been any children around here. It will be a nice change."

I exhaled in relief. "Thank you."

"Despite my godson's rudeness, we are quite grateful that you've come all this way to help us with the gardens. It's my understanding that you are exceptionally talented at restoring historic gardens, which is something we desperately need."

"I'm honored to be here, and I promise you that there is no one else who can do what I do."

"It will be an immense relief to finally have the gardens attended to by an expert."

Sam buried his face against my thigh. "I'm tired."

"Of course you are," Margaret said kindly. "Andrew, please show Sam and Julia to their room. You can meet us for dinner at six o'clock in the dining room after you've had a chance to freshen up."

"Thank you. That would be lovely."

We followed Andrew up the wide stairs to a long hallway lined with bookshelves. "I assume you will only need the one room," he said as he opened the door to reveal a bedroom that was simply furnished with a large bed and a white vanity next to the window.

"This is more than enough. And I really am sorry about your suit."

I couldn't tell from his curt nod whether all was forgiven or I was simply being dismissed. I expected him to leave us, but he hesitated at the door. "This project is deeply important to Margaret, and because of that, it's deeply important to me. It's vital it be completed with the utmost discretion and care."

There was a strange hint of vulnerability in his tone that stripped away my instinct to react defensively. "I wouldn't have it any other way."

"Good. If there's anything else you need, please let me know."

"We'll be fine."

"Then we will see you at six o'clock. The dining room is on the main floor just to the left of the entrance."

I shut the door and closed my eyes, letting out a shaky breath as the exhaustion from the long day finally caught up with me. This job was going to be so much harder than I'd thought.

A small tug at my pant leg shook me from my thoughts. I looked at Sam with his big round eyes and downy blond hair, still awed by how much I could love someone I had only known for such a short time.

I forced a small smile, knowing he was worried about me. "I'm okay. Just tired. What do you think about this place? Did we make a good choice coming here?"

He nodded eagerly. Whether it was to please me or because he genuinely meant it, I didn't know. But it would be okay. It had to be okay. I was going to fix this garden. And then, somehow, I would find a way to fix my life, too.

Chapter Two

Julia

Present Day

I woke with a throbbing headache and Sam's hand pressed against my cheek, his face just inches from mine. It used to unsettle me when he did this—sneaking into my bed at night to watch me sleep. Sometimes he would poke at my eyelids or tug strands of my hair. But I understood why he did it. It was because I looked so much like my sister.

Sam looked like her, too.

It made it so much harder to hold on to all my anger when I saw her in Sam's round cheeks and ocean-blue eyes.

I blinked a few times to adjust to the light streaming through the gap in the velvet curtains. The clock on the nightstand said seven o'clock. I confirmed on my phone that it was indeed a.m. We hadn't just slept through dinner. We'd slept right through to the morning.

There was a notification for two missed texts on my phone. Both from my former boss.

Please call me.
It's about the money.

I deleted the messages, vowing to block Ryan Hartwell's number as soon as I could figure out how. I had already paid back every cent my sister had stolen from Hartwell & Sons after I'd foolishly brought her on as my assistant when she was trying to get back on her feet. But that hadn't been enough. Rebecca's mistakes had cost me my career and reputation, too.

"I'm hungry," Sam muttered, distracting me from the raw ache in my chest.

"Me, too, buddy. Let's get you dressed and brush your teeth; then we can find something to eat."

Whatever inhibitions I had about sneaking around Havenworth were obliterated thanks to Sam. He ran ahead of me in the dark, narrow hall, opening three doors in a row before he found a bathroom. I sat on the narrow edge of the tub and scrubbed the brush up and down Sam's teeth, letting the foamy bubbles spill down his chin in a familiar routine we'd developed over the last few months. The space was tiny compared to the rest of the house, as if it had been tacked on as an afterthought. There was no shower, only an ancient claw-foot bathtub tucked into one corner. Sage-colored penny tiles lined the wall around it, and the sloped roof angled sharply above the tub, leaving just enough room for an adult to sit upright on one side. Nothing in the room, from the exposed pipes to the pedestal sink, appeared to have been updated in the last hundred years.

I couldn't help but wonder what kind of secrets were buried in the history of this place.

Sam spit a trail of minty foam into the sink. I turned on the tap to rinse it away. "Let's get you some breakfast."

After a few minutes of wandering, we found the kitchen deep in Havenworth's basement. The walls were painted a dull salmon color, making the shiny new appliances stand out even more. I hesitated when I saw Andrew at the stove, dressed down in a gray sweater and jeans that I instantly recognized as designer hiding behind a veneer of casualness.

I hadn't made the best impression yesterday. I hoped today would be a chance to start over.

"I'm hungry," Sam repeated, tugging me forward and alerting Andrew to our presence.

"You're awake," Andrew said with a practiced politeness that held no warmth. His shoulders stiffened before he turned around.

"Jet lag got the better of us," I said, hoping I didn't sound quite as defensive as I felt. Sam let go of my hand and wandered toward the wooden table at the far end of the room.

Andrew cleared his throat, the awkwardness thickening the air between us. "Look, I'd like to apologize for yesterday."

I blinked in confusion, uncertain I'd heard him right. "Oh, um. That's okay."

"No, it's not," he said. "I was called into the emergency department at the last minute yesterday, and it was a particularly stressful afternoon. My sister, Helen, was supposed to be here to greet you. Once I realized she had failed to show up, it was a bit of a scramble to get back here."

Judging by the strain in his voice, "stressful" might have been an understatement. "That sounds like a lot to handle."

He raked his hand through his hair. "It is. But as Margaret rather forcefully reminded me, it isn't an excuse for rudeness."

Apologizing wasn't something that came easy to me anymore. I'd been burned too many times by exposing myself to that kind of vulnerability. Perhaps that was why Andrew's straightforward apology caught me so off guard. "I know this job is important to you. It's important to me, too."

The kettle on the stove whistled, breaking the awkward silence between us.

Andrew shut off the burner. "Would you like some tea?"

Caffeine. The yearning overtook me as forcefully as a tidal wave. "I'm not much of a tea drinker, but I would love some coffee."

He retrieved a small tin from the cupboard. "Is instant all right?"

I fought the urge to wince. "Sure."

11

"I'm afraid we weren't prepared with any children's cereal," he said as he pulled the lid off the tin and dumped a heaping spoonful into a mug. "We do have milk, and I'm sure I could whip up some porridge for Sam."

"That's okay. Sam likes to eat toast in the mornings. Peanut butter would be a bonus."

"Why don't you have a seat and I'll see what I can do."

"Thank you."

Despite my insistence we didn't need anything fancy, Andrew proceeded to chop up some strawberries and add them to the plates he'd set out for us.

"We don't have peanut butter, but we do have raspberry jam. Would that be acceptable? I promise you it's quite delicious."

I looked at Sam, wondering whether his hunger was enough to overcome his aversion to new foods. He stared back at Andrew with outright suspicion.

"How about you give it a try, and if you dislike it, you have permission to spit it back onto the plate, and I promise no one will yell at you."

I wrapped my hands around the steaming mug and held my breath as Sam gingerly inspected the toast and took the tiniest nibble. Back home, I could get him to eat only plain white bread. The stuff Andrew served us was full of whole grains and seeds. Sam scrunched his eyebrows, considering the new flavors and textures. He took another bite.

Andrew pulled out the chair next to Sam and sat down, resting his forearms against his thighs. "Do you like it?"

Ever so slowly, Sam nodded.

"I knew it," Andrew said triumphantly. "I'll have the boy eating beans on toast next."

I sipped my coffee and forced a smile despite the bitter burn on my tongue. It should have made me happy to see even a hint of progress in Sam's eating habits, no matter who got the credit for it. "I was hoping to speak with Lady Margaret about her vision for the garden today," I said.

Andrew shook his head, and something that almost resembled a smile flashed upon his lips.

I frowned in confusion. "What?"

"Don't let her hear you call her 'Lady.' She abhors those kinds of traditions. You're better off referring to her simply as Margaret. Or even Maggie."

It was clear this man held great affection for his godmother, and despite our first encounter, he seemed to like Sam, too.

"Either way, it's important to know what she's envisioning for the gardens and what she's hoping to achieve. The sooner I know that, the sooner I can get started on the design plans."

"The vital thing is for the job to be done perfectly. We're hoping to open the gardens to the public next year to generate some additional revenue for the estate."

"Few things can be called perfect when it comes to a garden," I said. "It's a living thing that grows and changes with the seasons."

"Be that as it may, Margaret is absolutely insistent it be done exactly as it was in the summer of 1940."

It was the same request he'd explained over the phone when we'd discussed the job a few months ago, and still just as odd. Most clients had only vague ideas of what they wanted in a restoration that amounted to a nostalgia-driven return of its former grandeur. I usually discovered most of them valued their own ideas and preferences over the prestige of history. Which was why it was so unusual that Margaret had pinpointed such a specific slice of time she wanted restored. "Why 1940?"

"I'm not entirely sure. Margaret's always been a bit enigmatic, even to those who know her best."

"Was she even alive back then?"

"She was just a little girl when the war broke out, not much older than Sam. She doesn't like to talk about that period in her life, but I expect she remembers it vividly. She's always had a rather exceptional memory." He smiled to himself, as though disappearing briefly into some distant thought. "Despite her wealth, her life hasn't been easy. She

13

developed pneumonia when she was seven years old. It nearly killed her and severely weakened her heart. She spent much of her teenage years in and out of hospitals."

"Wow. I wouldn't have expected that."

"Defying expectations is something Margaret has always excelled at. Did you know she was one of the first women in the country to lecture in physics at Cambridge?"

I shook my head. The more I learned about Margaret Clarke, the more fascinating I found her. From my initial exchanges with Andrew, I knew that Havenworth was her family home, where she'd lived almost the entirety of her life. She was the driving force behind the garden restoration, but she was also the one who had allowed it to degenerate to this level.

"So why now? If she was such a rebel in her time, why does she suddenly care what others think about the gardens?"

From the way his expression darkened, I suspected this was a question he had asked her many times himself. "I don't really know. She's never given me a reason, but something changed last year, after her health took a turn for the worse. She's been on a mission since then to take care of all her loose ends. Whatever the reason is, it's clearly important to her."

"Would it be all right if I asked her about it?"

"You can try, but I can't promise she'll be any more forthcoming with you."

He was probably right, but it was worth a shot. "I'll also need access to any photographs and historic records of the gardens. Information about when they were first constructed and, most importantly, what Margaret's vision is for the restoration."

"Margaret doesn't usually wake until nine or ten o'clock most days, and it will be too much for her to show you around the grounds. But I have a few hours before I need to be at the hospital."

It took me an awkward second to realize he was offering himself as a guide. "That would be great."

He smiled tightly, as uncertain of our newfound détente as I was. "Very well. I'll meet you at the front doors in fifteen minutes."

After we finished breakfast, Sam and I met Andrew on the front steps. The stress of the last twenty-four hours had taken its toll, and I was eager to get outside and focus on the reason I was here.

We started with the front gardens. The space was large—nearly a full acre—but not huge in comparison with many of the more prominent English estates I'd studied.

The sodden ground squelched beneath my boots, filling the air with a strangely dank and musty odor. The previous day's rain had finally abated, leaving behind an overcast sky that still offered no hint of sun. I scanned the ground for any sign of shoots or stems. It was early spring. By now, the first hints of perennials ought to have broken through the earth, and the bulbs should have been on full display. "Do you know anything about what the gardens used to look like?"

"Margaret once mentioned the front gardens were for the adults. She preferred to play in the back, where things were wilder," he said. "Beyond that, I don't know."

I tried to visualize the space as it should have been—lush and green and inviting. But I couldn't shake the undercurrent of emptiness and decay from clouding my brain. The symmetrical hedge mazes signaled a more formal front garden, but I suspected the estate's borders had once been filled with vibrant shrubs and perennials.

We followed the dirt path along the side of the house to the back gardens. Before we rounded the corner, Andrew hesitated. "The back gardens are in worse shape than the front."

Despite his caution, I still gasped when I saw the grounds. Whereas the front gardens were barren and empty, the back was wild and abandoned. The architectural bones of what must have once been a magnificent garden were still visible beneath the mess of bramble and weeds. Just beyond an arched opening was a huge parterre encased in stone, the space filled with elegant pathways winding through the gardens. Instead of perfect symmetry, the west side was terribly damaged, with only the faintest traces remaining of what had once been there. Broken and missing pavers. A rusted iron arch. Even the ground that should have been perfectly flat was now filled with mounds of dirt. In the distance, I could see a collapsed greenhouse almost entirely overtaken by ivy and moss.

A space as magnificent as this should have been a gardener's dream, but instead it reminded me of a picked-over carcass. Everything was in much worse shape than Andrew had alluded to over the phone.

I had known this would be a difficult job, but this was so much worse than I'd expected. The cleanup alone would cost thousands of dollars and require a crew if there was any hope of getting any planting started this summer.

Andrew crossed his arms, staring out at the wilderness. Despite wearing an ancient pair of black Wellingtons, he somehow managed to look strangely regal. "It's quite a mess, isn't it?"

"Messes don't scare me."

He raised an eyebrow. "Isn't this the part where you're supposed to tell me you've seen worse?"

I laughed. "You don't strike me as the type of person who wants to be lied to."

"No, I suppose I'm not," he conceded with a wry smile.

Sam, bored by our conversation, wriggled his hand free from mine and ran ahead down the narrowed path toward the back of the estate.

I jogged after him, awkwardly navigating the overgrown path as I called for him to slow down. Luckily, the stone wall extended through this section of the garden, blocking Sam from traveling too far.

"That's odd," I muttered.

"What's odd?" Andrew asked, catching up to us a few seconds later.

"This section of the wall is new," I said. "Or at least newer than the rest of it."

Andrew came up behind me. "Why do you say that?"

"Look at the brick. It's larger than the other sections, and there's significantly less moss growing here compared with the rest. And the path we were on looks like it used to go straight through, like there was an opening here at one time." I ran my fingers along the rough edges. The newer section stretched out only a few feet in either direction, as if there had once been a door or opening of sorts that was now bricked over.

Andrew frowned. "I hadn't noticed."

"Most people wouldn't. It's my job to pick up on even the smallest details. At some point in the last half century, this section of the wall was repaired. So why not clean up the rest of the gardens?"

Andrew shrugged, clearly not finding this discovery as curious as I did.

"What's on the other side?" I asked.

"Woodlands. Margaret's family owned all the farmland surrounding the estate, but that was sold shortly after the war. They kept the forested area, however. Probably because there was no financial value in selling it."

"Do you think she's awake now? I'd really like to ask her some questions."

Andrew frowned and checked his watch. "Yes, it's about time I prepare her breakfast."

We found Margaret in the orangery later that morning. She was sitting in a rocking chair, looking out the floor-to-ceiling windows when we entered, oblivious to our presence. I tracked her gaze to see what had captured her so deeply. The gardens were no more beautiful from this vantage point.

Andrew cleared his throat. "Margaret, are you up for some company?"

She turned, a smile illuminating her face. "Of course. Please, sit down." She motioned to the love seat across from her. Sam squished up close to me, as he always did. I handed him his favorite dinosaur-themed sticker book, which I'd stashed in my bag to keep him occupied. He eagerly flipped open to the late-Cretaceous page, where he'd been setting up a battle between the velociraptors and a triceratops.

"I'm afraid I need to get to work soon," Andrew said, setting a cup of tea on the glass side table next to her. "Will you be all right?"

"Of course I will," she responded with a huff. "You needn't worry so much about me."

It was obvious from his pained expression that worrying was the only thing he would be doing. He kissed her sweetly on the cheek and said, "Call me if you need anything."

He looked at me with an unspoken plea. *Take care of her.*

I nodded, softening toward the man a little more.

With shaky hands, Margaret picked up her teacup and looked at Sam and me. "Did you enjoy your walk this morning?"

"Yes, thank you. Sam loved running through all that open space."

"I did, too, when I was his age. I used to get into so much trouble with Andrew and Helen's grandfather climbing trees and hiding in places where no one could find us."

Although she was well into her nineties, it was easy to picture Margaret as a young girl. There was still a mischievous, girlish spark in her eyes.

"Would this be a good time to ask you some questions about your expectations for the restoration?"

"What is it you'd like to know?"

"Well . . ." I smiled down at Sam, who was whispering sound effects for each of the ferocious creatures, before turning back to Margaret. "I need to know what your vision for the gardens is. What do you want it to become?"

"That's a simple enough answer. I want them to look exactly like they did when I was a child."

It was the same inscrutable answer Andrew had given me earlier. "What do you remember of the gardens? The kinds of flowers or plants—"

She waved her hand dismissively. "I was never good with that kind of thing. Not like . . . well, I'm sure you can figure it out. You're the professional."

"I find it best to work off historical sources and records. Do you have photos or designs or anything you can give me so I can re-create it as accurately as possible?"

"I'm not sure we have anything like that. So many things were lost over the years. But you are welcome to look. You can ask Andrew or Helen to help you search the house."

I fixed my smile in place, holding back any hint of the exasperation I felt. Most of the projects I worked on began with extensive records and documentation. In fact, it was usually the discovery of such records that prompted the desire for restoration in the first place—whether it was uncovering evidence that a renowned designer had originally created the gardens or simply a sense of nostalgia. "The garden is in a much worse state than I anticipated. There's very little left of what once was here. Without historical records, the best we can hope for is a re-creation, not a restoration."

Her thin eyebrows furrowed. "What is the difference?"

"Well, a restoration is a precise replica of an original garden. With a re-creation, we would take inspiration and cues from the era and style in which the gardens were designed to capture the feel of the original, but it wouldn't be a true restoration."

She shook her head so vehemently, wisps of gray hair slipped out from her bun. "No. It must be the exact garden that it was when I was a child. That's why we hired you."

Once again, I questioned how I was supposed to succeed if I didn't know what they expected of me. I wasn't going to get anywhere asking the same questions over and over. I needed to change my approach. I leaned forward, resting my arms on my thighs. "Margaret, what happened? It's obvious the gardens were once magnificent. How did they get so . . ."

"So decrepit?"

I nodded, relieved that she appeared more amused than offended by the question. "Exactly."

"The war."

I frowned. "What do you mean?"

"I was just a young girl then, but I remember so clearly how everything changed after that. My mother never cared much for the gardens and found them to be a terrible burden to maintain, especially during the war. She inherited Havenworth rather unexpectedly when her older brother passed away in 1926. She was much more interested in learning physics and maths than the finer points of running an estate, though she did her best."

"She was a scientist as well?"

"She wanted to be. She was a bit of an eccentric for her time. One of the first women to study physics at Cambridge, but she wasn't allowed to matriculate. It wasn't easy for women to find their way into academia back then."

I clasped my hands together on my thighs, fascinated by the glimpse into her history. "I can't imagine it was for you either."

She let out a small laugh as she shook her head. "No, it wasn't. But my parents never discouraged me from whatever I set my sights on either. My father was a professor of physics at Cambridge, you see. My mother worked with him in his lab for a time, but there was no room for her in the top-secret work my father did for the government during the war. So she did what most upper-class women did at that time and threw herself into the war effort. Havenworth became a hub of activity. We took on evacuees, and Mother even allowed the Women's Land Army to come and plant a victory garden. But then . . ." She pressed her lips together, inhaling a shaky breath.

"Margaret," I said gently. "What is it?"

She didn't respond. Instead, her gaze drifted to a stretch of land outside the window once more, her mind lost in thought.

"The Luftwaffe came," she finally answered. "London was hit hardest, but few places in the country were spared completely. The bombs fell in Cambridge in the autumn of 1940. Mother and I evacuated to a smaller country home in Gloucestershire for the remainder of the war. We left just days before Havenworth was hit."

I gasped. "That must have been terrifying."

"We were fortunate no one was hurt. It missed the house and landed at the edge of the back of the estate. We used to play there all the time." She gestured toward the area in the distance where she'd been staring earlier. "But much of the gardens were destroyed."

Sam, who had been slowly creeping away from my side as Margaret and I spoke, picked up something from the glass coffee table. Before I could see what it was, he threw it against the table. "Sam!"

The object—a small red rubber ball, thankfully—bounced up so high it nearly hit the ceiling. With shockingly quick reflexes, Margaret reached out and snatched the ball before it could crash against the table once more.

"I'm so sorry," I said with absolute mortification.

Margaret laughed. "It's a ball. What else is the boy supposed to do with it?"

She motioned at Sam to come closer. He looked to me for permission. I nodded, and he crept to her side, settling next to her chair on his knees.

"Do you know what this is?"

He shook his head.

"It's a game called jacks. I used to play it all the time when I was your age. Do you want to learn?" She spread out a handful of small silver jacks, then picked up the ball and let it drop against the table just as Sam had done seconds before. Before the ball landed, she swept her hand across the table, picking up one of the jacks. "I was the best jacks player in the entire county when I was young."

She handed the ball to Sam. "Now it's your turn to grab two."

He repeated her movements, bouncing the ball and picking up the jacks.

"How many did you get?"

Sam opened his hand to show her the two silver stars in his palm.

Margaret let out a boisterous holler I wouldn't have anticipated a woman as slight as her was capable of.

They spent the next few minutes playing, all but oblivious to my presence. Margaret seemed genuinely enamored with Sam's interest in the game.

"My goodness, you've won," Margaret said with delight, though I had no doubt she'd let him do so.

He beamed at her in response.

"Would you like to play again sometime?"

Sam looked at me once more for permission.

"Of course you can."

"Yes, please," he said eagerly to Margaret.

"Nothing would make me happier," Margaret responded, leaning back in her chair. Her energy was flagging. We'd taken up too much of her time already, but I still didn't have the answers I needed to move forward with any of the work she was asking of me.

"Margaret, if you don't mind, I just have one more question. Why now? After all the years, why do you want the gardens to be restored?"

She turned away from me once more, but not before I caught the sheen of tears in her eyes. "Because I made a promise to someone I loved a long time ago. Someone who hurt me very badly, so I let anger get in the way of that promise. But I don't have much time left in this world, and I don't want to spend it with regret. Restoring this garden is the only way I know to find forgiveness."

Chapter Three

Irene

May 21, 1940

I had just settled into my favorite spot beneath the Japanese camellia with my sketchbook when I caught our gardener unwittingly setting a curse on Havenworth Manor. The morning had been anything but peaceful, with a new group of Land Army girls bustling into the spare rooms of the house. Their excited chatter about the curving staircase and the portraits of long-dead relatives was wearing thin, and the prospect of sharing a bedroom with my half sister again was enough to push me to the edge. I was desperate for a bit of peace and quiet, but instead, I found myself rising to my feet and making my way toward Paul, our septuagenarian gardener, who was digging among the petunias in the annuals garden. "You can't plant petunias here," I said. "This is where the Queen Anne's lace always sprouts."

Paul adjusted the set of his cap and peered at me over the offensive purple bloom in his hands. His gruff demeanor and the gray scruff on his face did little to hide his short tolerance for my superstitions. "My shovel here says I can."

"Don't you understand what will happen if you do?"

"I understand that Lady Montgomery asked me to plant these petunias next to the front gate, and I don't want to lose my job."

"We both know Lady Montgomery has no business having any opinions on this garden." Despite his better intentions, Paul's lips twitched into a smile. He knew as well as I did my stepmother's taste left much to be desired. "All plants have meaning. And if you plant one that means anger and bitterness next to the one that represents our safe haven, it's as good as setting a curse on Havenworth Manor."

Paul raised an eyebrow. "Next you'll be telling me I can't have the lavender with the roses in the cutting garden."

A pairing that implied distrust of love. I couldn't say I entirely disagreed with that meaning. "They're both perennials. No planting required."

He placed his hands on the handle of his shovel and rested his chin on top. "So you do listen to my lectures."

"Every last word," I admitted. "But you never seem to return the favor. How many times have I explained that the meaning of flowers is just as important as their care? You can't ignore it."

"There's a war on, in case you've forgotten. We're lucky to have flowers at all. Now go back to whatever trouble it is you were getting up to."

I sighed. "How can I get myself into trouble when nothing interesting ever happens here?"

Paul nodded toward the wych elm, where Margaret was hanging upside down from a low-hanging branch, encouraging Charlie to do the same. The boy, still fearful of heights, remained rooted on the ground, wisely avoiding her taunts.

"Margaret Evelyn Clarke!" I shouted. "Get down from there before you break your neck."

She ignored me, her skirt tangled around her face as she swung like a pendulum. Horrified as much by the display of impropriety as the possibility she would get hurt, I ran to grab her, but she jumped down before I reached the tree, giving me a frightful start.

Bits of leaves were caught in her unruly curls, and her dress was streaked with mud. She had always been wild, but since Lady Montgomery had taken it upon herself to provide her education, she had become outright feral.

"I thought you'd fallen," I scolded.

Margaret rolled her eyes. "I know what I'm doing. It's perfectly safe up there." My half sister was only seven years old but had enough attitude for a century's worth of delinquency.

"You need to be more careful. And you," I said, turning to Charlie, "need to ignore her when she's up to no good."

Charlie cast a hesitant glance at Margaret, unsure. He was only one year younger than her, but the pair couldn't have been more different. He was thin and nervous, and still barely spoke to me, even after living here for almost nine months. Margaret had been wary of all the evacuated children when they first arrived last fall, treating them like servants she could boss about. But when they all returned to their families, leaving only Charlie behind, Margaret had taken him under her wing, teaching him all sorts of ways to get in trouble.

Charlie didn't respond to my instruction, but I sensed he was considering my words.

"Have you both finished your maths lessons?"

They nodded with so much enthusiasm I doubted they were being truthful, but I didn't have the energy to argue further.

"Then go on. And stay out of trouble."

They ran off toward the back garden, clearly intending to disobey me. But at least I finally had some peace. I settled down on my blanket once more and opened my sketchbook. I was determined to document every specimen within the extensive collections here.

Most of the camellias had long since finished their blooming seasons, but there were still a few lush flowers scattered across the ground, their petals browned and wilted. But one bloom had landed perfectly intact, still fresh from its descent. I picked it up and inhaled its scent before placing it next to me on the blanket.

Back in the early days, when Lady Montgomery had made an effort to speak with me, she'd told me that her great-grandfather, the baron of Havenworth, had traveled throughout Asia to amass the rare collection of camellias to impress her great-grandmother. From the way she told it, the gesture was more a display of ostentatiousness than grand romance, but that was because Lady Montgomery—despite her aristocratic upbringing—had no appreciation for courtship. Her wedding to my father had been a rushed affair in front of a magistrate with no guests other than her cousin Gwen to bear witness. I'd wanted desperately to be the flower girl waltzing down the aisle of a majestic church in a beautiful lace gown. Instead, I was forced to stand off to the side like a fly hovering where I didn't belong, not realizing it was a portent of how my existence would be tolerated for the next eight years.

With a sigh, I pushed that memory out of my mind and selected the blush-colored pencil from my tin, wishing I had more colors to choose from. The camellia's pale pink petals were almost obscene in their abundance as they fanned out in perfect geometry, making them a lofty challenge to capture. I greatly preferred my Faber-Castell coloring pencils, but Father had tossed them away the day after Britain declared war, saying it was unpatriotic to use anything produced by the enemy, no matter how superior it might be. My reminder that, as an American, Germany was not *my* enemy earned me a slap on the cheek. It was the first and only time he had ever laid a hand on me. The next morning I found a box of decidedly English coloring pencils on my vanity. I wasn't sure whether it was meant as an apology or a lesson in the superiority of British manufacturing, but it didn't matter. I would use whatever tools I could get.

The hours passed in a blur as I filled in the colors and shadows, until finally I had a near-perfect replica. With deep satisfaction, I wrote the words *Camellia japonica* below. *Blooms February through May.* All the scientific details I'd read in the botanical encyclopedias I'd found in Havenworth's library. At the bottom of the page, I added in practiced cursive the most important part of all: *Longing and desire.*

Of all the flowers, none better represented me than the beautiful camellia with its bittersweet meaning. Longing for something more, something better, was the only constant in my life. I wanted excitement and adventure, not the quiet, simple life that Havenworth offered. I wanted to travel the world and visit museums and galleries and gardens. I wanted to be the one making the choices about my future.

It was my mother who taught me the language of flowers. Back in Boston, she had worked as a florist, crafting arrangements for all the significant moments in people's lives. I had spent countless hours watching her at work—pink tulips for well-wishes, marigolds and geraniums to express sorrow, orange blossoms and roses for love. Each bouquet carried a special meaning for the recipient. Perhaps she hadn't possessed any true magic, but I liked to imagine she had.

Margaret's voice calling my name pulled me from my sketchbook. With a heavy sigh, I put down my pencil and rose to my feet. I didn't like being disturbed once I had fallen into the rhythm of sketching, but there was something endearing about how determined she was to draw my attention.

I followed the sound of her eager voice to the wisteria-covered back entrance of the house.

I set my hands on my hips. "What is it?"

Margaret waved a large letter in front of her face. "Post came for you. It's from America."

My heart jolted against my ribs. "Give that to me."

I reached for the envelope, but she held it just out of reach. "It says it's from Goldens." She drew out the last syllable in a taunting singsong.

"Goldings," I corrected, my heart beating like a sped-up clock. Goldings Institute of Fine Arts. The school I had dreamed of attending for as long as I could remember. "Hand it over."

Instead of complying, she held the letter tightly against her chest. "Why did they send you a letter? You're not going to leave Havenworth, are you?"

A pang of guilt shot through my chest. Havenworth wasn't my home, but Margaret was too young to understand that. It belonged to her family, not mine, and my presence had been a thorn in everyone's side from the moment I had arrived here eight years ago. I placed my hands on her shoulders and leaned down to meet her gaze. "Of course I need to leave. I'm eighteen years old."

"But this is our home. Who will take care of me if you go?"

I pulled her into an embrace so she wouldn't see the pained expression that came over me. Margaret almost never let her illness affect her, but these rare moments of fear reminded me of how young she still was. "You are going to be just fine without me. One day you will understand. I promise."

"I won't understand!" She leveled a fierce glare at me. "And I'll never forgive you if you leave."

"Margaret, please—"

"No!" She took off at a run down the gravel path, the letter containing my only hope of escape still clutched in her grimy hands.

I chased after her through the laburnum tunnel with its chain of delicate golden flowers cascading around me. When I emerged on the other side, Margaret was nowhere to be found. But there was only one place she would be.

The one place where she was not allowed to go.

Tucked behind the sprawling branches of an overgrown yew at the wild edge of the estate was a decrepit garden folly that had probably once resembled a miniature version of Havenworth but now sat abandoned and forgotten. No one in Lady Montgomery's family remembered why it had been constructed, so I could only presume the structure was beyond ancient, like everything else in this country. And terribly unsafe.

The structure itself was only half erect, thanks to a lightning-scorched tree trunk that had crashed into the back half, leaving a pile of crumbling bricks to be claimed by the forest floor.

"I know you're in there," I called from the darkened, moss-coated entrance, which rose only as high as my waist. Tiny yellow cowslips sprouted up in front—a terrible sign given their deathly meaning. "Give me back my letter!"

Her response was a loud shushing, as if that could somehow hide their presence. Of course Charlie was with her.

I took another step through the heavy brush that surrounded the decrepit structure. Something sharp jabbed into my shin, piercing my skin. When I looked down, a trickle of blood trailed down my leg. I pulled back the brush to reveal a small branch whittled at the end to a point that had been stuck in the ground right at the entrance. Not just one, I realized as I scanned the area, but almost half a dozen of these makeshift weapons had been hidden among the foliage. "What on earth?"

A collection of fist-size rocks had been piled just inside the entrance, as though waiting to be tossed at any intruders. Something had been scratched into the top of the entrance. Carefully, I leaned forward to inspect the words: KEEP OUT.

My hand flew to my mouth. "Oh, Margaret. What have you been doing here?"

It wasn't a question I expected her to answer, but the silence that followed made me all but forget the reason I'd followed her here in the first place.

"Please come out so we can talk. I don't want to have to come in there after you."

"You couldn't fit if you tried," she shouted back, abandoning all pretense of hiding.

Gingerly, I crouched down into the dark space, which was too narrow for anyone but a seven-year-old child, and took one tiny step inside. My throat seized. I hated small, dark spaces. Father called it an irrational fear, but what was so irrational about it? At any moment the rest of these bricks could come crashing down, trapping me inside—just like I imagined my mother, clawing and fighting to escape after her casket was lowered into the earth. She couldn't possibly be dead, not when she had promised she would never leave me. She must have battled against the heavy wood and suffocating layers of dirt, desperate to find her way back to me.

"Margaret, come out right now." I tried to sound firm, but I managed only a wheeze. "Please."

"Fine. We're coming!"

With relief, I backed away, letting my half sister and her companion in mischief exit the perilous structure. The boy was just as bedraggled, with a fresh hole at his knee, and I couldn't decide who to be more upset with. Margaret for stealing my letter, or Charlie, who had only two pairs of trousers to begin with.

I held my hand out expectantly. "My letter."

She scowled fiercely as she handed it back.

"Thank you," I said with the thinnest layer of calm, despite my racing heart. "But you know very well that the folly isn't safe to play in."

"We aren't playing in there," Margaret protested.

I set my hands on my hips, leveling my sternest look at her.

"We aren't," she whined. "This is our fortress."

"We were setting up a trap for the Germans," Charlie added with cloying earnestness. "We're filling it with rocks and sticks."

"There are no Germans here." I inhaled slowly, trying to keep my patience. It wasn't the boy's fault. He'd absorbed the same irrational fears and paranoia that had taken hold of everyone since Chamberlain's announcement of war nearly nine months ago. Panic had gripped the country, with people wearing gas masks and digging Anderson shelters in their yards. "We're safe at Havenworth. That's why your parents sent you here. So you wouldn't have to think about things like that."

It wasn't the right thing to say. The boy's lip trembled, and his brown eyes shone with tears. All the other children who'd been sent to Havenworth had returned to their homes when London proved just as uneventful as our sleepy country home. I'd never given much thought to why Charlie remained. Had his parents simply not wanted him to return?

"Well, if they do, we'll be ready for them," Margaret asserted.

"Come here." I dropped to my knees, despite knowing my dress would end up just as mud stained as hers. I wrapped one arm around her, the other around Charlie, and pulled them in close. "No one is coming here to hurt you. Havenworth is safe. I promise you."

"Then why would you leave?" Margaret asked in a quiet voice. "What if it's not safe in America?"

"Oh, Margaret," I sighed. "It's just a letter. I don't even know what it says. For all I know, they've written to tell me I have no business applying to their school."

It was a truth I hadn't wanted to admit, even to myself. I wasn't formally trained or anything of the sort. I had sent my application nearly a year ago, complete with a portfolio of my three best drawings and a promise to God that I would never ask for anything else. I'd assumed my chance of attending the prestigious art school was over because of the war, but this unexpected delivery offered a renewed hope. A chance to escape Havenworth. A chance to find my own way in the world.

She nodded, absorbing my reassurance as gospel, before running off with Charlie to find somewhere better to play.

I waited until they were out of sight before looking at the letter once more. The rumpled envelope, slightly torn at the corner, was emblazoned with a postage stamp of Martha Washington and a bright-blue airmail sticker signifying its urgency.

I tore it open and scanned the neatly typed words.

Dear Miss Irene Rosalie Clarke,
This letter is to inform you that your application to Goldings Institute of Fine Arts has been accepted.

Chapter Four

IRENE

May 22, 1940

Father didn't come home that evening—he had been working through the night increasingly often of late. He had always been overly committed to his work, but it had taken an extreme turn over the last few months, with him leaving before the rest of us woke for the day and returning well after we were asleep, if he came home at all. I couldn't understand it at first. If anything, his activities at the university should have slowed down with so many students enlisting. But that was before he let slip he was now chairing the Committee for the Scientific Study of Air Defence—a secret committee working on defensive technologies for the military. I tried not to be resentful of his work, but it was difficult when it consumed so much of his time that he barely had any left for me.

Lady Montgomery's presence at Havenworth had become equally scarce. She had once spent much of her time working alongside Father in his laboratory—an unusual pursuit for a woman of her standing, though it had never seemed to trouble her. My stepmother had always been far more comfortable with equations than with etiquette. But there was no place for her on the committee, so she had turned her attentions to the war effort at home, immersing herself in every other charitable endeavor and committee related to the war, and hosting displaced children with relentless determination.

The care of the children, however, largely fell to me, the only one in the household without other commitments. It was my duty to teach them, put them to bed, and ensure they wrote weekly letters home to their families. Yet, while my father and stepmother believed I was old enough for such responsibility, they still did not entrust me to make decisions about my own life.

When Father first told me we were moving to England not four months after Mother died, I was devastated. But he promised me we would be moving to a huge manor home with expansive gardens and a bedroom fit for a princess, where I would be welcomed and happier than I could ever imagine, with a new mother to dote on me. I'm not sure how it happened that I let myself believe my actual mother, resurrected from her grave, would be waiting for me, given I was far too old for such childish fantasies, but the idea sustained me during the long voyage across the Atlantic.

Nothing about my life had turned out as I'd been led to believe. Lady Montgomery had tried in her own way to be kind at first, but she hadn't the first clue how to be a mother to me. I suppose I didn't make it easy for her either. I resented the easy way she and my father got on in their rekindled romance. And it was rekindled. I hadn't understood at the time that the haste of their marriage was because of the romantic intentions they'd shared in their youth. Lady Montgomery's parents had forbidden her from marrying beneath her social class, but they had long since passed away by the time my father became widowed, giving him and my stepmother the freedom to finally be together as they had always wanted.

It wasn't until the next evening after I'd received my acceptance letter from Goldings that I heard Father's car pull up the drive just as we were finishing dinner. I raced to the front door and opened it before he had reached the front steps. His hair was unusually mussed as he stepped out of the vehicle, which only further emphasized the excessive gray strands that had appeared quite suddenly over the last year. His clothing, too, was rumpled and stained, as though he hadn't changed in days.

"Father, hello," I said as he walked past me, not appearing to register my presence at all. "There's something we need to talk about."

"Daddy!" Margaret streaked past me with her arms outstretched. He picked her up for a hug with an affection I'd never known from him.

"Margaret, my dear. What kind of adventures have you been up to today?"

"Charlie and I constructed a tiny raft from sticks we found in the forest."

"How very clever of you."

I waited for his attention to turn my way, clasping my hands tightly together behind my back to rein in my nerves. His smile was weary as he set her down. But instead of giving me his attention next, he strode past me as though I were not even there.

"Father, wait." I picked up my stride to match his as he continued down the long hall toward his office, my heart pounding thunderously with excitement. "I received a letter yesterday. One I've been waiting for."

"Could we discuss it later? I need to speak to your stepmother regarding an urgent matter to do with the war."

"But it can't wait."

"I'm sorry, Irene."

"Please, Father. The war can wait. Nothing has happened for months. We can't put our entire lives on hold for something that isn't real. That's what I need you to understand. I've been accepted to the Goldings Institute of Fine Arts. In New York."

He stopped walking, finally turning the full force of his attention to me. There was no kindness, no fatherly pride in his eyes. "What did you say?"

I sucked in a breath, trying to recall the speech I had rehearsed hundreds of times since the letter arrived. "The Goldings Institute of Fine Arts. They've accepted me."

"You are not going to art school in America."

"We agreed that once I turned nineteen, I could return to America as long as I was accepted to school. I'll be nineteen in November and—"

"That was before the war. It's no longer safe to travel."

I threw my hands up in frustration. "What war? Everyone keeps fretting about something that's happening thousands of miles away, but nothing ever happens."

"War is not a game. Nor is it a silly inconvenience. We all have to make sacrifices."

"Haven't I made enough sacrifices? All I've done for the past year is follow orders and take care of the children. I want to study art in New York. It's a wonderful opportunity and—"

"That's enough," he said, rubbing his forehead, exhaustion heavy in his voice. "It is not my intention to break a promise, but it would be a foolish risk to take."

Just then, a group of the young Land Army girls flitted brazenly through the front door, as comfortable as though they owned the place. I held my breath as they streamed past us, giggling and chatting and utterly oblivious to the seriousness of the conversation I was having.

"There is nothing foolish about wanting an education," I said as calmly as possible when the interlopers were finally out of earshot. "You of all people should understand that."

Father shook his head. "Art school is not an education."

"If I told you I wanted to study to be a scientist, you would let me go," I said, my voice shaking with bitterness. "You would be proud."

"Yes, I would have been proud. But I still would not let you go to America. It's not safe. There are German U-boats trolling the waters, just as eager to down a passenger ship as a naval vessel."

"You did it. You went to America for three entire months!" At the start of the war, he'd been called away by the government for a special mission. I'd begged to go with him, but he'd refused to take me along.

"And it was not without danger. You have no idea how close we came to being hit by a torpedo." There was a tremble in his voice. I had never heard my father sound afraid before. "It was a risk I took because I'm doing my part to end this war. Not for some lark. You are eighteen years old. It's time for you to grow up and take some responsibility."

My cheeks burned with anger and embarrassment. "How am I supposed to grow up when you keep me locked up in this prison with no escape?"

"You think Havenworth is a prison? Do you have no understanding of how fortunate you are? You want for nothing. I have provided you with a home, stability, all the clothes, books, and art supplies one could ever need."

Clothes and trinkets. As if those could replace everything I lost when Father forced me to move halfway across the world so he could marry Lady Montgomery.

"I want to go to art school and learn to draw properly. I want to have conversations with people who aren't seven-year-old children or servants. I want to make my own decisions about my life."

"You want to leave."

"I don't belong here."

I waited for him to correct me. To tell me I was being ridiculous. That of course I belonged in this family. But he just stared at me like I was an equation he couldn't solve. Each second of silence drove the invisible wedge between us deeper, until there was no way to ever reach across the chasm that separated us.

"I've given my answer. We are not discussing this any further." He stormed off down the hall, leaving me alone with only the tattered remains of my broken dreams.

◆ ◆ ◆

I didn't see Father again for the rest of the week. On the nights he was home, he kept his study door locked. Margaret wouldn't speak to me, either, though I wasn't certain whether she was angrier about my desire to leave or the fact I had strictly forbidden her from playing in the folly.

Havenworth had never felt lonelier.

A week after our last conversation, he finally sat down to breakfast with the family. I'd been waiting for another opportunity to confront him once more about the letter from Goldings. Now that he'd had some time to think it through, surely he could understand that it was a wonderful opportunity that I couldn't afford to pass up.

I waited until he had finished his coffee before I dared broach the delicate subject. "Father," I said as confidently as I could.

His intent gaze lingered on the newspaper a few seconds before he set it down and turned his attention my way. New frown lines had etched into the dull skin on his forehead. "Yes, Irene?"

I wish the sound of his voice didn't fill my chest with so much ache, but it was the first time he'd spoken to me in a week. "I wanted to ask if you've reconsidered your decision."

He raised his eyebrows, and my faint vestiges of hope began to splinter.

"Regarding Goldings," I added.

He picked up the newspaper once more, dismissing my request without a word.

"Please," I urged. "There are still steamships traveling out of Liverpool for New York. I could—"

"You are not leaving Havenworth," Father roared so loud that I fell back in my seat.

A chill spread through the dining room. Even Margaret and Charlie froze in their seats, quiet as church mice. I pressed my lips together, knowing the only sound my throat was capable of was a sob and not daring to let my father see me cry. Not when I was trying so hard to convince him to treat me like an adult.

It was my stepmother who finally broke the silence. "I've invited some of your father's colleagues and their families over for dinner this weekend," she said primly, as though Father hadn't just exploded in the middle of breakfast. "Uncle Edward and your father have been working so hard on the committee. Plus, your cousin Michael has some leave from the RAF. It will be a lovely opportunity to see him again."

My frustrations finally boiled over. I set down my fork, my appetite soured long before. As much as I craved excitement, the thought of an evening in the company of people with whom I shared no common ground was unbearable. Why was it that the only thing we celebrated anymore was the war? Neither my father nor stepmother had even acknowledged my acceptance into a prestigious art school, even if they had no intention of letting me attend.

"What's the matter, Irene?" my stepmother asked. "You've barely eaten."

"Nothing," I said. "I'm just not hungry."

Father sighed, his patience fraying. "I know you're upset, but that's no excuse for acting like a spoiled brat."

His words felt like a slap, stealing the air from my lungs.

No one said a word as I walked out of the dining room. I didn't belong here. Havenworth had never been a home for me; I was merely a reminder of my father's past regrets. So why wouldn't he just let me go?

I locked myself in my room. Not three seconds later, Margaret knocked softly at the door. "Irene?"

I ignored her. She tried again and again, rapping her small wrist against the door until I thought I might scream. Finally, she stopped. But she wasn't giving up. A slip of paper appeared under my door.

I saw no writing or markings of any kind. Just a blank page.

Despite my frustration, I reached for a pencil from my vanity drawer and shaded over the paper. Gradually, faint lines emerged, forming words against the graphite.

You're not a spoiled brat. Just a regular brat.

I laughed despite my anger. Margaret always knew how to dis-arm me, no matter my mood. One of the older evacuees had taught her to etch secret messages into paper with the tip of an inkless pen or the point of a safety pin or whatever reasonably sharp object she could find. For the better part of a month last year, the children were obsessively passing invisible notes to each other when they ought to have been learning.

I unlocked my door, and immediately a pair of fierce, tiny arms wrapped around my waist, a face burrowing into my stomach.

"I'm sorry Daddy was mean," Margaret whispered.

"Thank you, but it will all work out. He just needs some time to come around."

She squeezed me tighter. Whether it was to comfort me or her own way of keeping me from leaving, I didn't know and didn't care.

Chapter Five

IRENE

June 1, 1940

The dinner party turned out to be as dull as I predicted. Fewer than a dozen guests had been invited, none of whom had any interest in conversing with me. The invasion of France was on everyone's lips, setting a rather morose tone to the entire affair.

I had resigned myself to an evening of tedium and feigned politeness, but even that turned out to be too much to hope for. Lady Montgomery had seated me across from the one person certain to make the dinner as painful as possible: Deborah Howell. She might be my stepcousin, but I couldn't stand her. Deborah and I had been in school together, and she'd always been a terrible bully, teasing me for my "unusual and funny-sounding" accent and making sure none of the other girls would dare befriend me for fear of incurring her wrath. But thanks to our familial connection and the fact our fathers were colleagues, any rare social event I attended always involved their presence. Lady Montgomery was convinced we would become friends if we only spent enough time together, as if a mongoose and viper might become good chums if thrown into the same box.

Even now, I could sense her unfavorable judgment of my lack of makeup and out-of-fashion dress. Her face was overly done up, which had as much to do with flaunting the rationing as it did with covering her hideousness, and her hair coiffed into a rigid updo. I ignored her as best as I could, though with Margaret and Charlie seated next to me, my options for a stimulating conversation were limited.

I caught the pair playing jacks during the soup course when the little red ball splattered hot broth across my arm.

"You need to behave," I hissed. I snatched the ball away and tucked it against the fold of my skirt. Father and Lady Montgomery were too caught up in conversation at the far end of the impossibly long dining table to notice Margaret's poor behavior, but more than a few of the guests—Deborah included—glanced at us with disdain.

Charlie, at least, had the grace to look ashamed of his behavior, but Margaret crossed her arms in an unseemly pout. "Why?"

"One day you will be lady of this house. You need to learn the rules of decorum."

"When I'm lady of the house, there won't be any rules. We'll dance on the table if we feel like it and eat chocolate at every meal."

It took all my composure not to growl in frustration, even though I secretly agreed the house would be infinitely more enjoyable if Margaret were in charge. But my sister still needed to learn how to fit into the world in which she was born.

"Why Aunt Mary insists on the presence of children at such a gathering, I will never know," Deborah whispered to her sister, Pamela. My stepmother was too far away to hear the slight, but I wasn't.

"Yes, it would have been much more enjoyable if the ill-tempered children had been left at home with their nannies instead of forcing them to ruin the evening with their whining," I replied coolly, staring directly at her and Pamela.

Deborah shot me a withering look. "It's a shame you were always so obsessed with your silly doodles of flowers instead of learning how to conduct yourself like a civilized member of society. Perhaps then

42

you wouldn't be stuck here in this house, dependent on your parents for attention."

I balled up my fists beneath the table, unsure whether to be more offended at the insult or the claim that I counted Lady Montgomery among my parents.

"Irene's drawings aren't silly. They're remarkable," Margaret blustered. "She's the most talented drawer you'll ever meet."

"Quite certainly," Deborah said with a cruel smile. "Since I don't spend much time around children anymore, I doubt I'll be forced to encounter anyone's drawings until Rupert's and my children are in school." She waved her left hand in front of her face, flashing an unmistakable cushion-cut diamond on her ring finger.

"Deborah and Rupert are engaged," Pamela added fawningly.

"Congratulations," I said through clenched teeth. It was no secret that I had once harbored a crush on Rupert. For a time it had seemed more than mutual. We used to sneak out to meet each other after dusk at the abandoned barn in the sugar beet fields across the fen. The last time we'd met was nearly eleven months ago, when he stole a kiss and told me I was the most beautiful girl he'd ever known. For weeks afterward, I'd fantasized that he would propose and take me away from this place, though I knew it would never happen. He had always been destined to marry someone like Deborah. Someone who was born in this world and truly belonged.

It didn't matter how I looked or dressed, or even that I'd spent the better part of the past decade at Havenworth. I would always be the middle-class stepchild who did not fit in.

I set down my spoon, any sense of an appetite vanished and replaced with a burning pit of acid in my stomach. For the rest of the meal, I was forced to listen to Deborah and Pamela chatter about the upcoming wedding and how Rupert had insisted on proposing to her before he enlisted in the navy. Margaret and Charlie resumed their shenanigans, though with a bit more subterfuge this time. It seemed everyone had their place at this table except for me.

I'd resigned myself to spending the rest of the evening digging my fingernails into my palms when I spied a motor vehicle pulling up to the house through the large bay window.

"That must be Michael," Deborah said adoringly.

I didn't even bother to look up as Albert, our butler, escorted Michael into the dining room moments later—at least not until he announced, "Michael Howell and guest."

Michael stepped into the dining room along with a fellow uniformed man hobbling along on a pair of crutches.

Abandoning all decorum, Michael's mother—Lady Montgomery's cousin Gwen—rose to her feet to greet her son with a sobbing embrace.

"I hope you don't mind I brought my friend along," Michael said once he was finally released from his mother's clutches. "James serves in the RAF with me, but the poor chap's been banished to the nearby hospital for the last few weeks after his plane got clipped by a Messerschmitt. I thought an evening out to enjoy some of Ruth's delicious cooking would cheer him up."

"Not at all. The more the merrier," my stepmother replied politely, though anyone as familiar with her as I was knew she didn't appreciate last-minute changes unless she was the one orchestrating them.

I studied James as Albert arranged for an additional spot at the table. He was beautiful. There was no other word to describe him. He was tall, like Michael, but with dark hair parted fashionably on the side and slicked back with pomade, and eyes the deepest brown I had ever seen.

"Thank you so much for having me," James said to Father and Lady Montgomery as he took his seat next to Michael at the middle of the long table. "Havenworth is absolutely lovely. I've never seen such an impressive garden."

My stepmother blushed at the compliment. "That is very kind of you to say. We're just glad for the chance to see Michael after such a long time."

Michael took advantage of the mention of his name to break into a long description of his training schedule at the base, and the absolute thrill of flying a spitfire.

I pushed the boiled carrots around my plate with my fork; the sensation of being watched spread over my skin like flowing water. I looked up to see James staring at me. His smile was subtle—the kind that lifts only the corners of one's lips—but the gleam in his eyes made my heart somersault inside my chest.

I jerked my gaze away, perhaps a little too obvious in my perturbation. He was strikingly attractive, but he was an officer in the RAF. The last thing this evening needed was even more talk of the war.

I reserved some hope for enjoying the rest of the evening when we retired to the parlor, but Father did not even pull out the wireless for music. The women sat in a tight huddle, discussing the latest gossip, while the men all stood next to the fireplace drinking brandy. Margaret and Charlie had been excused to their beds for the rest of the evening, though they were more likely to be roaming the grounds for sightings of rogue German bombers than under the covers.

Fortunately, that left me alone and without scrutiny next to the bar, which served me just fine. I poured myself a glass of brandy and tossed it back the way I imagined dashing men with Clark Gable mustaches at gentlemen's clubs did. The cool liquid burst into flames inside my throat, scorching a trail to my stomach. I blinked away the rush of tears stinging my eyes and braced myself for another sip. After all, if I was going to develop a taste for such dreadful but necessary things in the real world, I needed to take advantage of every opportunity.

"The Germans were coming in hot and heavy, firing at us from all angles," Michael boomed to a rapt audience. "We thought that was it when we were hit, but I managed to get us home on a busted engine.

Landing was a little rough, but we made it, unlike so many others that night."

His mother made a dramatic strangled sound.

"How daring and brave," one of the older women fawned. "We're so fortunate to have men like you defending our shores."

"The RAF is strong, but we're no match for the Luftwaffe," Michael said with an uncharacteristic bitterness. "They have more planes, more technology, and they know how to find our weaknesses. If they decide to attack Britain with all their might, we won't be able to stop them."

I knocked back another glass of brandy to burn away all this talk of war from my brain. The way everyone went on and on about it, you would think they wanted the war to come to our doorstep.

"But surely Britain's radar defense system will hold," Lady Montgomery said to Father.

He nodded, his own glass of brandy still untouched in his hand. "The Chain Home is a crucial part of our defense, but Michael is right. There is much more work to be done if we are to retain our supremacy in the air."

"You're being rather humble," Edward, Michael's father, said. "The work of the committee to advance our radar capabilities is nothing short of astounding."

Father cut him a sharp, silencing look. Everyone knew the work they did was highly classified, not to be repeated even among family. But alcohol had a funny way of loosening lips.

"Our radar developments are only one step forward," Father said. "We need more funding. Ways to advance our agenda. Churchill's refused to give us any real support. He's focused entirely on arming the country for offense, not defense."

"And what would you have us do?" another man asked. "England doesn't have the capacity to scale up the design of any of our inventions to be effective."

"America does," Father said.

"What good does that do us?" Edward protested loudly.

The discussion had turned so heated that every other conversation in the room hushed.

"They're our allies," Father responded with a staunchness I recognized as anger.

"In name only. They're not our friends. America hasn't even joined the war."

"Why should they?" I asked impulsively.

All eyes turned to me, and I regretted opening my mouth.

"What on earth could you possibly mean by that?" Deborah asked with feigned innocence.

I should have been smarter than to respond, but the brandy had loosened my tongue, and I'd never been very good at ignoring my nemesis when she goaded me on to begin with. "Why should they join a war that has nothing to do with them? Why send their men into battle to be slaughtered? Perhaps they're simply learning from Britain's mistake—that there is no value in joining another country's war."

"You can't genuinely believe that," Lady Montgomery cautioned.

"Why not? After all, what good has it done Britain to join a war on the Continent? We can't drive anywhere. There's barely any food in the stores. Half the men that should be in college or starting families are trading bullets with Germans in some field in France. And for what?"

"Irene, dear, it's best not to speak on things you don't understand," Lady Montgomery said, as though I were a child not understanding the grown-ups' conversation. "War is a complicated matter."

My cheeks flushed with embarrassment. I drained the last of my brandy and made my exit, knowing well enough that I had overstayed my welcome anyway.

I took my sketchbook and coloring pencils to the moon garden, having no desire to spend the rest of the evening locked inside my room while the guests carried on about who was making the greater sacrifice to the gods of war. It was a special spot hidden away behind a round stone gate that only I seemed to ever appreciate.

The first buds on the hawthorn tree were beginning to unfurl, creating a mass of white that stood out against the dusky sky. There was something incredibly special about the grounds at twilight, when the plants and creatures that usually stayed hidden finally emerged from their hiding spots. The creeping phlox and jasmine, too delicate for notice in the daylight, sparkled like gemstones beneath the moon's glow. On lucky evenings, I might even spot an adventurous doe nibbling on the hydrangeas, though Paul considered deer a menace worthy of a shotgun.

It wasn't always this lovely, though. The moon garden had been all but abandoned when I'd first arrived. I'd begged Paul to let me help make it beautiful again. He let me choose all the flowers and plants, guiding me with gentle advice on how to ensure the garden would bloom all year round. When the early summer arrived, the white roses and lilies would put on a spectacular display. In winter, the snowdrops and white grape hyacinths would break through the gloom.

This was where I came when I wanted to feel close to my mother. It was she who had first taught me about moon gardens and the healing powers they possessed. Creating one at Havenworth allowed me to keep her memory here with me. Even at ten years old, I had known better than to tell my father and stepmother why it meant so much to me. My mother belonged to a past both of them preferred to leave behind.

But no matter how much time passed, I would never forget her. She smelled like jasmine and sewed the most beautiful dresses for me. But beneath her bright smile, she wasn't always happy. Father's long hours at the university left her lonely. Their marriage wasn't a particularly happy one. Mother never felt comfortable in Father's academic world, and I suspect she always knew she wasn't the true love of his life. When I would wake up from a nightmare, I often found her already awake, sitting by her bedroom window, staring at the night sky. She would tell me the moonlight helped her clear her mind. At the time I didn't understand what she meant, but I did now. There was a peace that could be found only in the quiet of the moonlight.

Drawing in the low light wasn't ideal, but the challenge was a welcome distraction from all the thoughts and frustrations still coursing through me. I sketched out the wide trunk of the magnolia first, then the length of the stone wall behind it. Delicate lilies of the valley encircled the base of the tree like a fairy ring.

The tranquility of the moment shattered when my white coloring pencil failed to capture the iridescence of the tiny blooms. I set the pencil down on the stone bench next to me with a huff and held up the sketch to examine the results more closely. I felt a prickle of awareness along my skin, signaling the presence of someone on the path behind me. I turned with every intention of chastising whoever it was for not respecting my personal space. But the words drowned in my throat when I locked eyes with James.

"What are you doing here?"

He leaned casually on one of the crutches. "Searching for a little solitude. The same as you, I suspect."

"Isn't the point of attending a party to avoid solitude?"

"I suppose it is. But you're the only person worth spending time with tonight."

A blush fell across my cheeks. "I thought you were Michael's friend."

"I've known Michael since we were seven years old and made to share a room at boarding school. Now that we're stationed at Duxford together, I know more about him than anyone should ever know about a friend. Besides, he has a captive audience for all his tales of bravery and daring. He'll be fine without me for a while."

"I didn't think anyone was immune to his charms."

"Personally, I'm more drawn to beauty and intelligence. Would you mind if I join you?"

Flattered, I inched over to make room for him on the stone bench.

He sat down, not touching me but close enough that I could smell the faint trace of bergamot from his aftershave. An easy quiet settled between us, letting the crickets fill the night air.

"This is a lovely spot," he finally said.

"It's a moon garden. Many of the flowers, like the angel's-trumpet, don't reveal themselves until after nightfall." I inhaled the intoxicating scent, unable to stop myself from the indulgence despite how silly I probably appeared.

"Is that why you came out here to draw?"

I pressed my sketchbook to my chest, hiding the drawing even though he'd already seen it. "It's not my best. These coloring pencils aren't any good for drawing, but Father refuses to let me use my Faber-Castells since they're German-made."

He shook his head. "Even with poor instruments, it's clear you have an incredible talent."

Another blush came over me. "Do you really think so?"

He nodded. "I would love to see more if you're willing to show me."

I bit my lip. No one had ever asked to see my drawings before, and the idea of it made me feel as vulnerable as if he'd asked me to shed my clothing. Slowly, I opened my book to reveal the hastily drawn sketch.

"Incredible."

I handed him my sketchbook and allowed him to flip through the pages, a fresh wave of nerves spilling over me with each image he inspected. "Have you considered selling your work for commissions?"

The question ought to have filled me with joy. Instead, it reminded me that a career in art would always be out of reach as long as Father refused to allow me to attend art school. "No. As I said, it's only a hobby."

I took the book back and closed it firmly, but that did not deter him at all. "Talent such as this shouldn't be wasted."

"There isn't any room for art when there's a war going on, no matter how far away it is."

"On the contrary. There is always room for art. After all, what are we fighting for if not that?"

"I'm surprised to hear an RAF pilot say that."

"We're not all warmongers and brutes."

"Then why did you enlist?"

I immediately regretted the question, fearing it might offend him. He stared out at the garden for a long time. Finally, he said, "I wish I could give you a proper answer that made me seem brave and honorable. The truth is, I signed up because of pride. All my mates were signing up. We thought it would be some great adventure. Flying planes and conducting raids all over the continent. I don't think any of us truly understood what we would be doing. The danger of it all feels rather far away until you're flying over the Channel with a dozen Messerschmitts firing on you."

"Was it terrifying when you were hit?"

"I was too preoccupied making sure I landed the plane safely to be terrified. It's the long nights in the hospital that have been the most difficult. Knowing I'm lying there useless while everyone else is doing their part."

"Will you go back?"

"If the surgeons clear me. Whether they allow me to fly again is still to be seen. To be honest, I'd volunteer for latrine duty just to get out of the hospital. But enough of my woes. I want to know how you've come to know so much about flowers."

I shrugged so as not to seem overly eager in my answer. "My mother was a florist. We used to visit gardens together all the time."

He furrowed his brow with the faint recognition of those who understood too well. "She died?"

I nodded. "From tuberculosis when I was ten."

"I'm sorry. I lost my parents, too. They were in a car crash last year while they were visiting Vienna."

I wrapped my arms around my waist, fighting the instinct to reach for him and offer the comfort I craved whenever I thought of Mother. Despite our easy rapport, he was a stranger. I couldn't let myself forget that. "You must miss them terribly."

He looked away, hiding whatever emotions came over him in that moment. "It's not easy to talk about, is it?"

"Who says we need to talk? Perhaps we can simply enjoy each other's company in silence for a little while."

"That sounds like a wonderful plan, save for one thing."

"What is that?"

He flashed a wry smile. "How am I to charm you without speaking?"

I sucked in a breath. "I suppose you'll just have to try even harder."

"How about this?" He cupped my cheek, drawing my face close to his. A flutter of anticipation danced in my stomach, like a million rose petals tumbling all at once. He was a stranger, and yet everything about this moment felt so perfect. So utterly right.

I closed my eyes, waiting for the press of his lips to mine. But there was no kiss. Only the sudden wail of an air raid siren erupting in the distance.

The sirens had never rung over Havenworth before. It was such a bizarre, unexpected sound that I didn't realize what it meant until James took my hand and urged me to my feet. He moved with surprising speed on his crutches, so that I had to run to keep up as we raced down the footpath.

James stopped abruptly as we approached the house and placed his hands on my shoulders, forcing me to look him in the eyes. "Irene, where's your shelter?"

It took me a moment to process the question amid the noise. "I don't . . . we don't have one. No, wait, we're supposed to go to the cellar."

He nodded grimly. "That will have to do."

Father was shuffling the rest of the guests into the cellar when we arrived. There were few lights in this part of Havenworth, and a frenzied energy took hold of the women as they stepped carefully down the dark staircase.

"Are we going to be attacked?" Lady Gwen cried out as she descended the stairs, clutching her husband's arm.

"We'll be just fine," Father responded calmly, placing his hand on Lady Montgomery's back to follow behind. "As long as we all hurry along."

Somehow the mix of hysteria and reason was even less reassuring than if everyone had been screaming in panic. I didn't know whose reaction to trust.

Charlie was shaking terribly, streams of tears along his cheeks.

I knelt next to him. "You'll be just fine. I promise. But you must go inside."

"Maybe you can help me," James said to Charlie, setting aside his crutches. "I'm not sure I can make it down the stairs by myself. We could be brave together."

To my relief, Charlie took his hand and disappeared with him into the darkness.

Finally, there was no one left but me.

The sirens still rattled my blood as I hesitated at the top of the stairs. Something wasn't right.

"Irene? Are you coming?" It was James, reappearing at the base of the stairs. "Everyone else is down already."

Not everyone. I gasped as the realization hit me. "Margaret! Where's Margaret?"

I didn't wait for an answer. I had to find her. The bedrooms were the first place I thought to look. I threw each door open, calling for her, but there was no answer. Panic grew inside me with each passing second. She wasn't in any of the rooms inside the house.

Because she wasn't in the house, I realized, cursing myself for my foolishness. There was only one place she would go.

I ran back outside, glancing up at the indigo sky for only a moment before taking off down the path that led to the forbidden garden folly. There were no planes overhead, and no signs of an attack. So why had the siren rung?

It was an error. A mistake.

At least that was what I told myself as I frantically called Margaret's name. There was no light to guide my way as I ran down the curving gravel path. It wasn't the first time I'd navigated the gardens at night. This place had always been my solace, and I knew them as intimately as my own thoughts. But could I say the same for my sister?

I slipped past the secret gate into the wilds of the forest. "Margaret? It's me—"

Something hard and heavy thwacked into my knee. I let out a shrill cry and bent over to clutch the aching joint.

"Irene? Oh no! I'm so sorry!" Margaret appeared before me, holding a heavy stick. "I didn't know it was you! Please don't be mad at me!"

"What on earth are you doing?" I asked, despite barely having any breath left in me.

"I thought you were the Germans."

I winced, pain still coursing along my knee. "And what would you have done if it were the Germans?"

She straightened her shoulders and raised her chin. "Defend Havenworth."

"Oh, Margaret. You're just a child."

"It's my responsibility. I'm going to be lady of the house one day."

This blasted war. A seven-year-old child should not have to feel this afraid all the time. "Come on. We need to get you to the basement."

"No! We can't leave! Who will protect Havenworth?" Her chin wobbled, fear lacing every trembling word.

"Listen to me. There is nothing to fear. No one is coming to attack us."

"But the sirens—"

"It's probably a false alarm."

"You don't know that," she said, doubt weakening her bravado.

"This war is nothing but a sham. A phony war meant to scare us all into submission. Mark my words. The all-clear signal will be rung in no time, and we'll all have a great big laugh about how much we panicked for no reason."

"You're certain?"

"Absolutely," I said with all the conviction I could muster. Still, I couldn't take any chances when it came to Margaret's safety. "But your parents don't understand that, and we don't want to worry them. That's why you need to go back to the cellar and let them know you're okay."

"All right."

On a whim, I plucked a rogue Astrantia flower from the ground. "Here, this flower means courage. Hold on to it and it will help you be brave."

She clutched the small starburst bloom to her chest. "Will it keep us safe?"

I swallowed hard. "Of course it will. I promise."

As soon as the words left my mouth, a silence fell over the night. The sirens stopped. A moment later, the all-clear signal rang out.

Chapter Six

JULIA

Present Day

The history Margaret had shared with me was an honor that weighed heavily on my conscience all afternoon. When I'd applied for the job, I'd been thinking only of Sam and myself. How much I needed the work and how a job like this would look on my portfolio and give us a fresh start.

Margaret's revelations were a reminder this job wasn't just about me. These gardens were part of her family's history. They meant something to her. I couldn't fail. I don't know who she made that promise to, but it was painfully clear that it was more than just a childhood fancy. It was her dying wish.

Sam and I spent the afternoon in the front garden, where I focused on mapping out the grounds and examining the soil for any signs of life. It was strange not to have a half dozen assistants to help with measurements and soil samples. I'd grown accustomed to the luxuries and perks of working for a big, prestigious firm. But that wasn't the reason I had gotten into this profession. It was passion. The skills I developed throughout my schooling and apprenticeships weren't lost just because my career was. I needed to go back to basics for a little while.

The back gardens had once been separated into defined sections. I decided to start with the smallest of the spaces—a moon garden near the back west corner behind the parterre. A round moon gate built into the stone wall gave the space the feeling of stepping into an entirely different world. The garden itself was tiny, barely eight feet long in any direction, but I could picture clearly enough how magical it must have been in its glory. Moon gardens were often believed to be deeply spiritual places where the barrier between the dead and the living thinned. They were a place for meditation and reflection. For memorializing those who have passed on.

I gave Sam a plastic spade I'd found in the old gardener's shed to occupy himself with, then sat down on the sturdy stone bench and opened my laptop, letting my imagination run wild. This was the part I loved best. Envisioning all the beauty and life that would burst out of the soil in the next few months. Figuring out the exact right combination of colors and textures. I still preferred my sketchbook for brainstorming, but the design software I'd spent the better part of my savings on was a necessary investment to succeed in this profession.

A rainbow of dirt flew across the screen.

"Sam! Be careful!" I shook the mess from the keyboard, praying it didn't ruin my computer. When I finally assured myself no permanent damage had been done, I turned to Sam. He looked angry. "Why did you do that?"

He didn't answer.

I let out a sigh. "I guess I've been ignoring you a bit, huh? Are you hungry? Do you want to go exploring?"

Still no reaction. I wished I knew how to translate his unblinking stares and subtle head tilts into words.

I rose to my feet with the most enthusiastic smile I could muster. "You know what? Maybe it would be better if we did this the old-fashioned way. Let's count how many steps are between each section of the parterre."

Sam led the way, counting his steps with careful determination. I let my mind wander to all the possibilities I could create here. I was eager to capture the ideas floating around in my mind into a 3D image I could share with Margaret. Maybe she just needed a gentle nudge to commit to a plan. Sam was happy enough turning over rocks and exploring every hidden corner for treasure for the rest of the afternoon, freeing me to make some headway on the inspiration boards for the garden. I created three different options—a classic English cottage garden filled with pink roses and purple alliums, another option relying more heavily on ornamental grasses for texture, and the third a more refined formal garden with neatly trimmed hedges and topiaries. Each style was beautiful but provided a completely different atmosphere. I hoped at least one of them would resonate with Margaret and give me a sense of direction.

"What do you think?" I asked Sam when I finished.

He scrunched his face, taking on the task of providing his opinion with the utmost gravity before pointing to the cottage garden.

"Great choice. I like that one, too. Why don't we go see if Margaret agrees?"

We packed up our stuff and brought it inside to go look for Margaret. Havenworth was large, but I suspected it would be easy enough to find her. Andrew had said the orangery was her favorite place in the house. She was still perched on her chair when we came inside, so deep in concentration while reading on her tablet that I wasn't sure she even noticed us enter.

"Good afternoon, Margaret," I said cheerily. "Do you mind if we come in?"

She harrumphed as she set down her tablet and lowered her reading glasses, making me hesitate at the door.

Sam had already raced over to the set of jacks on the coffee table, oblivious to any sense of formality or manners.

"Is this a bad time?"

"No, no. It's just this article I'm reading. 'Signal Processing in Airborne Radar Devices.'"

The words flew right above my head, and the confusion must have registered on my face, because she let out a bellowing laugh.

"Science, dear. I might be too old to putter around in the laboratory anymore, but I can still spot a bias in a methodology. What can I do for you now?"

"I wanted to show you some ideas I have for the gardens. Would you be up for that?"

Her energy dimmed, as though the question had blown a gust of air across her wick. She didn't outright refuse, but she didn't say yes either. Her gaze drifted to the window once more.

"We could come back another time," I said gently.

She shook her head. "It's fine. Best we get this over with so you can get on with your work."

This was painful for her. That much I could tell, but I didn't understand why. Why not leave the entire process to Andrew to sort out if she didn't want to be involved?

I opened my laptop and showed her the inspiration boards. She gave no comments, but her frown deepened with each image. "These aren't final designs or anything, just ideas to get a sense of what you like."

"It's not about what I like," she muttered angrily. "The gardens need to look exactly like they did before."

I grimaced in frustration. I'd missed the mark completely. She'd been kind to me and Sam so far, but how long would her patience stretch? Swallowing my worry, I said, "That's what I'm trying to do. But without any photos or plans, I'm not sure how to re-create the original gardens. Is there anything you remember about them?"

She sighed long and slow, then motioned for me to bring my laptop closer. "Show me that first one again."

I opened the image board of the cottage garden. She squinted through her glasses at the images. "The colors are all wrong."

I rubbed my temple. "Okay. But ignore that for a moment. What about the feeling you get?"

This was a tactic I'd used before with indecisive clients. People get overwhelmed by the details or fixated on a certain type of style. Taking them a step back to what they wanted from their space let me show them different options that they might not have ever considered by themselves. But Margaret wasn't a typical client. She was a scientist. A woman who had put up with more than her fair share of bullshit in her life. Feelings seemed to be the last thing she wanted to talk about.

"I remember I liked the patterns in the back gardens. It was like walking in a swirl of soft ice cream."

"The parterre," I said, and the tension in my shoulders eased a fraction as I visualized the space. "It was common to have winding paths through them. What else do you remember?"

She closed her eyes. "Past the first wall was a tunnel that felt like an explosion of color all around me. In the late spring, there were yellow flowers that hovered like raindrops above us." She shook her head as though not quite trusting her own memory.

"Laburnum," I said instantly.

The name didn't spark any hint of recognition, so I quickly typed the name into the search engine and pulled up a photo.

"That's it," Margaret said with delight. "The flowers were so vibrant but so fleeting. I remember our gardener scolding Charlie and me for playing with fallen petals. We would gather them up in huge heaps and throw them over each other until we were absolutely covered in yellow. The gardener would chase us off, but we always snuck back."

"That's probably because they're poisonous if you ingest them. But they make an incredible display in the late spring."

The memory was clearly a happy one for her, so I took my chances scrolling to a website that listed other types of flowers. She remained silent while I scrolled along through the images of irises and rudbeckia and sunflowers, giving me no further clues.

"Wait," she said, pointing to the screen where a dainty magenta flower in the shape of a starburst was displayed. "That one."

"Astrantia," I said. It was one of my favorite flowers for its simplicity and easy care, but often underappreciated in the gardening world.

"Courage," she whispered shakily.

I knelt down next to her. "Do you remember it in the gardens? It's also called masterwort."

She shook her head. "Courage," she repeated.

I bit my lip. "I'm sorry, I don't understand."

"It means courage," she said with obvious frustration. "That's what—"

"Hello, Margaret. What are you chatting about?"

I turned to see a woman standing in the doorframe. She was young—early twenties at most—with a bag of groceries on her hip. She had thick dark hair and a round, pretty face with a bright flush across her cheeks.

"Just some nonsense," Margaret said dismissively. "What have you brought me today?"

"A book, more of your favorite tea, and some more of the medication the doctor ordered," the woman said cheerily, setting the bag onto the coffee table. "Hello, I'm Helen. You must be the new expert gardener."

I rose to my feet. "Nice to meet you. I'm Julia, and this is Sam."

Helen glanced down at the boy. "Very nice to meet you, too, Sam."

Sam ignored her, but her bright smile remained.

Margaret's eyes narrowed. "Did you bring my biscuits?"

"Not until after you've had your dinner. And even then, it's our secret. No telling Andrew, okay? This stays between you and me and—" Her eyes widened as she seemed to remember me. "You won't tell Andrew, will you? He would positively murder me if he knew I'd brought Margaret sweets."

She spoke so quickly it was almost dizzying.

"Your secrets are safe with me," I replied. Mostly because Andrew didn't seem to have any interest in speaking with me at all, unless it was strictly necessary.

"That's a good girl," Margaret said, closing her eyes. Our little visit down memory lane had clearly exhausted her more than I anticipated. We had only just scratched the surface, but at least it was a start.

Chapter Seven

IRENE

June 1, 1940

The guests had all left by the time I coaxed Margaret back to the house. I tried not to let any feelings of disappointment take hold of me. James was a stranger, after all. An RAF officer I'd likely never see again. But how could I not feel dismay? In just a short conversation, he had recognized and appreciated my artistic talent in a way no one ever had since I'd arrived in this country. And he was beautiful. And now he'd gone without a proper goodbye.

Father and Lady Montgomery were pacing the main floor hallway when Margaret and I returned. My stepmother cried in relief and pulled Margaret into an embrace.

"Where on earth were you?" Father asked wearily, another crack in his stoic armor forming.

"I found her in the garden folly," I said, knowing his concern was entirely for my sister.

Father nodded, the closest I would come to an actual thank-you.

"Oh, Margaret, you know you aren't allowed to play there," Lady Montgomery said, running her hand along Margaret's tangled hair.

"I wasn't—" Margaret began to say before her voice cracked. She coughed—quietly at first, but it quickly devolved into a fit. Father and Lady Montgomery looked at each other with concern.

"Shh, darling," Lady Montgomery said. "We should get you to bed."

Her coughing didn't ease until she was tucked into my bed and I had rubbed her back until she finally fell asleep. I ought to have joined her but too many thoughts raced through my mind to allow for any true rest. Would my father have worried for me if I were the one ailing? I couldn't remember him ever showing such concern for me when I was younger. Not even before we moved here. It was my mother who tended to my wounds and comforted me when nightmares came. Father was always too consumed by his work.

I sat at my vanity and ran my brush through my hair. My mother had taught me to brush out my hair every night before I slept, no matter how tired I was. Perhaps it was silly, especially on a night like this, but it was another way I kept her memory with me.

A gentle tap sounded at my door, so subtle I might not have realized there was someone on the other side if they hadn't knocked again.

"Come in," I said softly, not wanting to wake Margaret.

My father entered, grimacing. "Irene, I know we're all exhausted, but we need to talk."

"It's late."

"And yet you're still awake."

With a heavy sigh, I rose to my feet and met him in the hallway, where we wouldn't disturb Margaret. "What did you want to speak about?"

My father glanced over my shoulder, still staring into my room. He was not an imposing figure—of average height, with a lean build and a face so plain and nondescript that it was easy to overlook him in a crowd. But those of us who knew him well understood the sharp intellect behind his deep-set, watchful dark eyes; they missed nothing. "You've changed your room again."

"I decided the vanity would look better next to the window. But I doubt you're here to discuss my design choices."

He shook his head. "It's your careless comments this evening that concern me."

"Why do you assume anything I do is careless?"

"Because it's far more frightening to assume you understand the implications of your ignorance."

Embarrassment heated my cheeks. Maybe I didn't understand much about the war, but I knew it had aged Father well beyond his forty-six years and forced Charlie to leave his family. It was the reason my sister was afraid all the time.

"The soul and freedom of this nation are in jeopardy, not just from Hitler but from those inside Britain who espouse fascism. We do not have the luxury of pretending the danger isn't real. Each one of us needs to decide whether our freedom is worth fighting for. Once this war reaches our doorstep, it will be far too late for regret."

It was a speech he'd recited before, but this time it was different. This time he said it as though I were the danger. The enemy.

Margaret was a bundle of energy when she woke the next morning. After stretching her limbs like a cat, she bounded out of bed with the declaration that she would be spending the day searching for butterflies among the milkweed. The only signs of something off were the rasp in her voice and the slight cough that grew more apparent as the day wore on. Otherwise, she was her typical stubborn self who refused to acknowledge the fear she'd shown last night.

For my part, I woke with a wretched headache and a heavy weight on my shoulders. Father's lecture had kept me awake all night, doubting myself. Had I been selfish for expressing my opinions? He had never chastised me for speaking my mind before. If anything, it was the one thing he had always encouraged. Just not about the war.

I didn't enjoy the feeling of being in the wrong.

It was approaching midday by the time I finally dragged myself downstairs. Late enough that I wouldn't have to face my father yet, but still early enough that there might be breakfast waiting for me.

Annie was in the dining room when I entered, clearing the dishes from the table.

"I hope it's not too late for breakfast," I said, glancing at the empty table, where the food had been cleared away.

She offered an apologetic smile. "Sorry. Ruth has already repurposed the leftovers for today's lunch. Bacon and vegetable soup. She's in a good mood today on account of her new grandbaby. Perhaps she'd give you some toast if you asked nicely."

"Thank you, I'll try," I said, managing a small smile. Ruth, our cook, was economical by nature, but since the rationing began, she had made it her mission to waste not a single crumb.

I turned to leave, but Annie called out once more. "Oh, wait! I forgot to tell you that a letter came for you this morning."

"A letter? From whom?" I immediately thought of the acceptance letter from Goldings. Had they written to rescind their offer? Not that it mattered, since Father had no intention of ever letting me attend.

A wry smile bloomed on Annie's lips. "It's from Officer James Atherton."

My heart soared like a bird taking flight. "May I have it? Please?"

She slipped it out of the pocket of her skirt and handed it to me. "I figured you might not want your father to know about this."

"Thank you," I breathed out, tearing the envelope open.

The note was written on monogrammed stationery with elegant cursive.

Dearest Irene,

I have not stopped thinking about our conversation last night in the garden.

If you are willing to see me again, I have some leave next Friday. I humbly ask if I may take you to lunch.

Signed,

James Atherton

Chapter Eight

IRENE

June 14, 1940

The day I was set to meet James for lunch, I spent the better part of the morning pinching my cheeks, hoping to coax some color into them. When that failed, I decided to head to the kitchen to find some beetroots instead, a tip I'd learned from *Vogue* magazine. But as I opened my door, I nearly collided with my stepmother, who stood just outside, her hand poised midair as though she'd been about to knock.

"Oh!" Lady Montgomery exclaimed as I came to an abrupt stop. "I was just looking for you."

"Is something the matter?" I asked.

"Your father left his important papers at home this morning. He needs them urgently at the university, but I can't go because the doctor is coming to see Margaret today."

"Why does Margaret need to see the doctor?"

Lady Montgomery waved her hand. "I'm sure it's fine. We're all just a little worried about her cough. That's the reason your father was so distracted this morning when he left. But he really does need this. Would you—" She cut herself off abruptly. "Never mind. I'll ask Albert if he can run it over."

I placed my hand on her arm to stop her. "You need me to take something to Cambridge?"

"Would that be too much trouble?"

"Not at all," I said. "I'm happy to help."

It wasn't exactly a lie. I was already on my way to meet James, and it was easy to detour to Father's office along the way. If anything, it gave me the excuse I needed to disappear without anyone asking questions about my absence. But the fact she was asking me as a last resort stung.

She let out a sigh of relief. "Thank you."

See? I wanted to say. *I'm not so selfish and useless after all.*

She handed me the folder but didn't let go when I attempted to take it. I raised my eyebrows in confusion.

"I'm sure I don't have to tell you this . . ." she began before biting her lip. "But this is terribly sensitive information. No one can know you have it or what's in it. It's imperative it not be lost."

It annoyed me that she thought I needed the caution, but I was determined to prove I was mature enough for the task, which meant swallowing my pride. "I'll take the utmost care."

She nodded, finally accepting the fact she was entrusting me with something so vital. "Don't forget your gas mask when you leave."

I carefully stuffed the folder into my purse and set off for the city later that morning. I tried accidentally forgetting my gas mask, but Lady Montgomery insisted on following the regulations to the letter of the law, meaning we had to drag the cumbersome masks with us anytime we stepped foot outside the grounds, even though we'd never had cause to use them. I would have ignored her, but she personally retrieved the mask from my bedroom and followed me out the gates before I could make my escape.

The pressure in my ribs eased the moment I stepped beyond the iron gates. It had been too long since I had ventured outside of Havenworth. The walk to the nearest rail line was nearly twenty minutes along the quiet country roads. There were no cars on the road thanks to the petrol rationing, and I appreciated the quiet while surrounded by the lush fens and endless fields. It had been too long since I'd experienced this kind of tranquility.

The city itself was much less peaceful. Bicycles zipped along the roads, and long queues of women clutching their ration books stretched down the pavements outside the shops. The tension in the air was palpable. But arriving on campus felt like stepping into another universe. There was no urgency here, no trace of war. Students strolled across the green, carrying stacks of books, chatting animatedly as though nothing had changed.

If such normalcy could exist at a university, surely there were other places in the world. Places I might go, if Father would allow it.

I'd been to his office only once before, but I remembered where it was: in the building with the ornately carved sculptures and crests above the grand entrance. First a left turn along the hall, then up the stairs and another left. The third door on the right.

I raised my hand to knock. But before my knuckles made contact, a shout from behind the door froze me in place.

"You can't be serious, John. Collaborating with Americans? It's madness."

I needed only an instant to recognize the familiar gruff voice. My stepuncle, Edward Howell. I hesitated at the door, unsure whether an interruption would be welcomed when they were obviously engaged in an argument. The last thing I wanted was to give Father any more reasons to be frustrated with me.

"What choice do we have? There's no way we can scale up the technology on our own. It needs more support than the committee can offer right now."

I leaned closer, nearly pressing my ear against the heavy door.

"If you've discovered a way for our planes to detect enemy aircraft from the air, that would be the most significant invention of the century. You cannot hand it to the Americans. You'd be giving away our most valuable tool. They will do nothing but profit off the technology. Our factories are more than capable of producing whatever you've designed."

"Not in enough quantity to support our military. Every factory in this country has been converted to the production of munitions. You know as well as I do Churchill will not spare a single one for something as unproven as new radar technology. He wants to dismantle the committee altogether."

"We would be giving England's future away," Edward pleaded. "Think of all the profits—"

"And if we don't, we will lose the war. What of that cost to England?" The ferocity in Father's voice made me rear back, shocking me so much that I dropped my purse. The contents spilled out around me. Coins, tissues, and, most worrisome, the papers inside Father's folder. I dropped to my knees and quickly gathered the items, shoving them back in my purse. But as I picked up Father's papers, I couldn't stop myself from peering at the contents.

On the pages were detailed plans for something called the cavity magnetron.

The door flew open just as I rose to my feet and Edward stalked out without even noticing my presence. I quickly stuffed the documents back in the folder.

When I stepped into his office, Father was pacing behind his desk. I had to clear my throat twice before he finally noticed me.

"Irene? What are you doing here?"

I held up his folder. "You forgot this. Lady Montgomery asked me to bring it to you."

There was no denying the relief in his expression as he took it from me and opened it. I waited silently for some kind of acknowledgment or gratitude, but the contents had already captured the entirety of his attention.

◆ ◆ ◆

The restaurant where James suggested we meet was undoubtedly one of the most elegant I'd ever seen. The spacious interior, with its soaring ceilings, radiated sophistication. Round tables draped in long white linens were impeccably set with gold-edged bone china and polished silverware that gleamed under the soft lighting. Father and Lady Montgomery preferred quiet suppers at home, and when we did dine out, my stepmother always chose more understated venues.

A wave of nerves rippled through me as I stepped inside, scanning the room for James. I could see I wasn't dressed appropriately for this kind of establishment. My simple yellow shift was perfectly fine, but felt hopelessly out of place among the other patrons' more formal attire.

"Do you have a reservation?" the maître d' asked, his upper lip curling as he eyed the gas mask dangling from my wrist.

"I'm supposed to be meeting a friend," I said, feeling rather sheepish. What if James couldn't make it after all? What if he'd simply changed his mind? "Officer James Atherton."

The waiter's demeanor changed almost instantly. "Of course. Please follow me."

He led me to the back of the restaurant, where James sat at a table in a quiet corner. My heart jolted the moment I set eyes on him. He was dressed in his uniform, just like the night we first met. Despite my feelings about the war, I couldn't help but appreciate the way his broad shoulders filled out the dark-blue jacket.

James rose to his feet with an eager smile that made my stomach flutter. "You came."

"Of course I did. It's not every day I'm invited to lunch by a mysterious gentleman. I had to see what awaited me."

"I hope I can live up to your expectations."

Despite his injured leg, he held my chair for me as I took my seat, then returned to his. I tucked my gas mask under my feet, feeling ashamed that I'd brought it. "You've already exceeded them by bringing me here."

James frowned, sensing the discomfort I'd tried to hide. "What's wrong? Do you not like French cuisine?"

"It's just that I'm not really dressed properly for this kind of place."

"You could be wearing a flour sack and still be the most beautiful woman here. Besides, it would be cruel to make me dine alone. Lunch is my treat."

My cheeks flushed from the compliment. "Well, how can I possibly refuse now?"

"You can't," he replied, leaning in conspiratorially. "I'm utterly irresistible. It's a proven fact."

A waiter passed by carrying a tray of plates. A symphony of aromas filled my nose. "Is that . . . chocolate cake?"

"Restaurants aren't subject to the same rationing rules as the rest of us common folk."

I laughed. There was nothing common about James. I didn't know much about him, but it was clear he carried the confidence of a man who knew he belonged in such a place. A confidence I wished I had. I hadn't grown up wealthy. During my childhood back in Boston, we'd lived in a one-bedroom apartment, barely surviving on Father's salary. The wealth that came from Father's marriage to Lady Montgomery had never felt like something that belonged to me. She provided for nicer dresses and proper schooling, but all the luxuries and niceties of our lives at Havenworth were things I merely experienced tangentially.

James ordered the steak. I found it much harder to decide between the poached fish in a lemon cream sauce or the herbed chicken with roasted potatoes, finally settling on the latter. I could barely remember the last time I'd eaten such rich food, and it took all my composure not to sigh aloud when the waiter set my plate in front of me.

I took a bite, savoring the flavor. But then a feeling of guilt came over me. "It seems so strange that restaurants can serve all of this while most people can't even buy bread and butter at the store."

James shrugged. "Perhaps. But few things are ever fair when there's a war on. And denying yourself pleasure will do nothing to change that. The government has already decided who wins and who loses in this war."

"What do you mean by that?"

He swallowed a bite of his steak. "I mean that it will be the governments who benefit and enrich themselves from the war, regardless of the outcome on the battlefields."

"Is that what they teach you at the RAF?"

He laughed. "Not at all. As military officers, we're taught to believe the world can be easily divided along simple lines of good and evil. Anything that benefits Britain is righteous and holy."

"That's exactly what my father and stepmother believe, too."

"But it's not what you believe."

I inhaled slowly, flattered to be asked my opinion. I'd never really given it much thought—at least not the kind of deep, sophisticated type of thought such a matter required. My notions of the war had emanated entirely from how it had impacted my life. It was rather selfish and immature, I realized now as I sat across from James. "No, I suppose it's not. I believe that good and evil exist inside of all of us. Rarely are our intentions ever truly pure, but even if they were, the outcomes never are. There is a cost to every decision, every choice. Even if this war is justified, there will be lives lost and families torn apart on all sides. How can anyone think that is a good thing? What is the point of this war if we are giving up all the things we are supposedly fighting to protect?"

His face broke into a satisfied smile. "Everyone is so quick to assume Hitler is the great evil of the world. And yet Britain is rounding up and interning thousands of its own people, all for the crime of having German heritage."

"That can't be true," I said, shocked at the assertion.

"But it is. The Isle of Man has been converted into a concentration camp. There are others popping up all over the country, filled mostly with German and Italian aliens. Even Jewish refugees escaping the continent have found themselves behind the barbed-wire fences."

"Why would our country do that? What harm could any of them possibly be causing?"

He tilted his head and looked at me like my question surprised him. "Most people are quite willing to sacrifice their morals in the face of hardships. We're all supposed to pretend that the war effort will unify us in our patriotism, when the truth is the wealthy look after themselves and average citizens are the ones making all the sacrifices."

The thought of innocent people forced into camps because of their heritage was almost too horrible to contemplate. "It's not right."

"Your naivete is quite refreshing."

I couldn't tell whether he was joking, so I kept my mouth shut, hoping the rush of embarrassment in my cheeks wasn't visible to him.

"The truth is, Germany's fascist government has given them every advantage over Great Britain. They've solved the problems of unemployment and increased their infrastructure and military capacity. It was a mistake for us to go to war with them when we're doomed for failure, but it's not the politicians who will pay for that decision." He shook his head. "I've been talking far too much. I apologize if I've been rude."

"No, it's fine," I said eagerly, not wanting him to think I wasn't capable of such sophisticated conversation. "It's important to care about the world around us."

He reached across the table and placed his hand over mine. "I've never met anyone like you, Irene. You notice things other people overlook. There are so many fools who walk blindly through life, never questioning anything."

I beamed at the compliment, even as I doubted its accuracy. What did I know of the world? I was stuck in Havenworth with no experience, no future. Would James still like me if he discovered how sheltered and naive I really was?

After lunch, we strolled along the streets hand in hand. He no longer needed his crutches, but his gait was undeniably changed by his injury. Some men might have been embarrassed by it, but James held his head high, seemingly unperturbed by his limp. His confidence made me only more attracted to him.

"I hope you don't think it's too forward, but there's something I wanted to give you," he said before we parted ways at the train station. He pulled a small thin box from his coat pocket.

My heart leaped with excitement. The green tin and gold lettering were instantly familiar, even though I hadn't seen them in months. "Faber-Castell coloring pencils?"

"You said they were your favorite."

"Thank you!" Gratitude overwhelmed me, and before I could stop myself, I threw my arms around his neck and kissed him. It was a fleeting gesture, but in that moment it felt monumental.

I pulled back quickly, my face flushing with embarrassment at my impropriety. But James held me close and smiled, as if nothing could have been more natural. "Talent like yours deserves the finest tools," he said softly. "It shouldn't be held back by anything less."

His words were everything I had longed to hear. It wasn't until much later that I found myself wondering how he had managed to acquire such an extraordinary gift in the first place.

Chapter Nine

Irene

July 11, 1940

James didn't have leave again for another four weeks. In the absence of physical connection, writing letters became our way of keeping in touch. He wrote to me of his daily life on base, never providing more than the vaguest details of his activities, lest the censors take issue and confiscate his letters altogether. But I could read beyond his words, scrubbed free from any true substance or insight, that he was worried about something. He'd hinted that the missions were increasing in frequency and, subsequently, danger.

There was no such excitement on my part to convey. My days blended together like clouds drifting in all directions. The only thing of significance was Margaret's worsening health. Her cough grew fiercer with each passing night, and though I tried to hide my worry, knowing it would only upset her, I couldn't help but fret. It was as though her once-vivacious spark had burned out. The doctor had given her a course of sulfonamide, which Lady Montgomery assured us would cure my sister soon enough, but so far it wasn't working. Of course, this was not the kind of news I wanted to share with James.

The written word was never my strength, and I'd never had anyone to correspond with before. So I sent James drawings along with my meager updates. Astrantia for courage. Eucalyptus for protection. Camellia for longing and desire—not that I was so bold as to reveal those meanings. But James had no hesitation expressing his affection.

> My dearest Irene,
> I have done little but dream of you since we last met.
> You are the light that guides me when the nights are
> dark and grey . . .

I kept each letter hidden inside my sketchbook, tucked beneath my mattress so I would have him close to me every night. I had never felt so strongly about anyone before. James and I were meant to be together—even the war wouldn't keep us apart forever.

On one particularly sunny morning, I made my way outside before breakfast, wanting to check on the newly planted rose I'd grown from a cutting of our established Baronne Prévost to make sure it wasn't drying out. Paul took great care of the gardens, but he had been without help this season since his sons had all enlisted. I filled a metal watering can from the outdoor spigot and carried it to the parterre, where I watered the thirsty young shrub. Almost immediately, the leaves seemed to uncurl and the pink blooms smiled up at me.

I sat down on the dry grass and pulled out the coloring pencils James had given me. The rich colors filled me with excitement as my hand swept over the page of my sketchbook. I lost myself in fantasies of James. The memory of his lips against mine had taken hold, consuming my thoughts and shocking me with its intensity. I imagined what it would be like to kiss him again—a real kiss this time instead of the brief peck I'd given him. What would it feel like to run my fingers through his hair while his mouth trailed along my skin?

"Why are you so happy?" Margaret asked me, casting a shadow over my sketchbook.

I set my pencil down and looked up at her. "Who says I'm happy?"

"You've been humming to yourself all week. It's quite annoying."

I laughed.

She threw her hands up in the air. "See? Even when I say things like that, you don't get mad at me like you usually do. You're happy." She spit the last word out like an accusation.

I tried my best to keep my expression serious, but it was impossible when she was so exasperated. "What's wrong with being happy? Would you rather I moped about the house like a wounded dog?"

"I don't want you to leave," she said sullenly.

"Margaret," I said slowly. "What are you talking about?"

"I overheard Mummy saying you want to go to school in America. That's why you're so happy, isn't it? Because you're going to leave."

I sighed and opened my arms wide. She wasted no time burrowing into them. "I'm not going anywhere. Father won't let me."

The tension eased from her tiny shoulders.

"Good. I would miss you terribly."

I stroked her wild curls. "I would miss you, too." She'd grown thinner over the few weeks from her illness. The knobs of her spine poked through the fabric of her dress as I ran my hand along her back.

"I never want you to leave."

"One day I'm going to have to grow up and experience life for myself. When you're older you'll understand that, too. But I won't leave without telling you."

"Promise?"

"Of course I promise."

She gave a gratified smile. "Good. Who else will play cat and mouse with us?"

"I can't right now. I need to finish this drawing." An involuntary smile tugged at my lips. Margaret's eyes narrowed, but I didn't offer an explanation.

I picked up my pencil once more, admiring the vibrancy of the hue. The colors blended so seamlessly I'd almost forgotten how much of a difference it made.

"Can I draw with you?" Margaret asked. She sank onto the picnic blanket next to me and reached for my case.

"No!" I batted her hand away before I could think better of it. She recoiled, clutching her hand to her chest. "I'm sorry. I didn't mean to do that. It's just . . . these coloring pencils are special. I'll get you my old ones to use."

I pulled the other tin from my bag, but Margaret wouldn't take them, her interest still fixed on the long, unbroken coloring pencils in my possession. "How did you get new ones? Daddy said we weren't allowed to ask for presents until our birthdays."

"Father didn't give them to me. A friend did."

"But you don't have any friends."

"That's not true. I have you. And now I have James." I tried not to grin ridiculously when I spoke his name, but my cheeks seemed to have a mind of their own.

"Who's James?"

"Michael's friend from dinner last month. Do you remember him? He's a pilot with the RAF."

She crossed her arms and stuck her chin out. "I don't remember him. He sounds boring."

I laughed. "Maybe to someone who spends her days inventing fairy tales and adventures like you, but I found him quite charming and refined."

She feigned retching, which made me laugh only more. "Why would anyone care about being charming? I want to be as wild as I can be."

"One day when you're all grown up, you will understand why these things matter, I promise you."

"Never!"

Whether she meant she would never understand or simply never grow up, I wasn't sure. But Lady Montgomery descended into the back gardens in a flurry of energy, calling for me.

"Irene! There you are," she said in a rush of breath. "The local orphanage is seeking donations of clothing due to the shortages in fabric. I was wondering if we could give them your old dresses?"

"All my dresses still fit me." Long before the war, Lady Montgomery had been in the habit of having us all donate anything that no longer fit to charitable causes.

"Yes, but with the changing fashions, it would be uncouth to wear such large, voluminous skirts. Think of all that wasted material that could be repurposed into two or even three new dresses for the children."

"Just because it doesn't follow government-regulated hemlines doesn't mean it's not fashionable. Besides, I like my clothing and I don't want to give any of it away."

"Would you at least consider it? I know it's difficult to do without, but we all have to do our part. We're donating all the old frocks Margaret's grown out of and a handful of my own as well."

I sighed, knowing I was being recalcitrant simply because it was my stepmother making the request. "Fine. I'll have a look in my wardrobe and see if there is anything I can spare."

I began to gather up my things, not wanting her to notice my new pencils. But of course my stepmother was always too observant of my every move, waiting for an excuse to criticize me. She picked up the pencil tin before I could hide it from her sight. "Where did you get these?"

I snatched the tin back. "It's none of your business."

"James gave them to her," Margaret said tauntingly. "He's her new friend."

"Shush," I scolded.

"Margaret, go find Charlie and tell him it's time to wash up for lunch," Lady Montgomery said.

"But—"

"Listen to your mother," I said in a rare moment of agreement with my stepmother.

Margaret threw her arms out in a huff and flounced off toward the house. Lady Montgomery and I waited in stony silence until Margaret was out of earshot.

Finally, when my half sister disappeared into Havenworth, Lady Montgomery turned her gaze back to the tin I gripped in my hands like a rosary. "Anyone who gives you German contraband is not a friend."

I rolled my eyes. "These are coloring pencils, not weapons."

"That's not the point. If your father were to find out—"

"No, please," I pleaded. "Don't tell him. He'll only make me throw them away, and what good will that do? The pencils already exist. It's wasteful to destroy something perfectly functional when there is so much scarcity."

She crossed her arms, pressing her lips so tightly together they nearly disappeared. I'd made a reasonable point, but she wasn't convinced.

"I'll give you my gray dress," I said quickly. "For the orphanage."

I loved the frock and its elegant wool fabric, but it was too warm for the summertime and surely this war would be over by the winter and I would be able to replace it soon enough.

"That's very generous of you. You can keep the coloring pencils, but please be smart about who you are associating with. Not everyone has your best interests at heart."

"Not everyone is evil either."

"I'm not trying to hurt your feelings. I care about you, Irene. I wish you could see that."

I wish you could show it, I thought unmercifully. "It's just a set of coloring pencils."

She sighed, all her disappointment in me gusting out like a windstorm.

The rumble of a motorcar's engine interrupted whatever chastisement was about to come. It was an unusual sound these days, with petrol rationing severely limiting travel. I followed Lady Montgomery to the front of Havenworth to see who the visitor was. The black vehicle was unfamiliar to me, moving quickly and spitting gravel as it pulled up the driveway before grinding to an abrupt halt.

Father stepped out of the passenger side. I knew instantly from the look on his face that something was terribly wrong.

"John? What are you doing home?" Lady Montgomery asked, rushing to him.

My father took her hands in his, those solemn eyes even more grave. "It's your nephew. Michael."

My stepmother's anguished cry cut through my chest, filling me with dread.

"His plane was shot down over the English Channel."

"Is . . . there a chance he's alive?" Lady Montgomery asked.

I knew before Father shook his head that any hope was misplaced. No one could survive the crashing waves and bitter cold of the wild seas.

A searing pain gripped my stomach, sharp and unfamiliar. The war that had seemed so far away, so abstract, had suddenly become all too real.

The next morning we drove to Edward and Gwen Howell's house, Father driving with Lady Montgomery in the passenger seat next to him, and Margaret, Charlie, and me mashed together in the back. It was strange being inside a car again after ten months of petrol rationing. It should have felt like a brief return to normalcy, but there was nothing joyful about this. The car was stifling hot, and my stepmother's shoulders heaved from her quiet sobs.

I felt awful for the pain she was in. I knew too well what it was like to lose someone. It was a pain I wouldn't wish on anyone. Michael and I weren't close, but he didn't deserve to die. And what was it all for? A war that Britain had no business taking part in.

Margaret rested her head on my shoulder as we drove, more stoic than I'd ever seen her. Charlie, too, silently hid his emotions, but I could sense the fear in his eyes. He was too young to understand any of this.

Edward and Gwen lived in a gated redbrick home on a posh, quiet street not far from the university. It wasn't anywhere near as large or stately as Havenworth, but few homes were. Still, my stepmother's cousin was a wealthy woman—not that wealth meant anything when it came to keeping one's family safe in these times.

I linked my fingers with Margaret's and Charlie's as we walked up the path to the front door, giving them each gentle, reassuring squeezes.

Edward, Gwen, Deborah, and Pamela were all seated in the parlor when we arrived, their heads bowed, too upset to greet us properly. The lights were dimmed, casting a somber tone over the room.

Lady Montgomery sat next to her cousin, putting an arm around her. "I'm so sorry, Gwennie. Michael was such a special boy."

"Is," Gwen corrected fiercely, refusing to look up from her tightly interlaced fingers at her lap. "He is a special boy. He is resourceful and strong, and he will come home to us soon."

Lady Montgomery and my father exchanged a glance.

"Stop it, Mother. Of course he's dead," Deborah spit out. "He was gunned down by a Messerschmitt over the North Sea. No one can survive that. We owe it to him to begin planning a funeral."

"There is no way for anyone to know for sure," Father said diplomatically. "But the RAF would not deliver a condolence telegram if they weren't fairly certain."

"You expect me to trust the RAF?" Edward countered. "They've been incompetent from the moment this war began. We've been sending those boys out to slaughter without any real form of protection. How many need to die before you finally share your bloody inventions with the rest of the committee?"

"Edward!" Gwen said, aghast. Deborah and Pamela began to cry loudly.

I pressed my hand to my mouth, shocked by Edward's accusation. I knew he and Father had been at odds, but Father was an honorable man who would never withhold his work without reason.

"It's true. For months, John's refused to share any of his work with the rest of the committee."

"Someone's been passing confidential information to Churchill before they're ready for the public," Father said, an accusatory note in his otherwise calm voice. "Our work is too important to risk any more leaks."

Edward's face turned a shade of puce. "You think I'm the one leaking information?"

The shouting and arguing were too much to bear. "Please stop fighting. It's not what Michael would have wanted."

"How do you know what Michael would have wanted?" Deborah said, her glare sharp enough to feel like a slap. "What are you even doing here? You're not part of this family."

My throat went dry. I knew I wasn't wanted here, but hearing it so plainly stung. I managed a polite smile. "If you'll excuse me, I think I'll take a walk." Keeping my composure, I reached for Charlie's and Margaret's hands, guiding them gently away. Whatever pain was being laid bare in that room didn't need young hearts to bear witness.

The bright, warm sun instantly calmed me as we stepped outside. I let out a deep exhalation. The children, however, seemed distressed, refusing to let go of my hands.

"Go on," I said to Margaret, gesturing to a spindly birch tree in the yard. "I won't be upset if you want to climb it."

She shook her head, too upset to consider her normal adventures.

I glanced around the garden for something that would lift their spirits. "Look over there. There's a tiny snail trying to crawl up the railing." I pointed to the iron railing where the little creature had fastened itself.

Charlie was the first to perk up. Margaret did, too, when the boy jogged over to inspect it.

I watched them play for the next half hour, giving my father and Lady Montgomery time inside. The iron gate creaked behind me, and I turned to see who it was.

My heart stuttered when I saw the navy uniform and dark, wavy hair. "James!"

I ran to him and threw myself into his arms, oblivious to whatever the children might think. He squeezed me tight against his chest. "I missed you."

"I missed you, too," I said, tilting my head to look at him. "But what are you doing here?"

"The RAF granted me an afternoon's leave to pay my respects to Michael's family."

"I'm so sorry. This must be incredibly difficult for you."

He swallowed hard, emotions seeming to battle beneath his calm surface.

"I should warn you, they're quite distraught. Edward even lost his temper and lashed out at Father. He practically accused him of being responsible for Michael's death."

"Edward has every right to be angry. Our pilots are sitting ducks up in the skies as soon as night falls, unable to see the enemy planes until it's too late." He shook his head in frustration. "But why would he blame your father?"

"My father is working on something—a device that could turn the tide of the war. But for now he's keeping it under lock and key."

James's brow furrowed. "He must have his reasons. Still, it's hard not to wonder. Is it something that could save lives? Ease the burden for the men risking everything up there?"

I hesitated, feeling the weight of his gaze, but I couldn't answer. "I . . . I'm not supposed to say anything."

"I understand, truly. But I can't help wondering how much more we might be able to do if there's something out there that could help. Just knowing someone's working on it would mean so much."

I twisted my hands together, squeezing until my knuckles turned white. I couldn't say anything about Father's work. I wasn't supposed to know anything. "I'm sorry. I can't."

His expression softened into something that looked like disappointment mingled with sadness. "I didn't mean to pressure you, Irene. I just . . . it's difficult sometimes, being out there and feeling so powerless." He sighed, turning slightly away. "Forget I asked. I shouldn't have put you in that position."

"Wait," I blurted, catching his arm. "It's called a cavity magnetron."

He stopped, his curiosity clearly piqued. "A cavity magnetron? What's that?"

"I don't know what it is exactly. It's supposed to allow the planes to have their own radar while flying."

"That's remarkable," he said, his voice laced with admiration. "Is that even possible?"

"If my father says it is, I wouldn't doubt it. You won't tell anyone about it, will you?"

He cupped my cheek. "Of course not. I promise this will stay only between you and me."

I smiled, grateful I had found the one person I could trust in a world that felt increasingly uncertain.

Chapter Ten

Julia

Present Day

"I hope you don't mind spaghetti and tomato sauce for dinner," Helen said, unpacking the rest of her groceries on the kitchen counter. "I'm not much of a cook." She looked a little embarrassed by the admission.

"Neither am I. Ever since Sam came to live with me, he's had to put up with peanut butter sandwiches for dinner every night." My job required so much travel, it was easier to rely on takeout for most of my meals. My last boyfriend had wooed me with wonderful home-cooked meals, but he'd never wanted kids and broken up with me the moment Sam entered my life.

Sam was sitting at the kitchen table, practicing with the set of jacks Margaret had given him, oblivious to our conversation.

Helen frowned. "He didn't live with you before?"

I winced, wondering how much to share. Helen's friendliness was disarming, but I'd only just met her. "He's my nephew. I became his legal guardian after my sister passed away."

"Oh. I'm so sorry to hear that."

"Hopefully you don't mind if he doesn't eat much," I said, eager to change the subject away from painful memories of my sister. "Sam doesn't do well with new foods. Although Andrew got him eating wheat bread and jam this morning, so maybe there's hope."

"Andrew has that effect on kids."

"I got the impression he didn't really appreciate Sam being here," I said, wondering whether Helen would react the same way.

She cocked her head with a wry smile. "Let me guess. He did his whole stern-and-serious routine with you?"

"You could say that."

She laughed. "Don't let him fool you. He's an absolute softie beneath all that gruffness. But kids are a bit of a sore spot for him. His last girlfriend had a teenage son that Andrew adored. She was a fellow doctor at the hospital where Andrew works. They dated for almost four years, but she ended things a few months ago when she accepted a new job in Australia, and he hasn't seen the boy since. I think that broke his heart worse than losing Amy."

"That's awful." No wonder he had reacted so strangely. I couldn't imagine Sam being suddenly ripped out of my life like that.

"The emergency department's been short-staffed since Amy left, and it's fallen to Andrew to cover her shifts until they can find a replacement. All this business with the gardens has been stressful, too. I think it's hurt his feelings that Margaret won't tell him why she's so set on fixing up the gardens now."

"It is odd. Most people I've worked with have really clear reasons for wanting a restoration."

"Margaret's not like most people. Fill that for me, will you?" She pointed to a pot she had just retrieved from the cupboard.

I filled the pot at the sink, then set it over the element. I fumbled with the stove's igniter, releasing a little too much gas before the spark took hold in a large burst that nearly singed my sleeves. I quickly adjusted the knob to lower the flame. At Helen's instruction, I added salt to the water and put the lid on the pot while she finished with the groceries. The last item she retrieved from her paper bag was a bottle of cabernet sauvignon.

"Fancy a glass?"

"Yes, please."

She uncorked the bottle and poured a generous amount into two long-stemmed glasses. "I can't tell you how much I needed this after the week I've had."

The wine was bold and spicy, coating my tongue with its velvety flavor. "You're an accountant, right?"

"A good, responsible job for a good, responsible girl." She sighed and took a hefty sip of the wine.

"You don't sound very convinced."

She laughed once more. "I like it well enough. Or, at least, I like the salary. But it sucks the soul out of me sometimes. There's a reason no kid Sam's age ever says they want to grow up to be an accountant."

"Not all jobs can be passion projects."

"Is yours?"

"Yes. It's the only thing I've ever wanted to do. But that doesn't mean it's always easy. There are parts of it that are hard and tedious."

"I can only imagine you've got your hands quite full with Havenworth. I don't think anyone's given the gardens any attention for decades." She set her wineglass down and peeked inside the pot, which was only just starting to boil.

"I'm used to working on large gardens. The challenge is not having a clear sense of what Margaret wants. She can't remember much about what they used to look like. Did she ever talk to you about that time in her life?"

Helen dumped a bag of spaghetti into the pot. "Sorry. Margaret never talks much about her past."

"Andrew mentioned Margaret is your godmother. Does that mean you grew up at Havenworth?"

She shook her head. "We grew up in Cambridge, but my grandpa Charlie was sent here during the war. He lived with Margaret's family for almost six years. He and Margaret were very close and remained friends for the rest of their lives even though they came from such different backgrounds. Our parents weren't particularly wealthy, but Margaret made sure we always had new clothes and that we were able to attend the best schools. Now that she's getting on in years, Andrew insisted on moving in to help her manage the household. I told him I could do it, but he doesn't trust me. As though I can't pay the gas bill or call a repairman. Anyway, Andrew works so much that he's got no choice but to rely on me to help. So if there's anything you need, just let me know. I can be around whenever you need me."

"Actually, there is something you could help me with," I said.

She raised a curious eyebrow. "What's that?"

"What I mostly need help with is uncovering the past. Old photographs of Havenworth or diaries written by Margaret's relatives. Anything that speaks to the history of the place."

"You want to go snooping." She said it with more excitement than accusation, confirming my instincts. In every project, the key was finding the one person who was eager to help, and Helen seemed more than up to the task.

I nodded. "Margaret said you might be willing to help me."

She polished off the last of her wine. "Let's go to the library after dinner. I know exactly where to start."

"I think they're in here," Helen said, leading me into a room on the second story not far from where Sam and I were staying. He had settled to bed easily after dinner, despite not eating much.

A wave of dust assaulted my nose as soon as I stepped inside. It looked like no one had been in this room in years. There was a single bed in the far corner of the room and a small dresser, but the room had clearly been used as a storage space in recent years, with dozens of Bankers Boxes stacked on top of each other along the floor.

"What's in all of these?"

"I'm not sure," Helen replied. "Mostly Margaret's work papers, I expect. The photo albums should be up here."

She opened the wardrobe and pulled out a stack of albums from the top shelf and set them on the bed. I sat down and opened the top one. A color photo of a young girl with unruly dark curls and the most mischievous smile I had ever seen. It was unmistakably Margaret.

Helen and I pored over the albums, which didn't seem to be organized in any discernible way, each one providing another peek into Margaret's storied life. Her graduation from Cambridge. The many awards she had received for her work and charitable efforts. Even snapshots of her with her parents. But not a single picture of the grounds.

"Oh, look," Helen said excitedly. "It's one of Andrew and me."

She angled the album to show me the grainy photo of her as a toddler and teenage Andrew standing stiffly with his hand on her shoulder. "He looks so serious," I said.

"He's always been that way. Too serious for his own good and always acting like the entire weight of the world rests on his shoulders." She laughed as she said it, but the undercurrent of bitterness was unmistakable.

"I can imagine it's quite stressful taking care of an estate of this size on top of his work as a doctor."

"He doesn't have to do it all alone, but he doesn't trust me or anyone else to help. I'm surprised he didn't attempt to take on the garden renovations himself, to be honest. I guess that's just big brothers for you, though."

I pulled out another album from the pile and flipped open the soft burgundy cover. The black-and-white image of a little girl with huge brown eyes and wild curls standing next to a serious-looking man with dark hair and wire-framed glasses, and a thin woman with a birdlike face, set off a spark of excitement in my belly. These photographs were older than anything we'd seen so far. "Do you think this could be Margaret?" I asked, showing Helen my discovery.

"Ooh, that could be. What's on the back?"

With painstaking care, I peeled back the plastic layer and lifted the photograph. *Margaret, John, and Mary Clarke, 1937.*

"She would have been just four years old there," Helen said. "She was born in 1933. And those are her parents: John Clarke and Lady Montgomery."

Margaret's resemblance to her parents was uncanny. Her dark hair and stocky build were so like those of the man next to her, but the pointed chin and pert nose were from her mother. Lady Montgomery wasn't beautiful in a typical sense, but she was striking, with pronounced cheekbones and fair skin.

I replaced the photograph and flipped to the next page. Unlike the other albums, which were stuffed with photos, this one was noticeably sparse. A single image at most adorned the pages, and some had none at all. All the photographs were of Margaret and her parents. A few included Helen's grandfather Charlie. Nearly all of the photos were taken indoors, with a few pictures of them on vacation at various beaches and landmarks.

"There are photographs missing from the album," I said, flipping to another page, where a brighter square of blue stood out against the faded backing. "Someone's removed them."

Helen frowned. "How odd. Why would anyone want to get rid of their own history like that?"

"Do you think we can ask Margaret about it?"

"I suppose we can try. She doesn't like to talk about her past much, though. Especially the war."

"I've noticed that."

"I think it's true for their entire generation. My granddad was the same. We knew he was sent to live here as a child to escape the bombing in London, but he would never talk about it. Andrew told me I wasn't to ask him because it made him sad. But I never understood it. He and Margaret remained friends their entire lives, and after his dad and siblings died in the war, Margaret's parents supported him and my great-grandmother. Andrew said it was a traumatic experience for him, being ripped away from his parents at such a young age like that, no matter how well he was treated by Margaret's family.

"The thing is," Helen continued, "it makes sense that my grandfather was so hesitant to talk about his past after all the loss he experienced. But why Margaret? Her father was a scientist at Cambridge University. By all accounts their life wasn't upended quite as much as so many others, who didn't have as much wealth or privilege."

"Maybe it was the bombing," I said.

Her eyebrows scrunched together in confusion. "What bomb?"

"Margaret told me that a bomb fell on the far end of the garden. It's why that part of the wall was replaced. They had to move to a country home for the rest of the war."

"She never told me that." She looked down at her hands, seeming hurt that I'd known something she didn't.

We flipped through the rest of the album in silence, searching for more clues of what the estate had been like in the past. I suspected Helen was searching for something entirely different from what I was, but, regardless, there were no photographs of the gardens.

"I'm sorry," Helen said, closing the final album. "I was sure we would find something."

I looked around the dusty space. How could a home this old have so few memories of its past? Surely there must be some ghosts still lingering. I stood up, needing to settle my restless energy. "Do you mind if I look around some more?"

Helen shrugged. "Suit yourself. Don't know if you'll find anything other than dust mites and lab notes."

I opened the vanity drawers and peeked inside the boxes. Helen was right. There was nothing here. On a last, desperate whim, I looked under the bed. The floor was empty save for the decades' worth of dust bunnies. But there was something tucked beneath the mattress, against the metal frame. "Helen, get up," I said excitedly.

"What is it?"

I lifted the thin mattress. "This." A thick hardcover book the color of a robin's egg was hidden beneath.

"Maybe it's someone's diary," Helen said excitedly. "Open it."

The spine creaked ominously. The pages inside were shockingly delicate and crumpled from age, but I was greeted with the most incredible sketch of a daffodil, the details meticulously captured in the sharp lines and gentle shading. Below, details about the flower were written in precise cursive.

Narcissus.

Blooms February through April.

Meaning: Unrequited love.

The sketch itself was dated March 12, 1937. Havenworth Manor. I carefully paged through the rest of the book. It was filled with botanical sketches—some of single flowers, some collections of plants, and, more importantly, some landscape sketches of the gardens.

"What is it?" Helen asked over my shoulder.

"A florilegium," I said, my voice rising with excitement.

"Come again?"

"It's a collection of drawings of flowers," I explained, turning the pages carefully. "It was a way of recording all the plants in a garden."

I studied the detailed illustrations, feeling a growing sense of wonder. This wasn't just a keepsake; it was a record of Havenworth's gardens in their prime—a blueprint for bringing them back to life.

"I wonder who made these," I whispered, still entranced by the incredible details.

"I doubt it was Margaret," Helen said. "She's the only person I know who could walk by a Van Gogh and not even turn her head for a second look."

"Do you know who lived in this room?"

"It's been a storage room for as far as I remember, but I think my grandfather stayed here during the war. He didn't have an ounce of artistic ability, though. Maybe it belonged to one of the other evacuees."

"The dates don't line up. This was done in 1937. See?" I angled the florilegium in her direction. A photograph slipped out from between the pages, landing in my lap. Inside the yellowed edges of the square frame was an image of two girls with their arms wrapped around each other. The young one was clearly Margaret, staring up at the other with unabashed reverence. The other girl was at least a decade older, with long blond hair and a dazzling smile.

"She's beautiful," Helen said.

"Do you know who she is?"

She shook her head. "No, but they must have been close."

"A nanny, maybe?" Even as I said it, it didn't feel right. The affection between the pair was too uninhibited. "Why would it be folded up like that?"

"Who knows? Maybe they meant to throw it out."

The sound of footsteps echoed in the hall.

"That must be Andrew," Helen said. "He was supposed to be home hours ago."

He appeared in the doorway a moment later. "What are you two doing in here?"

It would have been easy to assume he was annoyed by the tone of his voice, but his face told an entirely different story. There were deep purple bags under his eyes and a sag in his shoulders. He was exhausted.

Helen walked over to him with the bent photograph. "That's Margaret as a little girl, right? Do you recognize who the other one is?"

He took the photograph from her and studied it closely. "I haven't a clue. Where did you find it?"

"We were searching the old photo albums for pictures of the gardens," I said. "I thought that would be easier on Margaret than trying to get her to remember the details."

He nodded. Was that a sign of approval? His reactions were so guarded, it was almost impossible to read into them.

"We found a florilegium under the bed, too," I added. "It's full of sketches of the garden. This photo was inside it."

"We should ask Margaret if she recognizes the girl in the photo," Helen said.

"I don't think that's a good idea," Andrew replied.

"But look how happy she is," Helen pleaded. "I bet she would love to remember whoever this is."

"All right," he said with a sigh. "Let's go see what she has to say."

Margaret was sitting in the orangery reading when we came in. She raised a finger without looking up, indicating she was determined to finish her page before brooking any interruptions. Finally, she set her book face down on the quilt draped across her lap. "Why do I have the feeling that the three of you coming in here together means you've been up to no good?"

"Because you're so accustomed to stirring up trouble yourself that you assume the rest of us are, too," Andrew said teasingly.

She chuckled. "All grown up and you still haven't lost one ounce of that cheekiness. If not for trouble, then what are you here for?"

"I was showing Julia the old photo albums in the storage room, and we found this picture of you," Helen said, handing the photo to her godmother. "It was inside a sketchbook with a bunch of drawings of flowers."

Margaret gasped, the memory clearly a shock.

Andrew rushed to her side and squeezed her hand. "Margaret? Are you all right?"

She nodded.

"You recognize her," I said gently.

"Yes."

"Who is she? Was the florilegium hers? Whoever created it clearly loved the gardens."

Margaret swallowed, still visibly shaken. "Irene. My half sister."

Helen's gaze whipped to Andrew. A silent exchange passed between them.

With his lips pressed into a grim line, Andrew crouched down next to Margaret. "What happened to her? How come you never told us you had a half sister?"

She stroked a trembling finger along Irene's image. "We weren't supposed to talk about her. That's why Mummy made us throw out all the photographs of her."

"Why would you throw away her photographs?" Andrew prodded gently.

Margaret was silent for a long time before finally speaking. "Because she was a traitor. She betrayed our family by spying for the Nazis during the war. She ran off to Germany during the Blitz, and I never saw her again."

I froze, stunned by the weight of Margaret's revelation. I had pressed her for answers—it was the only way to do the job Margaret had hired me for—but I never expected to unearth something this devastating. The shock on Andrew's and Helen's faces sent a ripple of guilt through me. I wished I could spare all of them the hurt this secret had caused. But I'd known from the moment I walked through the front door that Havenworth was a place filled with long-buried stories. If I was going to see this restoration through, I had no doubt more secrets would come to light.

Chapter Eleven

Irene

August 17, 1940

The dry heat carried through the summer at Havenworth, but the mood remained as dour as it had been on the day of Michael's funeral. Father threw himself even deeper into his work, while Lady Montgomery traipsed about like a ghost with red-rimmed eyes. But the worst was Margaret. My spirited younger sister no longer ran wild through the grounds on adventures concocted by her boundless imagination. She was consumed by real fears.

Her cough had returned, too.

I tried not to worry, since the one thing I knew for certain about my stepmother was that she would ensure Margaret received the best possible care, but it was difficult to ignore her wheezing and the way her clothes hung loose on her skinny shoulders.

The gardens had suffered, too. Half the parterre had already been destroyed by the Land Army, replaced with square vegetable patches. I'd been working to save what I could of the irreplaceable peonies and irises and other precious species being ripped out, but it was too much for one person. What was left of the flower gardens required daily irrigation.

Lately, I'd been spending the mornings helping Paul with the tedious task, transporting watering cans all over the gardens.

Today was no different. I no longer had to manage Charlie and Margaret's schooling, since Lady Montgomery insisted they would return to their former selves with a summer break, so laboring alongside Paul was the best way to calm my nerves and pass the time until the afternoon, when James was coming to pick me up. He had made arrangements to borrow a car so that we could go on a proper date. We were set to visit the Cambridge University Botanical Gardens followed by a trip to the cinema.

I'd just finished putting away the watering cans in the greenhouse when I saw the Land Army girls sauntering down the path toward Havenworth in their green sweaters, laughing about something I couldn't make out. They kept to themselves for the most part, but they'd been around long enough that I knew their schedule. It must be nearing five o'clock in the evening if they were done with their shift.

James was meant to pick me up at six. I cursed myself for losing track of time. I still needed to bathe and pick out an outfit and do a million other things before he arrived.

I had just finished the quickest bath of my life when I found Margaret sitting on top of the blue frock I had laid out on my bed.

"Be careful with that," I said sternly. "I don't want the skirt to wrinkle."

She scooted over but crossed her arms so I would know she didn't appreciate it. "Why do you care if it's wrinkled? It's not like anyone here is looking at your clothes."

"Because I'm not wearing it for anyone here. I'm going on a date."

Her eyes narrowed suspiciously. "With James?"

I sat down at my vanity and ran a brush through my hair. "Yes. With James."

She harrumphed, an exaggerated sound that might have been comical had there not been such purple shadows beneath her eyes. "I don't like him."

"You don't know him."

"I don't want to know him."

"Then it's a good thing you aren't the one going on a date with him." I opened the glass jar of perfume I'd made by infusing vodka from Father's liquor cabinet with crushed rose petals from the garden, and dabbed a light amount against my wrists. In the absence of real perfume, I'd come to prefer my homemade concoction. The smell, so pure and fresh, reminded me of my mother.

"Where's he taking you?"

"To the cinema." I didn't know what film was playing, but I hoped it would be a comedy. I wanted to laugh and be entertained.

Margaret opened her mouth to say something, but only a cough came out. Within seconds, she was overtaken by a fit of coughing that turned her cheeks bright red.

I ran to her. "Are you all right?"

She nodded when the fit finally subsided. "I'm fine," she insisted with no small amount of annoyance.

I pressed my hand to her forehead. She didn't feel clammy or particularly hot.

"I'd like to go to the cinema one day. Will you tell me what it's like?"

"Of course I will. But you'll get to go when you're old enough."

She feigned a retch, showing signs of the vibrant girl she used to be. "I don't want to go on a date."

"You don't ever have to go on a date if you don't want to. I'll take you one day."

"You will?"

I put my arm around her narrow shoulders. "There is nothing I wouldn't do for you. You must know that."

She nodded solemnly. "Fine. Then I suppose you can go with James tonight so you can be prepared for when you take me."

"How generous of you," I teased before shooing her out of my room so I could change in peace.

By some miracle, I managed to have myself completely coiffed and ready with minutes to spare. I decided to wait outside, knowing the sight of James might dredge up painful memories of Michael for Lady Montgomery.

Nearly half an hour passed before I began to worry something had gone wrong. I popped inside briefly and asked Annie whether anyone had called, then returned to the stoop. Surely James hadn't forgotten about me? But when another hour passed with no sign of him, and then another, I had no choice but to admit the truth.

James wasn't coming.

◆ ◆ ◆

Margaret was in my room when I woke the next morning, sitting on the edge of my bed in her pale-white nightgown.

I perched up on one elbow and rubbed my eyes. "What are you doing? It's barely six o'clock."

She had always been an early riser—springing from her bed with too much energy for a single earthly being—but we had struck a truce years ago in which she would allow me to sleep until a reasonable hour and I, in turn, wouldn't tie her pigtails to her bedpost.

"I'm here to warn you," she said in an exaggerated whisper.

I moaned, in no mood for her wild beliefs and exaggerated stories. I'd slept terribly, unable to stop thoughts of James from creeping in every time I closed my eyes. Had he forgotten about me? Or had something even worse happened to keep him away? "About what?"

"Daddy's furious."

That knocked the sleepiness out of my body. I sat up straighter, staring at her intently. "Why?"

She shrugged. "I tried to hear what he and Mummy were saying, but Annie caught me listening through the door and sent me away. I think it's because of you."

"I'm sure it's nothing," I said, trying to convince myself as much as Margaret. "They're always mad at me for something."

I sent Margaret off so that I could get ready for the day, determined to be dressed up to face my inevitable dressing down. My appearance was my only armor, feeble as it was, so I selected my favorite blue shirtdress and brushed my hair into a neat chignon.

Father was in the dining room with Lady Montgomery when I came downstairs—an uncommon occurrence, even for a Sunday. But what truly set me on edge was the way he looked up from his newspaper to acknowledge me as I approached. It made me wonder whether Margaret had been right after all.

"Irene, have a seat," Father said impassively, setting his newspaper down.

"We've saved some of the strawberry preserves for you," Lady Montgomery said with a false cheeriness. "I know it's your favorite."

I glanced at the array of scones and preserves, more confused than ever. We hadn't had anything but simple toast and eggs for breakfast in months. Why would they have asked Ruth to cook something special this morning if I were in trouble?

Lady Montgomery smiled stiffly as I sat down and filled my plate. I eyed her curiously for a moment before asking, "How are you this morning, Father?"

"Tired," he said in his overly frank way.

"Is that because of your work?" I asked.

He exhaled heavily through his nose. "It's because of a phone call I received late last night from Edward Howell."

My stomach clenched, the bite of toast I'd just taken turning sour. "What phone call?"

He looked to Lady Montgomery, a secret conversation happening between them. Finally, Lady Montgomery nodded.

"James Atherton was arrested last night," Father said.

I dropped my fork, letting it clatter against the porcelain plate. "What?"

"His name was among those listed as belonging to a secret fascist sympathizer group. The military intelligence service subsequently raided his quarters and discovered he'd stolen classified information regarding the RAF's offensive operations."

My head spun as I tried to process Father's revelation. James couldn't be a fascist. There had to be some kind of mistake. "Is he okay?"

Father's lips hardened into a straight line. "He was released this morning. The charges were dropped, no doubt thanks to the influence of his family's connections."

I set my hands on the edge of the table and released a heavy breath. "Thank goodness."

"Irene," Father said with enough force to make me look up once more. "I don't think you understand the gravity of this situation. This boy you've been seeing is a Nazi sympathizer—"

"That's not true!" I shouted. Father shot me a look that made my blood chill. I forced myself to calm down and said, "James isn't a Nazi sympathizer. He's interested in ideas and debate and hearing all sides of the issues. There's nothing illegal about that. Besides, if the charges were dropped, then surely he isn't guilty of anything."

"There is no debate!" Father bellowed. "What is wrong with you that you do not understand this?"

I flinched, a rush of tears stinging my eyelids. "He was Michael's friend."

In desperation, I turned to Lady Montgomery for support. Instead, she offered only a pitying look. "People like James can be incredibly charming and convincing. We aren't blaming you for being ensnared by him. But think about the gifts and—"

"Don't," I said. "You promised you wouldn't say anything."

Her frown deepened. "I'm sorry, Irene. But I can't keep that promise in light of the circumstances. He gave you contraband German goods. No one acquires those kinds of items through legitimate means. You need to accept the facts in front of you. That boy may have been Michael's friend, but anyone can make an error in judgment. Even you. I'm afraid we have no choice but to forbid you from seeing James again."

"What? No! Please, Father. You can't do that."

Father shook his head. "It's for your own good. One day you'll understand."

I bit back the molten anger burning inside me, desperately clinging to my composure. But I couldn't accept Father's orders. "And if I refuse to listen?"

His eyes narrowed. "Then you will no longer be welcome in this home or this family again." The coldness in his voice was unlike anything I'd witnessed before. I knew without a doubt that he was serious. If I attempted to see James again, I would be disowned.

I excused myself from breakfast and locked myself in my room for the rest of the morning, finally letting the torrent of anger and frustration spill out with the tears I shed into my pillow. Father didn't come to check on me, but Lady Montgomery did. She knocked softly at first, then more forcefully when I didn't answer. "Irene, I know you're upset, but you must understand your father and I are only acting out of concern for you."

Her attempt at consolation made me want to scream. I buried my face in the pillow, damp from tears. Her desire to talk with me was clearly as feeble as my interest in listening, and the echo of her footsteps disappearing down the hall came moments later. Margaret turned out to be harder to ignore when she pounded on my door, complaining of boredom. It took over fifteen minutes for her to give up, and even then she returned a few times over the morning to try again, until Lady Montgomery rounded her and Charlie up for church.

I finally emerged from my bedroom when the house was empty. It was unusual that I found myself in such solitude at Havenworth. If I weren't so miserable over James, I might have appreciated it. Instead,

I only felt hollow. I didn't want to believe the accusations against him. James had only ever been good and kind and honorable. But there was a whisper of worry deep inside me. What if Father was right?

The telephone in the main floor hallway rang as I passed by on my way to the gardens. I considered letting it go unanswered. But the telephone rarely rang these days, and when it did, it was almost always for something direly important.

"Hello?"

"Irene? Thank god." James's voice came through the line. "I've been worried sick about you all night."

"My father told me you were arrested."

He exhaled heavily. "I'm so sorry you had to find out that way. I wanted to explain everything to you myself. It was all a terrible mistake."

"They said you had classified documents in your possession."

"I did, but not for any malicious reason. There's a perfectly good explanation."

I held my breath as I waited for him to continue.

"Since my release from the hospital, the RAF reassigned me to the operations team. My role was to maintain contact with the Observer Corps along the coast to warn of any incoming raids. It's not where I wanted to be. I wanted to be back in the air, doing my duty, but they refused to clear me for that. Every night I watched as we sent our men out on increasingly dangerous missions, knowing we're completely outmatched. Michael isn't the only good man we've lost." He paused for a moment. "Lately, there's been talk among the commanders that the Germans were going to go on the offensive. We were all working around the clock, desperately trying to antic-ipate any future attacks. One night, I took the maps of our radar stations to compare with the key targets of interest to the Luftwaffe so that I could work through the evening. That was the night I was raided. It was all a simple misunderstanding. Once they realized my intentions, they released me."

I swallowed hard, wanting to believe him. But I needed to know for sure. "My father said you were released because of your wealth and connections."

James laughed bitterly. "I suppose that's true. If it weren't for my uncle intervening, I would still be in jail, awaiting my chance to defend myself. But that doesn't make the outcome any different. I was innocent. That's why I was released."

Relief settled over me like falling snow. It all made perfect sense now that he'd explained it. I cradled the phone against my face, wishing it were his hand caressing me instead of the cold brass. "Are you okay, though? Were the police terrible to you?"

"It wasn't pleasant. They treated me like a criminal, denying me even the most basic dignity. I had no food or water. I wasn't even given the chance to contact a lawyer. Thankfully, a friend at Duxford alerted my uncle to my predicament."

"I'm so glad you're okay."

"Irene . . . there's something else I need to tell you." The way he said my name—soft and gentle, drawing out the sound—made me brace myself. "I'm returning to London this weekend."

My stomach dropped. "For how long?"

"For good. Despite my innocence, they've discharged me from the RAF. They've no use for an injured pilot whose name has been tainted by suspicion. I've no reason to stay here any longer."

The ground seemed to shift beneath me. "I . . . I understand."

"I want you to come with me," he said quickly.

"What?"

"Come with me," he repeated, more urgently now. "To London."

"But . . . but where would we live?" I stuttered, my head spinning. "Father would cut me off."

"I have more than enough money for both of us. I'll take care of everything. I promise. We can live at my flat and you can pursue your art while I go back to work for my uncle. I can introduce you to other artists and gallery owners."

"Live together? But what will people think? We aren't even married."

"We could be," he said in a voice so quiet, I thought I had misheard. "I mean, if you would consider marrying me, that is."

My breath caught in my throat, unable to form a coherent thought, much less an answer. Marrying James was a fantasy. A dream. But I had never contemplated it would happen so quickly.

"I can't bear to be without you, Irene. My train leaves tomorrow at eleven o'clock. Say you'll be there."

I held my breath. This was everything I had ever wanted. An escape from Havenworth. A chance to pursue my dreams with the man I was falling for, fiercely and irrevocably. But if I left Havenworth, it wouldn't just be a temporary departure. It would be forever. There would be no forgiveness from Father. No chance of ever returning.

No Margaret.

"Please, Irene. I love you."

My heart stumbled, taking down the last of my defenses with it. "I'll be there. I promise."

Chapter Twelve

JULIA

Present Day

I stayed up far too late poring over the florilegium. I'd taken a class on botanical illustration in college and been taught that the objective was to provide the most scientifically detailed renderings, highlighting anatomically unique characteristics against stark white backgrounds. Irene's illustrations were different. Even with my lack of artistic ability, I could see the emphasis was on the plants' beauty. The delicate curves of a calla lily, the perfect symmetry of a dahlia. On nearly every page of the thick book was a featured flower, interspersed with incredibly detailed sketches of the gardens. As a restoration gardener, this was an absolute gold mine.

But the most interesting part wasn't the drawings themselves. The text below each illustration, written in impeccable cursive, included not only the basic information about the flowers, but also their meaning.

Iris.

Blooms late spring to early summer.

Wisdom, valor.

The language of flowers had been a craze that swept through the Victorian era, with secret codes and messages imbued in every posey and nosegay gifted among friends and lovers and sometimes even enemies. But the language of flowers had been almost entirely forgotten by the time Irene Clarke was alive.

How could someone with a passion for something as pure and innocent as flowers turn into a traitor against her country?

I set the florilegium down on the nightstand and picked up my phone, scouring the internet for any reference to Irene Clarke. There were endless news articles and posts about Margaret's family. The media lauded her father's role in developing radar technology instrumental in stopping the German air raids during World War II, and her mother was well known for her philanthropy. But no mention of Irene. It was as if she had never existed.

I had nearly fallen asleep by the time I found a single newspaper article referencing her disappearance.

> James Atherton, age twenty-five, of London, and Irene Atherton (née Clarke), age eighteen, of Cambridge, have been formally charged with treason. The known fascist sympathizers stand accused of sending classified information to the Abwehr through coded messages hidden inside shipping cargo. It is believed the pair fled to Germany to evade arrest.

Could this be who Margaret had made her promise to all those years ago? A fascist sympathizer? It was no wonder her family had tried to cut all reminders of Irene's existence from their lives.

I glanced down at Sam curled up next to me in the giant poster bed, his mouth parted as he slept, making him look so incredibly young. I couldn't imagine excising Rebecca from our lives, no matter how much pain she'd caused our family. But Rebecca wasn't a traitor. She was someone whose pain and struggles had been too powerful to overcome.

What had made Irene Clarke go down a path like that? From what I could see, Margaret had grown up wealthy and loved. Surely her half sister had, too. So why throw it away for something so vile? It was easier to find information on James Atherton. He was the son of a wealthy industrialist who was a known Nazi sympathizer. His mother had been an Austrian national whose loyalties remained with her homeland, though both of his parents died shortly before the war. James made a small fortune profiteering from selling contraband goods on the black market and passing secrets to the Abwehr before MI5 caught wind of his activities. Suspicions, however, quickly turned to Irene, his charming but ruthless wife, as the true mastermind of their network of traitors. According to one account, the pair escaped to Germany on one of their acquaintances' merchant ships. MI5 caught James in 1967, when he attempted to return to England under an alias, and he spent his few remaining years in prison. Irene was never heard from again.

When I realized it was well after midnight, I forced myself to put my phone down and get some sleep. The jet lag was still messing with my internal clock, but now that I had a vision for the gardens, I needed to make some headway.

The next morning, Andrew and Helen were both in the kitchen when Sam and I made our way to breakfast. I could hear them arguing in hushed voices from down the hall.

"Why can't I ask her about it? She's my godmother just as much as yours."

"The last thing she needs is a reminder of a past that is clearly painful for her."

"Just because things are painful doesn't mean we shouldn't talk about them."

They quieted as soon as I came into the room, the angry tone of their conversation still lingering in Helen's crossed arms and Andrew's scowl.

"Good morning," I said tentatively. "We can come back if this is a bad time."

"No, no. It's fine," Andrew said stiffly.

I wondered whether the man ever relaxed. "I have a tentative projection for the work, and I'd like to discuss the budget and timelines with you."

He nodded. "We can discuss it after you've had breakfast. Meet me in the parlor when you're done."

He sent a sharp look to Helen before disappearing from the kitchen. Whatever conversation they had been having clearly wasn't over.

Andrew was on the phone when I entered the parlor. The room was large, with green wallpaper and velvet-tufted couches that looked as old as Havenworth itself. A piano sat in one corner near a huge fireplace. It was the kind of space that immediately transported a person back in time.

I was about to retreat to the hallway to give him privacy, but he waved me inside, indicating with a finger he would be only a minute.

"You cannot keep asking me to cover these shifts. We need a proper replacement," he said, the edges of his composure fraying. "I'll be there shortly. Surely you can manage until then."

He ended the call and rubbed his forehead before turning his attention my way.

"That sounded stressful," I said.

"It's part of the job. At least until we hire another doctor to take on some of the load. One of my colleagues left recently, and we've had a difficult time finding a replacement."

An ache of sympathy welled in my chest when I remembered what Helen had said about why the hospital was short-staffed. He wasn't just overworked, but heartbroken as well.

"If you would rather discuss the gardens at another time, it can wait," I said, despite hoping otherwise. Delays meant unnecessary costs, and there was only a small window to get the work done before I needed to return to America so Sam could be enrolled in school. But more than that, no one knew how much time Margaret had left.

"It's fine," Andrew said to my relief.

I showed him my tablet, where I had the full estimate laid out in a spreadsheet. "The biggest up-front cost will be the soil amendment, which isn't a surprise, given how long the gardens have been fallow. But the cleanup requirement is going to be larger than I initially expected. I'm suggesting we hire a crew who can do the work more quickly. Otherwise, we might not be able to get much planting done until next spring."

The flat line of his lips grew harder. "This is a bit more than I was anticipating."

"Havenworth sits on twelve acres of land. You have crumbling hardscaping that needs to be repaired, which means matching stone that was manufactured hundreds of years ago. And you asked for this to be done in an impossibly tight timeline. So, yes, it's expensive. But that doesn't mean I'm ripping you off or trying to cheat you in some way." I pressed my lips together to stop myself from saying any more. Nothing good would come from losing my cool. Andrew knew nothing of the reason why I was fired from my position with Hartwell & Sons. Getting defensive would only raise suspicion.

"I never suggested you were," Andrew responded calmly.

I took in a breath to calm myself. "I'm sorry for overreacting. It's important to me that you know I take this job very seriously. I know how much it means to Margaret, and I want to do well by her."

The chill between us thawed a few degrees. "It's difficult not to worry about her. This entire business with the gardens is dredging up some painful memories when she's already quite weak."

"Her body might be weak, but her mind's as sharp as a tack. You have to trust her to know what she's doing."

He sighed. "You're right."

I grinned despite myself. I hadn't thought he was capable of admitting I was right about anything. "The price of the plants will likely change over the course of the work, but I'll do my best to keep costs minimal. But the sooner we make headway, the better. Buying young plants early in the season will be less expensive than full mature ones. Now that I have the florilegium to work with, I'm going to start drawing up plans for the actual designs."

"The book of drawings by her half sister who became a German spy during the war?"

I ignored the distaste dripping from his tongue. "It's not just drawings. There's information about their growing cycles, their origins, and even their meanings."

"Flowers have meanings?"

"Some people believe so."

"Do you?"

"Not in any intrinsic way, but flowers have always been powerfully symbolic in almost every culture. I've seen in my work how certain flowers can emotionally impact people. Even with Margaret, I can see how the garden is helping her remember things."

"Have you shown this book to her yet?"

"Not yet, but I'd like to."

"I think it's best if we hold off for a little while. I'm afraid it could be too much stress for her heart."

I understood Andrew's reasons, but he hadn't lost a sister the way Margaret and I had. Margaret's parents had tried to erase Irene's memory, and that decision had clearly haunted Margaret for the rest of her life. The same way reminders of Rebecca were everywhere, no matter how much I wished I could forget her. But it wasn't my place to say anything. "Of course. I understand."

Chapter Thirteen

Irene

August 18, 1940

I packed my suitcase while the others were still at church, taking only the few items I couldn't live without. The necklace that once belonged to my mother. My coloring pencils. My florilegium. I made sure to leave enough of my clothing behind that no one would immediately suspect anything.

I just needed money. I crept into my father and stepmother's bedroom next. Lady Montgomery kept a small stash of money in her otherwise unused jewelry box. A brief moment of guilt invaded my mind as I pilfered a handful of bills. In all the years I'd known about the money, I'd never been tempted to steal like this before. I had never wanted for material things at Havenworth. The holes in my heart were burrowed entirely by loneliness and rejection.

I took only the amount I needed to see myself safely to London and left the rest. If there was a god judging my sins, I would have to hope it was a forgiving deity that understood my reasons. The family would be better off without me. Their black sheep would be off to a different pasture, where I would no longer embarrass them with my unwanted opinions and lack of intelligence. They could finally be the perfect happy family, something Lady Montgomery would no doubt willingly pay more than a few quid for if given the choice.

I scanned the room for anything else I might need, and my eyes caught on something atop Father's nightstand. A folder that looked like it belonged in Father's office rather than a bedroom—though given his office had been taken over as a spare bedroom for the cadre of nurses still residing at Havenworth, it made sense an important document would be here instead. The folder was tucked beneath a stack of books. Instinct told me to pull it out and peer inside. There were no top-secret markings or special committee designations, but I knew the moment I opened it and saw the contents that it was important.

Operation Josephine.

There were no details as to what that meant. Only a travel itinerary.

Tuesday, October 15, 1940—London to Liverpool via train.

Thursday, October 17, 1940—Liverpool to New York via ocean steamer.

The tickets were attached to the itinerary, each one bearing the name John Clarke.

My father was going to America. After all his warnings and recriminations about my desire to go, too. He was going and he wasn't taking me with him.

A white-hot rage lit inside me, burning away any lingering doubts or fears I had about leaving Havenworth.

I left my suitcase in the garden, tucked out of sight behind the wych elm. When the following morning arrived, I sneaked out before anyone else had awoken to retrieve it so I could make my way to the train station before anyone knew I had left.

I felt no guilt leaving my father and stepmother without a word, but I dreaded leaving Margaret and Charlie the same way. I wrote a note for my sister before I left. Not one anyone else would be able to read. Using a hairpin, I scratched the invisible words into the page the way she had taught me.

> Dear Margaret,
> I'm sorry I've run away. One day you will understand. I have to follow my heart. James and I are in love and he has asked me to go with him to London. Take care of Charlie. I promise to write to you soon.
>   Love always,
>   Irene

On the other side, I drew a daisy for Margaret.

Daisies always reminded me of Margaret. Not just because of her name—"Marguerite" being the French word for the flower—but also because of the meaning it carried: childhood innocence. There was no one more innocent and pure than my sister. I hoped it would be enough.

It had to be enough.

I slid the paper through the small crack of space under her door. I brushed away my tears and quickly made my way down the stairs and out the door. My suitcase was exactly where I'd left it, undisturbed. I gave the gardens one last glance. Even in their dissolved state, they were truly spectacular. Would I ever see them again?

With a heavy sigh, I dragged my suitcase down the pathway toward the road.

"Where are you going?"

My breath hitched at the unexpected sound of Margaret's voice. I turned around to see her standing in her nightgown, her dark hair in a tangle of curls around her face. My note was clutched in her tiny hand.

There was no point in lying to her when she already knew. "I'm going to London with James."

"But you can't go!"

"I know you're upset, but it's for the best. I'm an adult now. I'm supposed to leave and follow my own path. One day you will, too."

She threw herself at me, wrapping her arms around my waist. "But who will take care of me and teach me to be a lady?"

The ache in my chest was almost unbearable as she sobbed into my skirt. I set my hands on her narrow shoulders. "Listen to me. You are going to be just fine. You are so smart and capable and strong. Do not let anyone tell you otherwise."

"Take me with you! Don't leave me here by myself."

I brushed my hand along her hair. "I would love nothing more, but Havenworth is your home. Your mother and father would miss you terribly. So would Charlie. This is where you belong. One day you will be the lady of this house."

"I don't want to be here without you."

Tears of my own tracked down my cheeks. "Promise me something, okay? Promise me that when you are lady of this house, you will take care of this garden. That no matter what happens, you will make sure it remains as beautiful as it is today. If you promise me that, then I promise you I will return someday."

She nodded solemnly. "I promise."

I hugged her tightly, then grabbed my suitcase and walked out the front gates, knowing that despite my promise to Margaret, I would never return.

James was already at the train station when I arrived. He didn't notice me at first. Butterflies danced in my belly as I walked across the platform toward the bench where he sat with his nose buried in the pages of a newspaper. The headline **Hitler Orders the Surrender of Britain** splashed across the front page. We were almost toe to toe by the time he lowered the paper and noticed me.

"Irene! You came?"

His reaction startled me. "Of course I came. I promised I would."

He rose to his feet, erasing my worries with the heat of his touch. "You seemed so hesitant on the telephone. I was afraid you might change your mind."

I let myself surrender to his warmth, my breath hitching against his chest as I exhaled my relief. "It wasn't easy. I had to sneak away. Father would have locked me in my room for a year if he knew I was leaving. He told me if I left Havenworth, I was never coming back, but I don't care. I'm tired of letting him control everything. I want to make my own decisions."

James traced his hand along my back. "You're going to love London."

I was really doing this. I was running away to London to follow my passion with the man of my dreams. The thought sent a rush of exhilaration and desire through me, leaving me breathless and giddy with anticipation.

The train pulled up to the station shortly after. Once we settled into our seats, James looked at me with a rather serious expression. "There's something I need to ask you."

I frowned. "What?"

"There are implications for a young woman like yourself running off with a man like me. I want to make sure you have no regrets."

"Of course I won't," I insisted, despite the tiny thread of doubt creeping through me as the train began pulling away from the station. I had never done something so bold. So daring. And as the familiar sights of Cambridge grew distant in the window, the weight of my decision sank into me. I had promised Margaret I would return to her one day, but it was a lie. Father would never forgive me for running off. I would never be welcomed back to Havenworth.

"Good, because I don't want to wait any longer to do this." He reached into his pocket and pulled out a small box. "Irene Clarke, will you do me the greatest honor of becoming my wife?"

I gasped as he opened the box to reveal a stunning diamond-encrusted band.

"I promise I'll replace the ring with something better soon. It's all I was able to acquire on short notice."

"No," I said fervently. "It's perfect. Of course I'll marry you."

He slipped the ring on my finger. It fit perfectly. In a fit of boldness, I kissed him. Fellow travelers cheered, but I ignored them. This was my and James's moment.

◆ ◆ ◆

The rest of the train ride passed in a blur. James suggested we elope immediately after arriving in London, so that there would be no time for anyone—least of all my father—to interfere. I didn't have the strength to admit out loud that my father wouldn't care. He did not issue empty threats. The moment I'd left Havenworth, I had ceased to exist as his daughter.

But the fact I was only eighteen was a problem. I was not yet old enough to marry without my father's consent. Just as I couldn't go to school or do anything else without his permission.

"An unfortunate complication, but not one that will defeat us. Trust me," James promised.

I did trust him. That was why I didn't ask him how he would find a way around the law. It was easier to lose myself in his assurances and the excitement of my newfound engagement. James promised me a real ceremony later, when I'd had the chance to settle in, but if we were married in the eyes of the law, I would be free.

Despite the lingering limp from his injury, he insisted on carrying my suitcase when we arrived in London. Almost immediately, I noticed a shift in him, as subtle as a gentle breeze that flutters the leaves on the trees while still too light to feel on the skin. His energy was different here. An undercurrent of excitement that matched the faster pace of London flowed through him.

We headed directly to a registry office, where James found a simple solution to our problems: money. The registrant was more than happy to overlook my age and our lack of appropriate paperwork for a few pounds.

There was nothing fancy or formal about the ceremony, but I was too giddy with excitement to care. Instead of a grand white gown, I was dressed in a simple blue skirt and blouse, my face bare of any cosmetics and my hair a mess from the train ride. Dozens of people were queued around us at the long wooden service desk of the registry office when we signed the certificate of marriage. The clerk—an older man with a pinched nose and small round glasses that sat low on his nose—quietly pocketed another stash of pounds before declaring us officially wed.

I was no longer Irene Clarke—the simple girl from Havenworth who never did anything exciting or daring. I was Irene Atherton. A married woman with my entire life ahead of me.

James took my hand as we walked out of the registry office. He paused at the top of the steps, turning me to look at him. "How do you feel, Mrs. Atherton?"

I wrapped my arms around his neck. "Like the luckiest woman in the world."

He kissed me and it felt like the entire world disappeared.

"What do we do now?" I asked when he released me.

He smiled. "We go home."

Home. What a wonderful thought.

His flat in Mayfair was just a short tube ride from the registry office. I couldn't help but gasp as we approached the large white stone building. The stunning Edwardian architecture stood out like a centerpiece among the rest of the buildings on the street.

The inside of his flat was just as luxurious as the outside, with high ceilings, marble floors, and dark wood furniture.

"It's a little dusty," he said sheepishly as he set my suitcase down on the floor.

"I'm not afraid of a little dust," I said. "And I do remember how to use a duster."

"I would never ask you to do such a thing. You are my wife, not my housekeeper. This is now your home as much as it is mine."

It wasn't that I wasn't accustomed to such opulence—Havenworth was, after all, the epitome of excess. But I had spent the first decade of my life in a cramped one-bedroom apartment where spiders were frequent visitors and water stains tarnished the cracked walls. I expected James's place to be similarly modest. There was nothing in our time together to suggest he possessed this kind of wealth. A part of me was greatly relieved that I hadn't impulsively rendered myself destitute, but I couldn't shake the uncomfortable feeling that I had just married a man I didn't know all that well.

I pushed those fears and doubts aside. I had made my choice—rash as it was—and there was no turning back.

I excused myself to the bathroom to freshen up while James put the kettle on for tea. The space was equally elegant to the rest of the flat, with a large claw-foot tub and porcelain pedestal sink. I splashed water onto my face and brushed my hair.

This wasn't just where I would be living now. It was where I would be sleeping, too. Next to James. It was something I had been thinking about nonstop for the last twenty-four hours—mostly with excitement. But now that I was here, the thought filled me with anxiety.

"You're a married woman," I scolded myself. "It's fine."

The girl staring back at me in the mirror looked less convinced. She was young and naive and afraid.

I decided a hot bath was exactly what I needed to calm my nerves.

It was only once the warm water hit my shoulders that I realized how tired I was. The train ride from Cambridge was less than two hours, but it felt like I had traveled a thousand miles.

When I finally emerged, clean and fresh from my bath, I found James in the bedroom with my empty suitcase on the bed, my florilegium in his hands, opened to a drawing of daisies I had done last year.

"What are you doing?" I asked nervously.

He looked up with a rueful smile. "My apologies. I didn't mean to snoop. I thought I would help unpack your things to make you feel more at home."

It was a sweet gesture, but one that made me feel exposed. "That is very kind of you." I took my florilegium back and shoved it in my suitcase.

"Is everything all right?"

"Of course," I said in my cheeriest voice. "It's just that the sketch you're looking at reminds me of my sister. She was quite angry when I left this morning. I'm not sure she'll ever forgive me for leaving the way I did."

"She will one day. I'm certain of it. But there's no point dwelling on things we can't change. Especially not when we have plans."

I raised my eyebrows. "We do?"

He nodded. "We cannot waste your first night in London. I suggest you put on your best dress."

"Where are we going?"

"To celebrate our wedding, of course."

Chapter Fourteen

JULIA

Present Day

The florilegium became almost an obsession over the next week. The book was so thick and richly detailed, I had gotten through only a fraction of it. I pored over each page as though it contained an entire universe in those detailed pencil strokes. It wasn't just a blueprint to the gardens, though. The book read almost like a diary from the time she was a girl until adulthood. I could feel Irene's moods and personality in each drawing. She was precise and serious, but at times whimsical and irreverent. The gardens at Havenworth needed to reflect that.

That was the entire reason Margaret wanted the gardens restored. She wanted to reconnect with the sister she lost all those years ago.

The same sister who had gone on to do some terrible things. I understood why Andrew was so reticent to reach into the past. He was scared the memories would dredge up the old trauma and hurt the Clarke family had tried to bury all those years ago. But he was wrong. You couldn't erase the people you love. Love didn't stop because of hurt or pain or betrayal. It thickened like scar tissue around the heart, until the muscle was too stiff, too inflexible, to work properly again. Margaret had been forced to bury the memories of her sister for decades, but they were always there inside her. Just like Rebecca would always be with Sam and me, no matter how much I wished I could forget.

Sam hadn't asked about her for a few days now, though. The newness of Havenworth had been a distraction, but that would last for only so long.

We had settled into a good routine this week. In the mornings, while I worked on the designs, Sam would play with his toy dinosaurs or color. In the afternoons, we explored outside. Each section of the gardens needed to be surveyed for slopes and angles, making sure the drainage was appropriate and the soil properly amended. Sam's presence made the work slower, but infinitely less lonely. I was used to working with teams of people in this phase. I couldn't bounce ideas off Sam the way I did with my coworkers at Hartwell & Sons, but he still nodded along and took interest when I talked aloud to myself.

The evenings were the hardest. Sam liked to visit Margaret when she was feeling up for a visit, and they had gotten into the habit of playing a mean game of jacks. But on the days when she needed rest, I had to settle him down with the tablet so that I could catch up on all the other things I needed to do—like paying my overdue credit card bills. I'd been putting that unpleasant task off for too long. I couldn't risk another interest charge. Andrew was paying me in installments to cover the work, including the part that would go to my salary. I had put the entire initial payment into a separate business account. Paying off my debts was tempting, but I needed to ensure there was enough to cover the work itself. I settled on extracting just enough to cover the monthly amount due, knowing I was only dragging out my problems for another day.

Sam tugged on my sleeve as I sent the payment through. "Just a sec, buddy."

He tugged again.

"Just wait," I snapped, immediately regretting it when his bottom lip trembled. I winced in frustration. It wasn't Sam's fault I was in a financial mess. "I'm sorry. What did you want to show me?"

He didn't say anything, but there was a set of jacks held tightly in his hand.

"Did you manage to pick them all up?"

Still only silence.

I glanced at my phone. "It's almost time for bed. Why don't we get your teeth brushed?"

The fact he didn't protest made me feel even worse.

After brushing his teeth, I helped him change into his pajamas and settled him into bed. He didn't want a book, so I made up a story about an adventurous boy named Sam who climbed the tallest tree in the world. His eyes fluttered closed just as I finished the part where Sam saves a stranded kitten on the tallest bough.

Rebecca had loved animals just like Sam did. Growing up, she had begged our parents for a kitten, but they never allowed it. They said she wasn't ready for the responsibilities of owning a pet. They were probably right, but it devastated my sister nonetheless. I would've loved to give Sam a furry companion, but I couldn't do that without some stability in our lives.

My emotions were too jumbled from memories of my sister to focus on bills now that he was asleep. I settled on the bed next to him and opened the florilegium to a random page. The image wasn't what I was expecting. It was a drawing of a wilder, forested area. Giant yews, with their distinctive thick, gnarled trunks, rose up majestic as mountains, with lush ferns carpeting the ground around them. But tucked in the bottom right corner was something that made me blink. On first glance, it looked like Havenworth Manor, but that made no sense. The architecture was similar, but the building in this drawing was smaller and sunken into the earth.

It was a garden folly. They were common ornamental features in gardens like these throughout the eighteenth century. Wealthy estate owners built them as tributes to ideals of beauty from around the globe. They served as focal points in the gardens and often were meant as places to reflect or relax. It would only make sense for there to be one at Havenworth, but I hadn't seen it anywhere on the grounds.

I paged through the rest of the florilegium but found no other references to it. But something else did make me pause. The last entry to the book was dated October 14, 1940. It was a bouquet of tall asphodel spires, elegant columbines, thick purple hyacinths, and a single white daisy. It took a moment for the logical side of my brain to catch up to what my instincts had already latched on to. Every flower Irene had drawn until this point was accurate to the season. They were a reflection of her surroundings. But none of these flowers would have been in bloom during the early autumn.

I flipped back through the last few pages. All the entries from September 8, 1940, onward seemed to be done out of memory with flowers that would have been out of season. Based on the locations she included in her sketches, she had been in London since August of that year. The drawings during that late-summer period were mainly of the gardens around Hyde Park and Buckingham Palace.

My curiosity was too strong for any chance of falling asleep. I searched through the book until I found her detailed entries for each of the flowers to decipher their meanings.

Asphodel: regret.

Columbine: foolishness.

Hyacinth: please forgive me.

A heaviness settled over my heart. She had chosen these flowers for a reason. Margaret had said she'd been spying for the Germans. Was this drawing a sign of her doubt and regret? Or was the drawing a way for her to cast those emotions aside?

It took me a while to find her entry for daisies near the beginning of the book. Irene had still been developing her artistic skills when she drew the narrow white petals and bulbous yellow center. The rendering lacked the sophistication of her later sketches, but it still embodied all the cheerfulness I associated with the flower.

Compared with the other flowers, the meaning Irene had assigned to the daisy was jarring.

Childhood innocence.

The combination made no sense, and for a moment I wondered whether I had gotten it wrong. Maybe it was just a random sketch. I set the florilegium on my nightstand and glanced at Sam before turning off the lamp. His hands twitched slightly against his chest, like he was having a nightmare.

I curled up next to him, brushing his soft curls. He was so sweet. So innocent.

A thought drifted into my mind just before sleep overtook me. Margaret couldn't have been much older than Sam when Irene disappeared. Her name meant "daisy" in French.

That last sketch wasn't just a drawing.

It was a message.

I woke with a start from the sound of an owl hooting outside the window. At first I thought it was part of my dream. Owls had been Rebecca's favorite animal, and I'd dreamed about her nearly every night since her death. She was always angry in my dreams. Always questioning how I could've betrayed her the way I had.

I blinked my eyes open, trying to adjust to the dark. I slipped my feet out from the blanket and walked to the window to see if I could spot the bird, but the quarter moon offered too little light. The owl's presence was a good sign, despite the commonly held belief they represented death. This was the first true sign of life in the gardens since I arrived at Havenworth.

An eerie feeling crept over me as I padded back to the bed. Something was wrong. I stilled for a moment before I realized it was the sound of Sam's gentle breathing that was missing. He wasn't in the bed.

"Sam?" My voice echoed in the empty room as I fumbled for the light switch.

The bedroom door was open.

A thousand fears erupted in my brain. He could have wandered anywhere. What if he'd gone outside? What if he was hurt?

I raced through the hall, searching for signs of him with my phone's flashlight. I descended the stairs three at a time and wrenched on the front door. It was still locked, thank god. Sam had to be somewhere inside. But where? Havenworth was so big there were millions of places a five-year-old boy could hide.

A faint but familiar sound floated down the hall, overwhelming me with relief. Sam was down here somewhere. Giggling.

I chased the sound to the kitchen. Sam was at his usual spot at the table, with a rose-patterned china cup in front of him. Andrew sat across from him, wearing expensive-looking navy pajamas that made me suddenly very aware of my ratty, oversize I'D RATHER BE GARDENING T-shirt and bare legs.

I crossed my arms in front of my chest and watched as Andrew leaned closer to Sam and said, "Do you know how to make a skeleton laugh?"

Sam shook his head.

"You tickle its funny bone."

I watched in awe as Sam threw his head back as he let out another fit of giggles. He hadn't laughed like that in so long, I almost couldn't believe what I was seeing.

Andrew's eyes met mine for the briefest moment, silently reassuring me everything was okay. "All right now. Best finish up and get back to bed before your aunt Julia realizes what's in that cup."

My legs still trembled with adrenaline as I walked into the room and sat next to Sam, unsure whether I ought to be more angry or relieved to find him here. He looked at me with so much guilt in his eyes, I couldn't bring myself to scold him. Instead, I said to Andrew, "Anatomy jokes? Isn't that a little too on the nose for a doctor?"

"I find them rather humerus," he replied with a grin. "Sam likes them too."

"What's the fastest part of your body?" Sam asked me.

I narrowed my eyes. "Hmm. I don't know. My feet?"

He shook his head, delighted to have stumped me. "Your nose, 'cause it's always running."

I laughed in spite of myself. "Very clever. Especially for a boy who should be in bed right now."

"Sam was having trouble sleeping. I was, too, so we decided a drink might help," Andrew said.

My eyes stung with tears that I refused to shed in front of Sam. How had I not noticed him disappear in the middle of the night? It was my job to keep him safe.

Sam tipped the cup to his mouth and tilted it all the way up, finishing his drink. When he set it back down, there was a light-brown mustache above his lip. "I'm tired now," he said with a sleepy yawn.

"Let's get you back to bed." I picked him up so he could rest his head on my shoulder. He curled into me, still so small and sweet. Andrew followed us, shining his phone so I wouldn't trip in the dark. Sam didn't even make it up the stairs before I heard the gentle sigh of sleep from his lips. I settled him into bed and tucked him tightly under the covers.

He was okay, I told myself. He was safe.

When I was certain he wouldn't wake again, I went back to the hallway to face the scolding Andrew no doubt had in store for me. His flashlight app was still on, but he kept it pointed toward the ground so that his face was shadowed.

"Thank you for taking care of him. He's never wandered off like that at night before and—"

"Julia, take a breath." He put his hand on my shoulder. "I'm not upset."

"You're not?"

"Why not join me in the kitchen so I can finish my drink and we can talk. You look like you could use a drink, too."

"But Sam—"

"Sam isn't likely to wake for the rest of the night, but you won't get a wink if you don't let out some of that stress." When I hesitated, he added, "Doctor's orders."

I exhaled deeply. "Okay."

I checked on Sam one more time before following Andrew back to the kitchen. He didn't ask me what I wanted to drink. He turned on the kettle and pulled an orange jar from the cupboard. It was strange to see a man moving so comfortably in the kitchen. My dad had refused to so much as pour himself a glass of water, insisting my mother cater to his every whim once he walked through the front door after work.

The lean muscles in Andrew's forearms flexed as he poured the hot water into the cup and stirred the drink. My cheeks heated with embarrassment when I realized I'd been staring. Seeing him being so silly and sweet with Sam made it impossible to ignore how incredibly attractive he was.

He set the cup in front of me. "I promise you'll like this."

I sniffed the milky brown liquid, unable to place the scent. "What is it?"

"Ovaltine. Chock-full of magnesium. Great for sleep."

I knew of the drink but had never actually tasted it before. It was less sweet than I anticipated, with a faint chocolaty flavor that somehow tasted the way it felt to put on a cozy sweater.

"I'd have offered something a little stronger, but we don't keep the whiskey in the kitchen," he said.

"This is perfect, thank you. And I'm sorry about Sam."

"I was already awake when I heard him coming down the stairs." His brow furrowed like there was something else he needed to say but he didn't have the right words for it.

My stomach clenched, waiting for him to tell me that I had been irresponsible letting Sam run off in the middle of the night.

He scrubbed a hand over his jaw, where days-old stubble had covered the skin. "Sam's clearly been through a lot, but he's a good kid. I'm sorry I gave you a hard time about him when you first arrived."

My hands stilled with the cup poised at my lips as my brain struggled to believe I'd heard him right. "I thought you would be angry."

His lips quirked into a small smile. "Believe it or not, I'm not usually an angry person. Having Sam around has been a nice change."

"You're good with him."

"I always wanted kids of my own," he said. "But it's never quite worked out. Medical school and residency didn't leave much time for a personal life. I was dating a woman last year who had a child. A boy named Henry. He was a great kid. They had come up from Australia because Amy accepted a position at the hospital where I work. But a few months ago, she decided to return to Australia. Amy didn't think a long-distance relationship would work and thought it would be best to end with a clean break for Henry's sake."

"I'm sorry. That must have been incredibly hard for you."

"I suppose that's why I was reticent about Sam at first. He reminds me of Henry." The muscle in his jaw flexed with barely restrained emotion. "But I'm glad you're here."

His eyes met mine. A subtle heat spread through me. I cleared my throat, knowing it was silly to read anything into it. "It's been good for Sam. And me. Havenworth is a special place."

"It's been good for Margaret, too. Despite her age, she's always had a little bit of childlike mischievousness about her, and I think she's found a kindred spirit in him."

"Sam's never really had any grandparents. It's nice for him to spend time with her."

"Are your parents not around?"

An uncomfortable lump lodged in my throat. "They don't have much to do with Sam. My sister struggled with addiction her whole life.

My parents didn't know how to handle it other than to cut her off. She ran away when she was eighteen, and none of us saw her again until she banged on my front door ten years later with Sam in tow, asking for a place to stay. Sam was already four years old at that point."

Andrew let out a breath. "That must have been a shock."

I cupped my hands around my drink and nodded. "Every few years, I would get a text from her asking for money, but she never gave me any details about her life. She was in a bad place when she showed up again. I couldn't turn her away because of Sam, so I let her in. She swore she was clean and just needed some help getting back on her feet. I tried to help her. I hired her to help with one of my contracts, and it seemed like it was working out at first. She worked hard and seemed happy for the first time in a long time. It felt like I finally had my sister back. But after a few months, I found out she was using again. She had stolen money from the company I worked for, too. She didn't want to go to rehab, but I didn't give her the choice. It was that, or I turn her over to the police. I paid for the best facility I could find. I thought it would help, but she still managed to get her hands on something while she was there and ended up overdosing. She passed away and Sam was left in my care."

I couldn't stop the tears from falling now. I rubbed them away with the back of my hand, knowing I must look like an utter mess. "I'm sorry. I don't know why I'm telling you all this."

Andrew reached over and squeezed my hand. "Maybe because you needed to."

The physical contact was so unexpected, but I couldn't bring myself to pull away. I had been on my own for so long—just me and Sam against the world—that I'd forgotten what it was like to be comforted by another person. It would have been so easy to confess everything that came after. To relieve myself of the heavy secrets I had carried with me for the last six months. The way I had tried so hard to help my sister, only to make everything worse. And because of that, Sam would never have his mom back.

But Andrew's unexpected kindness didn't change the fact I worked for him. I couldn't risk him finding out anything more about my past. Not if I wanted any hope for a better future.

I slipped my hand free and cleared my throat. "You never told me what you were doing awake at this hour."

He shrugged. "Just your typical midlife existential dread."

"Are you worried about Margaret?"

The pain that flashed in his eyes was so visceral, I felt it all the way to my bones. "Always. She's been the guiding light in Helen's and my lives for so long. I'm terrified of how we'll get on once she's gone."

"She's an incredible woman."

"That she is. Though she would hate it if she knew we were talking about her this way," he said with a wry smile.

"There was something I found in the book I wanted to ask you about," I said, trying to ease us back into professional territory despite the fact we were dressed like children racing downstairs on Christmas morning. "There was a sketch in the florilegium of a garden folly. I think it must be somewhere on the grounds, but I haven't seen it."

His shoulders stiffened the way I knew they would when I mentioned the florilegium. "I don't ever recall seeing a folly."

"In the sketch, it's surrounded by yew trees. It could be on the other side of the stone wall at the back of the property. Does Margaret still own that land?"

"I believe she does."

"I'd like to go exploring and see what's there."

"I have some time in the morning, which is coming sooner than either of us would like."

As if on cue, a yawn rose up through my chest. Andrew escorted me back to my room, where Sam was still sleeping peacefully. Neither of us spoke as we parted ways for the evening, but something had changed between us. Something I wasn't quite ready to admit to myself.

Chapter Fifteen

IRENE

August 18, 1940

With no hints other than to wear my best dress, I followed James into the warm summer evening to celebrate the first night of our new life as a married couple. The streets of London buzzed with life—people elegantly dressed, coming and going from restaurants and galleries and nightclubs.

James led me down a narrow street that reeked of rotten fish. I had to tread carefully, avoiding the strange puddles and piles of garbage. The thought of any respectable establishment hidden back here was incongruous, but I didn't question it. I trusted James implicitly. A metal door marked only by a bronze number loomed at the end of the alley.

"I know it doesn't look like much, but you'll be pleasantly surprised when you see it."

As soon as he opened the door, a wave of smoke and music flowed out. A broad-shouldered man in an ill-fitting suit stood inside, but he didn't say anything in greeting. He simply nodded at James, allowing us through. We descended a short flight of stairs into a huge room filled with round tables and dozens of people dancing and drinking everywhere I looked. At the far end was a stage occupied by a band playing some kind of music that sounded like jazz.

"This is incredible," I said, having to almost scream the words over the noise. "I can't believe this is hidden down here."

My arm was tucked inside his, and he squeezed it tighter. "There are so many wonderful things hidden from plain sight if you're willing to look."

The venue was so crowded, I collided with a man stepping back from the bar, knocking over the pint glass in his hand.

"Watch it," he said, scowling as the beer spread along the front of his shirt.

"I'm so sorry," I said quickly.

The man's gaze raked over me like I was little more than a piece of trash in his way.

"If you ask me, you look better that way," James said.

"I didn't ask—" The man's anger seemed to vanish almost instantly, replaced with a hearty laugh. "James? You son of a bitch, what are you doing here? I heard you were rotting in Holloway with all the other traitors and sinners."

James let go of my hand and embraced the man in a quick hug. "Nothing a little money and influence can't smooth out. But the RAF discharged me from my duties."

"Dishonorably, I hope," the man said with a booming laugh.

"Is there any other kind?" Turning to me, James said, "Roger, this is my wife, Irene Atherton."

"Nice to meet you," I said, hoping to start afresh.

"A new girl already?" Roger said, barely bothering to look at me. "Quite impressive."

I looked to James in confusion. He shook his head with an amused grin. "Ignore him. He's an oaf."

"And proud of it," Roger said. "Come on, we're at our regular spot."

An oaf, indeed. Despite feeling as welcome as a cockroach, I refused to let this Roger character sour my mood. This was my first night out in London, and the music was infectious. I was going to enjoy every second of it.

We followed Roger to a dark corner, where a dark-haired woman in a slinky black dress with impossibly elegant long limbs and a cigarette dangling from her red lips sat at a table covered in empty glasses. Next to her were two men—one of whom looked to be as old as my father, with salt-and-pepper hair and an impeccably sharp suit, while the other was passed out with his head on the table.

"Irene, meet my cousin, Catherine, and my friend Leslie, and whoever was unlucky enough to think he could keep up with him tonight."

Catherine jumped to her feet, balancing precariously on her sky-high heels as she threw her skinny arms at me in a hug. "I'm so excited to finally meet you! James has been telling us so much about you," she practically squealed.

"It's wonderful to meet you, too," I said earnestly.

Leslie shoved the younger man off his seat. "Make room for the lady."

He fell to the ground in a drunken stupor before stumbling away.

"That's not necessary," I said in horror. "Really. I'm fine to stand."

"I was tired of him anyway. I'll get you a drink. Sidecar?" He disappeared before I could answer.

The bandleader announced they were taking a short break. The din quieted to a more tolerable level as people streamed off the dance floor to refresh their drinks and rest their feet.

"So," Catherine purred. "James's letters said you're an artist."

I was grateful the darkness of the club concealed my blush. "I am. At least, I'm trying to be."

"Perhaps you could take her to some of the galleries while I'm working," James interjected. "She's never been to London before."

"Never?" Catherine's eyes widened. "What a shame. You absolutely must visit the National Gallery, but first let me take you shopping. You haven't lived until you've spent obscene amounts of money at Harrods."

"You mean your father's money," James said teasingly.

Rather than be offended, Catherine shrugged. "You don't expect me to spend my own, do you?" She winked at me, as though we were sharing a joke.

Leslie returned with a handful of drinks, setting them down on the table. "Finally, we can toast to the bride and groom."

Everyone clinked their glasses, except Roger. He lifted his tumbler only the barest fraction to avoid being called out for rudeness. It was clear he and James were friends. I couldn't understand why he seemed to dislike me so instantly. Surely he ought to be happy for his friend's marriage?

I took a sip of my sidecar. The mix of sour and sweet was unexpected but strangely delicious. I savored the warm burn of the brandy before licking the sugared rim.

"Enjoying that, are you?" James teased.

The alcohol gave me an extra dose of courage. "Almost as much as I enjoy being your wife."

"Young love is so sweet, my teeth are practically rotting from all of this happiness," Leslie said, taking another sip of his wine.

"Jealousy doesn't suit you," Catherine chided playfully.

Leslie sighed exaggeratedly. "Fine, fine. I wish you all the joy in the world. Better?"

"You always were a sentimental one," James said with a laugh.

"How did you two meet?" Catherine asked.

"James was a friend of my stepcousin Michael," I said, choking a little on his name. It still hurt to think of him in past tense.

"May he rest in peace," James said solemnly.

For a reason I couldn't explain, my gaze shifted to Roger. He was staring back at me with a blank expression, as though he had no emotion at all. But the slightest tic in his jaw suggested otherwise.

"Did you know him, too?" I asked before I could think better of it.

"We were all schoolmates," James said.

"A long time ago," Roger said before downing the last of his drink.

I wondered whether he was truly so heartless as to feel nothing in this moment. But people grieved in their own ways, I supposed.

"Why are we talking about depressing things when tonight is supposed to be a celebration?" Catherine asked. She pursed her red lips and glanced at the stage. "I want to dance."

As if on cue, the band returned to their instruments.

I looked to James excitedly before quickly realizing my mistake. Of course he couldn't dance on his injured leg. He might never be able to walk properly again, much less perform a foxtrot.

"Go on," he said. "I'll be fine over here."

Catherine grabbed my hand and pulled me onto the dance floor just in time for the band to start a new song. We weren't the only women dancing together. The ratio of women to men, as in every other place in this country, was grievously skewed. A handful of uniformed men lingered next to the bar, with a few others making the most of their time off on the dance floor.

Eventually, Leslie joined us, demonstrating the perfect technique for the rumba. Catherine picked up the steps easily. I was certain I looked like a clomping elephant next to her, but I didn't care. The more the alcohol flowed, the slipperier my worries became, losing all traction in my mind. I danced until the early hours of the morning, taking short breaks to refill my glass and spend time with my new husband whenever my feet needed a rest.

If it bothered James, he didn't show it. Every time I glanced his way, he was busy talking to someone new, as if everyone in the night club wanted their turn with him. He was enjoying himself. That was what mattered.

I was alone when I woke the next morning. It was the absence of another heartbeat next to me that alerted me to that fact well before I opened my eyes. I'd become so used to Margaret's soft whimpers and tiny breath that it was strange to hear only my own. But that wasn't the only thing that was different. The din of cars and people just beyond the window. The cotton sheets and thin pillow that smelled like a man's cologne.

Untethered memories of last night flashed in my brain, like scattered pieces of a puzzle I could barely fit together. But then, with a gasp, I did remember. We'd kissed passionately. Recklessly. I'd let James take off my clothes and lay me down on the bed. He'd lain on top of me, with nothing between us but our skin. I sat up, wincing from the light, and felt a jolt of pain between my thighs.

In a panic I called James's name, but there was no answer. I forced the covers back and rose to my feet, only to be greeted with a new horror. Blood had dripped down my thighs, leaving a dark stain on the sheets.

I tore the sheets from the mattress and scrubbed them in the bathtub until the stain faded to a dull pink. I cleaned my own body next. My legs were so tender, even the graze of soap against my skin caused an unbearable sting. Where had James gone? How could he have left me alone after last night? This was our first morning together as a married couple. He was supposed to be here to hold me and tell me he loved me.

I fought tears as I dressed myself and searched the kitchen for something to eat, hoping that might quell the roiling in my stomach. There was no food at all. Not even a box of crackers or tea.

Of course not. James wasn't the type of man who cooked for himself. He'd mentioned on our first date that he didn't believe in suffering through ration-compliant meals when he could afford to dine at the ritziest restaurants.

A knock sounded at the door, disrupting my spiral of worries. Before I had the chance to open it, the knock came again, rather more insistent this time. I opened the door cautiously to find Catherine on the other side.

"There you are! I was beginning to worry you had forgotten about our date today." She was dressed in a sharp red suit that set off her dark locks and pale skin.

The excited pitch of her voice made my head throb even worse. I winced, trying to remember what promises I had made and cursing myself for doing so.

She sighed. "James has given me strict instructions to take you shopping. I'm not taking no for an answer."

"But I don't have any money."

"Darling, you do not need to worry about money. James has arranged for everything. We'll start with Harrods, then Selfridges. After that we can visit some of the smaller boutiques."

Relief coursed through me. How silly I'd been not to trust James. He hadn't abandoned me on my first day in London. He'd taken care of everything, just like he'd promised. "Could we start with lunch instead?"

"Of course!" She linked her arm through mine and urged me out the door.

Despite my wretched state, lunch with Catherine proved to be exactly the distraction I needed. We dined at the Ritz, where they served every type of pastry and fruit under the sun—not that my stomach would allow for anything but plain toast. She gabbed so easily throughout the entire meal, oblivious to my relative silence. I didn't mind, though. It was exciting hearing about her life, and it allowed me to eat my lunch peacefully. If she judged me unfavorably for my American accent or lack of worldliness, she didn't show it. If anything, she seemed happy to have an audience for her stories.

Catherine was at least a decade older than me and had grown up wealthy, like James. In her youth, she embarked on a career as a dancer with a prestigious ballet company, traveling the continent to perform. "But the schedule was just too grueling. At one point, we were billeted in a tiny inn that required us to sleep four to a room, with only one bed. I quit that very day and became a model instead. Much less arduous. And what about you? Have you always been an artist?"

"Oh." I set my fork down, unprepared to speak after listening to Catherine for so long. "It's all I've ever aspired to be." I didn't want to explain that I was only eighteen and had spent my life until this point chasing unruly children.

"Well, don't be surprised if Leslie insists you pose for him at some point. You have rather lovely bone structure."

"He's an artist, too?"

"All of James's friends are. He seems to attract them like flies to honey, despite not having a lick of talent himself."

"Even Roger?" I couldn't help but shudder at the memory of his hostility toward me.

"He aspires to be a writer. His work isn't half bad, to be honest. I convinced him to read some of his poetry for me one morning. I recall it was good, but I admit, it's difficult to focus when a man is reading poetry to you while sitting naked in a lounge chair."

"You and Roger . . ." I couldn't finish the sentence. The thought of them together was too incongruous to contemplate.

She waved her hand dismissively. "We're not together. But we've enjoyed a dalliance once or twice over the years. Usually after a long evening of drinking and dancing, when we both realized there was nothing better to be found."

I stared at her in disbelief.

"Oh, don't tell me you're prudish about such things. This is London, darling."

"Of course not," I lied. "It's just hard to imagine Roger with anyone."

"He's a very generous lover, but such a boor sometimes. You'll get used to him eventually."

"I doubt that. He acted as though he outright reviled me even before he knew my name."

"That's just his way. But we shouldn't talk about him when we have something much more important to discuss." She set her arms on the table, looking at me expectantly.

I tilted my head with curiosity. "What would that be?"

"Your wardrobe. It's Leslie's birthday in a few weeks, and he insists that everyone abide by the dress code. This year the theme is gilded innocence."

"Gilded innocence? What does that even mean?"

She lifted her champagne flute. "Whatever you want it to."

I didn't understand how she could consume alcohol again so soon after last night's debauchery. My head spun at the thought of another sip, but I didn't dare mention that to Catherine, lest she think of me as a child. "What will you be wearing?"

"A gold cocktail dress. Unfortunately, there's nothing innocent about me, so the sweetheart neckline will have to do."

"That sounds incredibly glamorous."

"It's a party, darling. It's supposed to be glamorous. That's why we need a proper day to shop. Hurry up and finish your meal."

Unlike my stepmother, Catherine had no shame in enjoying her wealth and privilege. We were privately assisted by a saleswoman at Harrods who collected items for me with ruthless efficiency. Shoes, stockings, gowns, and even underwear. James, it appeared, had prearranged for this outing, calling ahead to open an account for me and leaving precise instructions that I not leave without an entire wardrobe. After an hour, I had everything I could possibly want and more. Except for a dress for the party.

I had no idea where to start. Catherine and the saleswoman brought an array of options for me while I waited in the fitting room, but none of them felt right. I didn't want a boring dress that even Lady Montgomery would have approved of. But despite my desire to break free from my past, I didn't feel comfortable in the risqué gowns Catherine favored.

Finally, I'd had enough of waiting for the dresses to be brought to me. I slipped my shirtdress back on and wandered outside the fitting room, determined to find something on my own. Even walking through the women's clothing department was a luxurious experience unlike anything I had ever known. I marveled at the ornate ceilings almost as much as I did the vibrant colors and textures of the clothes.

"Irene, there you are!" Catherine said, a pile of gowns draped across her arms. "I was wondering where you went. I found this most perfect gown. I'm certain you'll love it."

She held up a frothy concoction of lace and tulle. I bit my lip, not wanting to offend my new friend with yet another rejection. But as I looked around in desperation for an excuse, my gaze fell upon the most beautiful dress I had ever seen. "That one," I said in a breathy gasp.

It was knee length in an elegant shade of blush pink that reminded me of the peonies that grew every summer at Havenworth. The dress had a tasteful straight neckline with a tulle overlay covered in delicate gold appliqués in the shape of roses.

When I tried it on, even Catherine agreed that it was the perfect dress. "James is going to absolutely love it."

I beamed at my own reflection. In this dress, I was a woman.

At the sales counter, we added it to the pile of items. As the saleswoman packaged everything in clover-green garment boxes, my eye was drawn to a small yellow hair ribbon on a rack nearby. It immediately made me think of Margaret—always losing her ribbons and having to borrow mine whenever her mother forced her to dress for an occasion. The bright yellow would look spectacular against her dark hair.

"Can we add that, too?" I asked impulsively.

Catherine raised a curious, well-arched brow. "It's a little juvenile."

"I know. I'd like to send it to my sister. She's only seven."

"How sweet. She'll love it."

We weren't the only ones out shopping in the streets of Knightsbridge that day, but few people had quite as many bags in hand as Catherine and I, which drew more than a fair share of raised eyebrows. Guilt made my parcels suddenly feel terribly heavy. I'd been so entranced by the luxury and opulence of the shops that I hadn't stopped to consider whether it was appropriate to indulge so extravagantly.

"What's wrong?" Catherine asked, noticing my changing mood.

"It's just . . . there's a shortage of fabric right now. It feels a little wrong to have so much when there are so many people going without."

She looked at me as though I had grown a second head. "What was so wrong about it? The clothes were there to be sold. Besides, it's not like you have anything else to wear. You needed a new wardrobe."

"You're right," I said, even though I wasn't fully convinced. "I was being silly. Besides, my stepmother has probably already donated every shred of clothing I left behind."

"Exactly," she said. "It all equals out."

We were only a few blocks from James's flat when Catherine waved excitedly at a handsome man approaching us on the street. "Arthur! It's been ages. How are you?"

"Quite well, thank you. Though much better now that I've encountered the two most lovely ladies in London."

"How sweet of you to say." Catherine's demure expression was so put on, I had to stop myself from laughing. "Though you do say it every time we meet."

"And I mean it every time."

"Just as you meant it when you promised to take me on a proper date soon?"

Their brazen flirtation left me agog.

Arthur glanced at his wristwatch. "I suppose it is getting to be time for supper. Perhaps you'd like to join me?"

Catherine turned to me suddenly. "You don't mind, do you?"

"Not at all," I replied. In truth, I was surprised she even remembered that I was standing there.

"You're such a doll. Oh, wait. Can you give this to James?" She reached into her purse and pulled out a small, nondescript envelope.

"What is it?"

"Just a letter for James that was delivered to my place by mistake." She stuffed it into my purse.

She kissed me on the cheek and went off with her new beau, leaving me to navigate the rest of my journey home. I soaked up the warm sun as I walked, the remaining fragments of my headache finally abating.

It was almost a shame to go inside, but I needed to set these bags down before my arms grew too weary.

An elderly couple stepped into the lift before I reached it. "Please hold on," I called out, but the doors closed too quickly. With a sigh, I contemplated waiting for the lift to return, but our flat was only three stories up.

The staircase was narrow, with windowless walls. I'd made it up the first flight when I heard a faint echo of footsteps behind me. I glanced behind, but there was no one there. Perhaps my ears were playing tricks on me.

I continued my climb, and this time I was certain someone was following me. "Hello? Is there someone there?"

No answer came except for the sound of footsteps stomping even more quickly.

I was probably overreacting, as there were plenty of other people in this building who had reason to use the stairwell. But my instincts were screaming otherwise. I sped up until I was practically running. The footsteps behind me got quicker, too. By the time I reached the last flight, the person was right behind me. It was too difficult to open the door exiting the stairwell with all my cumbersome bags. I dropped them to the ground and wrenched the door open.

Whoever was behind me had gotten so close, I could feel their hand brush against my shoulder as I slipped into the hallway. The door slammed shut behind me.

"Is everything all right, dear?"

I turned to see the elderly couple from the lift, standing at the far end of the hall. "Everything's fine, thank you. Those stairs were a little harder than I expected."

The woman smiled kindly before disappearing into her flat along with her husband. My hands shook as I fumbled with the keys to our flat. When I finally made my way inside, I leaned against the door and let out a huge sigh.

"Irene? What's the matter?"

My eyelids flew open at the sound of James's voice. I cleared my throat and forced a smile. "I didn't expect you home."

He rose from the couch and came over to me, setting his hands on my shoulders. The scent of his cologne filled me with comfort. "I felt terrible having to leave while you were still asleep, but there were some important matters to take care of. My uncle has asked me to take on a position in his parliamentary office."

I dropped my forehead to his chest. "I completely understand. You have responsibilities."

He ran his hand tenderly along the back of my head. "I wanted to be there for you. Last night was special."

Heat spread through my chest at the memory of our first night together. The feel of his skin against mine. "It was for me, too."

"You weren't too lonely today?"

I didn't want to burden James with the truth. "Catherine stopped by and took me shopping—" I let out a groan.

He cupped my face, forcing me to stare up at him. "What happened? Please don't lie to me. I can tell something's wrong."

"I took the stairwell up just now. There was someone following me—or at least I thought they were following me." Embarrassment welled in my chest. It sounded so foolish now that I was saying it aloud. "I dropped all my bags in the stairwell."

The alarm in his eyes darkened to something more. Something deeper and angrier. "I'll kill whoever it was."

He reached for the doorknob. I placed my hand on his forearm. "I just want my parcels. Not murder."

I held my breath as James made his way to the stairwell while I stayed inside the flat. I knew he was more than capable of defending himself despite his limp, but my nerves still hadn't settled. He returned within minutes carrying the green bags I'd dropped. "There was no one there."

"Maybe he ran off," I said feebly, doubting myself.

James set the parcels down on the coffee table. "Or maybe you were just spooked. Moving here's been a big change for you, and I left you all alone today. It's no wonder your nerves were rattled."

I exhaled slowly, trying to reconcile James's words with the reality I'd experienced. "I was just being silly."

He kissed my temple. "Exactly. Now why don't you find something suitable for an evening at the Café de Paris from all these outfits you've purchased."

"I thought we might stay in tonight," I said. "We've barely spent any time alone since we arrived."

His exhalation was slow and heavy, and for a moment I thought I had disappointed him. But he rubbed my back reassuringly and said, "Of course. There's nothing I would love more than to spend a quiet night in with you."

We spent the rest of the evening curled up on his couch, sharing more about our pasts and talking about all the things we would do when the war was over. He promised to tour me around the continent, while I told him of all the places in America we could visit. That night, he made love to me again until I fell asleep in his arms. It was everything I pictured our life together as a married couple to be.

But in the morning I awoke alone once more. I occupied myself by finally arranging all my new clothing in the closet, reminding myself to be grateful for such luxuries rather than petulant that my husband had to work.

It was only when I finished hanging the last dress that I realized the yellow ribbon was missing.

Chapter Sixteen

Julia

Present Day

Despite the late night, I woke up with the sunrise the next morning. The sky was a brilliant golden shade, showing none of the signs of rain. It was the kind of morning that made me eager to get outside, but Sam was still asleep.

I found myself reaching for the florilegium again. The eeriness of those last few pages still gnawed at me. The drawings inside had been consistent in style and purpose for years, right until September of 1940. The date was a familiar one, but I couldn't recall why. I typed it into my phone, only to feel like a fool when the results came through. That was the start of the Blitz, Germany's eight-month reign of terror over London, during which they relentlessly bombed the city night after night. The number of civilian fatalities was enormous, and the psychological torture people suffered unfathomable. Irene had been in London by that time. Had the Blitz changed her perception of the war? Had it made her regret her choices? Or was it the catalyst for her treachery?

In my own notebook, I wrote down the meanings behind the drawings from September onward. There weren't many. The first drawing was a combination of begonias, lavender, and foxglove, along with a single daisy.

Warning. Distrust. Secrecy.

The next was monkshood and hardy geraniums, and, at the center, still a single daisy.

It took me a long time to locate their meanings. Irene had listed the flowers under their less common names: aconite and cranesbill.

Deceit. Falsehoods. Treachery. Beware.

A shiver spooled down my spine. This was Irene's personal florilegium, but this combination of meanings felt more like a warning. I tugged the elastic out of my hair and combed my fingers through the tangled strands before pulling them back into a tight bun. None of this made sense. If Irene was already estranged from her family by the summer of 1940, how did the florilegium end up back at Havenworth?

I wished I could have asked Margaret about it, but I couldn't risk upsetting her. Raising these kinds of questions about her sister would only cause her more distress.

Sam stirred next to me, flailing his leg across the mattress. He blinked one wary eye open, then quickly shut it again after deciding he wasn't quite ready to face the day. But after rolling around a few more times to escape the morning light, he finally sat up and rubbed his eyes.

I set the florilegium aside and went to fetch him some clothes.

"What do you think, Sam? The blue shirt with the trucks or the green one with the dinosaurs?" I turned back with a shirt in each hand. "No, Sam! Don't!"

I dropped the clothes to the floor and snatched the pencil from his hand. In the split second I had turned my back, Sam had gotten a hold of the florilegium. I extracted the book with more delicacy, and exhaled in relief when I realized I had caught him before he'd done any damage to the brittle pages.

"That book is not for coloring. Why don't you use this one instead." I handed him my notepad, flipping it over to a new page.

"It *is* for coloring," he said. "Someone colored all over it."

"That is a special book that belonged to Margaret's sister. It is very old and very precious. We have to take extremely good care of it, okay?"

His bottom lip jutted out in a pout.

The rest of the morning was little better. He refused to change out of his pajamas. I didn't bother to fight about it. I was too tired from the late night to face his stubbornness head-on. But when I told him we were going on a short adventure with Andrew, his demeanor changed from grumpy to excited. I tried not to read too much into it, but I couldn't help but feel a twinge of jealousy. Sam hadn't had any real male role models in his life. Rebecca never said anything about his father, other than he wasn't in the picture.

It was good for Sam to open out of his shell, even if it wasn't with me.

With the florilegium tucked safely into my satchel, we went to meet Andrew at the front gate after breakfast. The sun was out, bringing a hint of late-spring warmth to the air. Summer was around the corner.

Andrew smiled as we approached, seeming genuinely happy to see us. I found myself smiling back. I worried it would be awkward between us this morning, but if he shared that worry, he didn't show it. "Good morning. I'm glad to see you've got your boots on. It's a little more unkempt where we're headed."

He wasn't lying. Most of the land around Havenworth had been cleared for agriculture, but the area behind the estate was still deeply forested. A carpet of bluebells was in bloom, creating a stunning sealike effect.

Watching Andrew navigate over the untrodden underbrush was the only time I had seen him look anything but graceful. I wondered whether he had ever come out here as a child, or if he had always been too serious for the kind of reckless fun that came with exploring nature and climbing trees.

After a few minutes I spotted a slight clearing in the forest floor. The remnants of a pathway were just visible through the slightly thinner growth.

"Over here," I called out. The stone gravel beneath our feet matched the paths in the Havenworth gardens. Sure enough, the trail led directly to the stone wall enclosing the grounds, confirming my suspicion that there had once been a gate leading out to this area.

I held tight to Sam's hand as we set off down the trail in the opposite direction until we found the folly. The front of the structure was sunk so deep into the ground, only a person of Sam's size could reasonably fit through. There was something off about it. Something different from the drawing that I couldn't quite put my finger on. I approached it cautiously, suspecting the entire thing could tumble over from the faintest touch.

"This is incredible," Andrew said, his hands on his hips as he took in the folly with sheer awe. "It looks just like Havenworth."

Sam tugged at my hand. "Can I go inside?"

"No, buddy. It's not safe."

Despite my warning, I couldn't help myself from exploring more closely. I instructed Sam to stay with Andrew, then made my way around the side of the structure. The sight that greeted me made me gasp. A huge crater roughly ten feet in either direction had formed in the ground behind it, causing the back of the structure to crumble into a heap of bricks and rubble. Only the thinnest layer of vegetation had sprouted over the top.

"What happened here?" Andrew asked from behind me, Sam hanging off his neck in a piggyback, neither of them able to resist their curiosity.

I bit my lip. "I think a bomb fell here."

Andrew didn't say anything. The heaviness of it was probably too much to take in.

"There's a sketch of the folly in the florilegium. I thought I might be able to restore it for Margaret, but this might require an expert remediation to make sure there's no unexploded ordnance here."

"You say that like you've encountered this before," Andrew said wryly.

"No, this is definitely a first. But I did have a college professor who mentioned discovering a Civil War–era cannon in a client's garden. Legal and Regulatory Considerations for Historic Garden Conservation. It was a painfully dull class, except for that day."

"Can't have been as dull as a three-week learning module on diagnosing pustular rashes."

I laughed. "We'll have to agree to disagree on that. Can you keep an eye on Sam while I take some photos of the area?"

Andrew nodded. I pulled my phone from the back pocket of my jeans and snapped shots from different angles while my mind set off on its own journey, imagining a young Margaret running through these woods, so carefree and innocent. Would she be disappointed if the restoration didn't include this part of the land? Or would raising the issue cause her unnecessary distress?

I crouched down to photograph the folly's entrance. Still lost in my musings, I didn't notice the low branch from a nearby tree jutting out at a sharp angle above me. When I stood abruptly, I smacked my head against it and let out a hiss of pain.

"Are you all right?" Andrew asked.

"I'm fine," I said, more embarrassed than anything. But as I reached up, I realized my hair had snagged on the rough bark. I tugged at it gently.

Andrew approached me. "Hold on. You're going to make it worse."

With a sigh, I relented and let him slowly untangle the snarl of my bun from the branch. He worked with careful, precise movements, showing no signs of impatience, despite Sam's giggles and my cheeks flushing with embarrassment while I had no choice but to stand there like a helpless child.

It felt like an eternity before he finally freed the last strand. "There. All done."

"Thank god. Please tell me it's not as bad as it looks."

I reached for my hair, hoping to restore some of my dignity, but Andrew caught my wrists. "Hang on. I think you've cut yourself, too."

He stepped even closer, brushing his thumb along my cheekbone. "Just a slight surface wound, but we should clean it out."

I wanted to tell him that it was unnecessary, but the look he gave me left no room for negotiation on the matter. Fifteen minutes later, we were back at Havenworth. I left Sam to visit with Margaret while Andrew sat me down at the kitchen table with his first aid kit.

"This might sting a little," he said, dabbing at my cheek with some kind of antiseptic.

I winced, rearing my head back. "A little?"

"I did warn you." He cupped my chin with one hand in a gesture that was somehow gentle and authoritative all at once. I knew it was just his clinical training, but I couldn't help my heart from stutter-stepping in my chest. It had been ages since I'd been this close to a man. I didn't realize until this moment how much I'd missed it.

Andrew was my employer, I reminded myself, even more embarrassed at my reaction than when I was caught in the tree.

I pulled out my phone to distract myself while he treated the cut, and I inspected the photos I had taken of the folly. It was such an odd structure. Most follies were designed as feature pieces in the gardens, but this one was tucked away—a secret hideout rather than a central focal point. It would be so much easier to leave it be, but whoever had designed it clearly meant it as an homage to Havenworth. How could I ignore such a vital piece of its history?

A pop of yellow next to the folly's entrance in one of the photographs caught my eye. I zoomed in closer to see what it was. "Huh."

"What is it?" Andrew asked.

"Cowslips. I didn't notice them anywhere else in the forest." They were a common wildflower in England, with tiny yellow bell-shaped flowers blooming at the end of a long calyx. There was nothing odd about finding them in a spot like that, but I couldn't shake the heavy feeling settling in my gut.

"All done," Andrew said. "Next time, try to be a little more careful with your head. After all, I'm paying you for all that expertise inside of it."

I smiled, though cringing inside at the reminder ours was nothing but a professional relationship. "Thank you for your excellent medical service."

"Speaking of, I need to get to the hospital now."

Once he left for work, I detoured to my bedroom to finally inspect the state of my hair in the vanity mirror. It was worse than I expected. It was a disaster. Some kind of sticky residue had glued needles and bits of bark to my hair. I groaned with embarrassment at my reaction to Andrew's touch when he was probably looking at me like I was radioactive.

My attempt to brush out the knots was futile. With a frustrated sigh, I gave up on the brush and opened the florilegium. At least when it came to gardening, I was a competent, capable human. It would have been easier if the book were in some kind of order or came with an index. But this wasn't a textbook. It was someone's personal artwork. A book that was likely never meant to be shared with anyone.

Some of the meanings Irene ascribed to the flowers were logical. Roses for love. Rue for regret. But others were a surprise. Beautiful, showy dahlias representing modesty and carnations for heartache. The language of flowers wasn't something taught in any classes. There was no official dictionary or definitive guide. And yet every meaning I read in the florilegium somehow felt so real. I couldn't imagine the flowers holding any other significance.

As I paged through the book, I landed on a drawing of cheerful yellow flowers. Cowslips, just like those growing next to the folly.

Irene was quite young when she had drawn them—barely a teenager—but the details of the delicate flowers and long tubular calyxes were utterly mesmerizing. I let my gaze travel down to the details.

Cowslips.

Primula veris.
Blooms in spring.
Meaning: death.

It was just a flower. Not an omen. But I couldn't help but think of all the lives lost during the war. How much fear and desperation the people here must have felt.

Margaret had been only a child back then. But even at Havenworth, she hadn't been safe from the devastation.

Chapter Seventeen

IRENE

September 7, 1940

The next weeks passed in a blur. In the evenings, we would sneak off to another nightclub, drinking and dancing until we could barely stand straight. James's social circle was as wide as the entire city. People knew him in every room we walked into, greeting him with handshakes and jovial slaps on the back.

It was exhilarating.

At least until the sunrise came and James disappeared once more. I knew I should be grateful for those quiet hours when he was at work. That was the time for me to focus on my art. Here, I had all the peace and quiet I needed to dedicate myself fully to my craft. Except that every time I picked up my pencils, I found myself utterly devoid of inspiration. I told myself it was because I didn't have the exquisite beauty of Havenworth to spur my creativity, but that wasn't quite true. There were stunning gardens all over London.

It wasn't Havenworth I was missing. It was Margaret.

Would she ever forgive me for leaving?

I had written to my family only once to tell them I was alive and well. I thought, perhaps, with enough time passing, they would come to understand my reasons for leaving. I was an adult now. It was time for me to find my own path in life. But no one had written back. It seemed Father had meant it when he said I would no longer be welcome in this family.

On one particularly lonely afternoon, when I had nothing to distract me from thoughts of my sister, I found myself reaching for my florilegium and coloring pencils. I let my mind drift aimlessly as the tip of my pencil swept across the page. But the drawing itself was not aimless. When I finally set my pencils down, I realized I had sketched a fresh bunch of daisies emerging from a garden bed.

I set my florilegium aside, not ready to deal with the feelings the image of my own creation unearthed. It wasn't until the next morning that James spied it on the coffee table while I was preparing a quick breakfast for us. "Daisies?"

"They remind me of my sister."

I tried not to allow the longing to seep into my voice, but James noticed anyway.

"You miss her."

I nodded. "But it's for the best. This is where I'm meant to be."

"I think you should write to them again. I can see you miss them."

"My missing them doesn't mean they miss me."

"I expect your sister does."

I smiled weakly. "I don't think I'm quite ready to face any of them yet. The only person I want to think about today is you."

He came up behind me, wrapping his arms around my waist and nuzzling into my neck. I allowed myself a moment to revel in his touch. "If you're not careful, I'm going to burn these eggs. There'll be time for canoodling later."

There was something about his disappointed sigh that made me believe there was more than just his usual desire for affection at play.

I shut the heat off on the stove and crossed my arms. "What's the matter?"

"My uncle's asked me to come back into work today."

Despite my best effort to hide my disappointment, I winced. "We were supposed to spend the day together." We were meant to visit Kew Gardens together. James had promised me days ago that he had secured the time off.

"Please don't be upset with me. It's the war. Germany's been increasing its attacks on British radar stations. The war cabinet has been relentlessly busy, and my uncle needs my help."

"Of course I'm not upset," I lied. "But promise me you will at least be able to make it to Leslie's party tonight. Catherine swears it will be the party of the year, and you know he'll be miserably disappointed if you aren't there."

"I promise I'll be home in time," he said.

I adjusted the knot on his tie. "Make sure to ring the telephone if you're going to be late."

He picked up his briefcase. "Remember what I said about writing to your family. It might do you some good."

It would be easy to assume my husband was simply concerned about my loneliness, but something in his voice made me question whether there was more going on. "What aren't you telling me?"

"It's about your father," he said solemnly.

I stiffened. That was the last thing I expected James to say. "Is everything all right?"

"For now. I'm not supposed to say anything. It's all privy information." His lips pressed together in a hard line as his gaze shifted away from me toward a blank space on the wall.

A lump hardened in my throat, making it difficult to breathe, much less beg for information. "Please, James. I need to know."

"I overheard my uncle speaking with a colleague in the war cabinet yesterday. Apparently, your father's work with the committee has fallen out of favor with Churchill. The prime minister doesn't believe the technologies being pursued by the committee have any value. If your father is still planning on collaborating with the Americans, it's not with the prime minister's blessing."

A strange numbness crept over my skin. "My father is a smart man. I'm sure he has a reasonable plan."

"The Germans have already made it nearly impossible for our cargo ships to pass through the English Channel. Recently, they've been increasing their attacks in the Atlantic, attacking merchant and civilian passage ships alike. If your father is planning on traveling to America soon, it might not be safe anymore."

"Surely the government wouldn't let him travel if it were dangerous."

James rubbed his temple. "If you wrote to him or even called, perhaps you could find out when he's leaving. My uncle's connections might be able to help him ensure safe passage at the very least."

"Thank you."

"Try not to worry. It will all be fine." He kissed me on the cheek before leaving.

I stood in the foyer for a long time, haunted by the unwelcome thoughts of my father, knowing I would never speak to him again. I had no doubt John Clarke was capable of looking after himself, or that James would do everything in his power to help. So why had I not revealed that I knew exactly when Father was traveling?

James did arrive home in time for the party, just as he'd promised. His mood was considerably lighter than when he'd left for work that morning. I couldn't say the same for myself. Thoughts of my father had plagued me all day. Surely he wouldn't still be planning a visit to America if conditions were unsafe. But there was no way to know for certain without asking him.

I didn't have the courage for a telephone call. Instead, I made my way to the post office and sent a telegram.

Do not go to America. Not safe.

I didn't know what else to say. I had no facts or details to provide. But at least I hadn't done nothing.

Thankfully, the excitement leading up to Leslie's party was a welcome distraction. The dress fit perfectly, the hem hitting just above my knee. I'd never worn anything so short before, but as Catherine said, youth lasted for only so long. If I didn't enjoy a dress like this now, when would I ever?

James appeared to share that sentiment the moment I stepped into view. His eyes widened as he took me in, a heady mixture of lust and admiration flashing across his face. "Absolutely gorgeous."

"Thank you." I beamed from the compliment. "I see you've made the minimum effort."

James was dressed in black trousers and a crisp white shirt. "That is because you are my gilding."

I raised an eyebrow. "Does that make you the innocent one?"

"Absolutely."

I laughed as he led us out the door. The late-summer air was beginning to cool, but I didn't want to mar my meticulously planned outfit with a coat or jumper. Luckily, Leslie's townhome was only a short walk from our place, which made it easier to memorize the directions and potential hazards for our return. The nightly blackouts had turned the streets into a perilous journey, the white-painted curbs doing little to help pedestrians safely navigate.

The home itself was much larger than I'd expected, though knowing what I did of Leslie, nothing ought to have surprised me. He was unconventional in every way, and his living space reflected that. The walls were painted a deep cobalt blue, a striking contrast to the historic building's intricate millwork. The furniture was an eclectic mix, each piece seemingly plucked from a different era. A green Victorian fainting couch was positioned next to the ornate fireplace, flanked by an orange armless cocktail chair, while the rest of the decor leaned decidedly toward art deco. To some, it might have seemed chaotic, but I could tell nothing about it was accidental.

There were over a dozen people already inside when we arrived. Some I recognized, like Catherine and Robert, while many others were new faces—part of Leslie's revolving social circle. James immediately wandered into the crowd to chat with someone he recognized, leaving me to fend for myself.

Fortunately, I didn't have to wait long before Catherine waved me over. She whispered something to the dapper gentleman at her side before greeting me with an air-kiss, as had become our custom. "Thank god you finally arrived! This party has been dreadfully dull."

"You look like you've been occupying yourself well enough." I gestured to the man who had been speaking to her moments before.

"Oh, Reginald? He's a painter," she said, infusing the term with a hefty dose of disdain. "He's handsome but painfully conceited."

"How is it he wasn't conscripted yet?"

Catherine threw her head back and laughed like I'd just recounted a joke. "Because he's the son of an earl. His daddy made sure his precious heir wasn't sacrificed for king and country."

I frowned, thinking of Michael. I knew it was naive to be surprised that so many healthy young men from well-to-do families were able to avoid conscription, just as James's connections had quickly pulled him out of Holloway. But it ran so counter to how Lady Montgomery wielded her wealth and power. She viewed it as her duty to do everything to support the war effort, no matter the cost. Then again, the cost for her wasn't the life of a child.

"I'm weary of talking about men. They're all a terrible disappointment. Let's get you a drink, and you can tell me more about growing up in America." She linked her arm through mine.

The first time she asked me about my childhood, I'd assumed she was simply making polite conversation. But over the past few weeks, I'd come to realize she was genuinely curious. It would be easy to dismiss her as flighty at first glance, but she listened intently to my stories, as dull as they were, and always seemed to want to know more.

I recounted the story of the time my mother let me stay home from school so I could help her prepare the floral arrangements for a fundraising gala at the mayor's house. We decorated the entire ballroom with dark-blue and purple hydrangeas offset by white orchids. The mayor's wife was so impressed, she invited my mother and me to stay for the dinner. We were woefully underdressed, but I still found it to be the most magical evening of my life.

I had just finished telling Catherine about how the waitstaff had sneaked me so many chocolate truffles, I'd nearly retched, when I felt someone's gaze land on me. A prickle formed along my skin. I scanned the room. Roger stood alone at the bar, sipping a pint of ale, watching me.

"Ignore him," Catherine said.

"He hates me."

"He hates everyone. He's been utterly miserable since he was a child."

I shook my head. "The way he stares at me, though. It's like he thinks I'm an insect he wants to squash with his boot."

"Don't be so dramatic. No one can possibly know what any man thinks. Half the time, I'm not sure they're capable of intelligent thought at all. It makes absolutely no sense that Roger and James are even friends. James was terrible to him growing up. He bullied Roger relentlessly, and yet, somehow, they're now the best of chums."

"Surely James wasn't cruel as a child," I said, unable to reconcile the image of my husband as a schoolyard bully with the man he was now.

"James was whatever he needed to be," Catherine said with a shrug. "Oh, there's Arthur. I've been dying to see him again after our date the other week. We'll catch up later."

Alone once more, I settled into my seat and searched for a friendly face among the partygoers. The only face I saw was Roger's. He started walking in my direction, never once letting his hard stare falter. My heart pounded quicker. What could he possibly want from me?

I didn't care to find out.

I quickly rose to my feet and took off in search of the bathroom. I climbed the curving iron staircase and found myself wandering a long hallway with a handful of doors to choose from. I reached for the knob of a random door on the right and cracked it open.

"Please don't open that," a man said behind me.

I wrenched my hand back. It was Leslie. I hadn't seen him all evening, despite this being his home. He was dressed in a dramatically long cape made from some kind of gold lamé. "I'm very sorry. I was just looking for the bathroom."

"Seems to me you were looking for an escape."

I bit my lip, unsure how much to confess. "I still don't feel like I quite fit in."

He tilted his head, offering a kind smile. "To be honest, sometimes I don't either. But at least I have the benefit of age, and the wisdom to not care."

"Is that why you were hiding at your own party?"

He studied me closely for a moment, then said, "Come with me."

To my surprise, he led me through the door that he'd forbidden me from opening just moments before. It was not a bathroom or even a spare bedroom, as I'd anticipated. The room was dark save for a strange red glow. Tables lined the walls, cluttered with strange contraptions and trays filled with liquid. My mind spun with confusion before the pieces finally clicked together.

"This is a darkroom," I said in wonder.

"I'd be happy to show you how it works sometime."

"Really?"

He nodded. "There are few people I trust to have the patience and appreciation for this kind of work, but I suspect you would be the one to surprise me. The most important rule is to never, ever open the darkroom when you are not meant to."

"Does that ruin the pictures?" I asked, worrying that I may have destroyed Leslie's work.

"Not to worry. The trays are empty at the moment, but yes. Developing photographs is all about balancing the light with the dark."

"The same can be said for human beings," I mused.

"Spoken like a true artist."

I sighed ruefully. "I can hardly call myself that. I've barely found the inspiration to draw at all since I arrived here. When I was at Havenworth, all I wanted to do was leave so I could pursue my art. But now that I'm here, it's as though I'm too afraid to try."

"Perhaps you just need to dig a little deeper for inspiration. Some of the greatest art comes from times of struggle and challenge."

I cast my gaze to a photograph drying on a line above me. It was an image of a mother gripping a small child's hand tightly as they stood in a queue for a train. The child reminded me of Charlie—so vulnerable and yet brave in the face of such uncertainty.

"Hopefully that will be the case for me. The entire reason I came here was to pursue my art."

"And here I thought it was for love."

"Of course I love James," I said quickly, realizing how my words sounded. But something about Leslie's quiet compassion made me want to confess the truth. "It's just . . . James promised we would be starting a new life together in London, but he's so busy working all the time we never seem to spend any time together."

Leslie picked up a small towel lying on a nearby table and wiped his hands. "James has made many promises to a lot of people lately."

"What do you mean by that?"

"Only that you have to be responsible for your own destiny. You can't rely on anyone else if you truly want to be happy."

"Is that why you aren't married?"

He laughed. "No. The reason I'm not married is because I'm a terrible scoundrel who can't possibly be expected to endure the boredom of a single person when there is a veritable feast of possible lovers out there to enjoy."

I giggled, still not accustomed to his licentious ways. "Speaking of which, I should probably let you get back to your party."

"Mmm, yes, there is a pinup model out there I've had my eye on." He reached for the door, then paused and turned to face me with a serious expression. "The offer still stands. You're welcome to come by anytime."

"Thank you."

I followed Leslie out of the darkroom, determined to not let his wisdom go to waste. James was my husband. There was no reason for me to be afraid of him or of expressing my feelings.

I returned to the party, searching the crowds with each step. I didn't see Roger, to my relief. Perhaps the oaf had finally grown tired of pretending to be a civilized human being and had gone home. But I couldn't find James either.

I found Catherine flirting shamelessly with an entirely new man. I tugged her elbow to pry her attention away. She swayed clumsily, nearly toppling over before her prospective lover caught her around her waist.

"Have you seen James?" I asked.

"He's probably outside having a cigarette," she slurred. "Leslie is so ridiculous about not allowing anyone to smoke inside."

"The only vice that man does not approve of," the man added with a snicker.

Despite a trickle of worry about Catherine's drunken state, I left her in the man's company to go search for James, figuring she could take care of herself for a little while longer. It was pitch-black outside, and the night air was shockingly quiet. Most people had no doubt retreated to their beds by this hour. With any luck, James might even be willing to head home instead of returning to the festivities.

He wasn't anywhere in sight of the front entrance. I found myself torn between concern for his whereabouts and frustration at his disappearance. Lately, it seemed like he was distancing himself from me at every party and nightclub we attended, choosing to spend the time exchanging a few words or a laugh with every familiar and unfamiliar person he encountered. But what kind of wife was I to question him when he had taken me in and helped me escape Havenworth?

The sound of voices coming from a nearby alleyway caught my ear as I walked. When I turned the corner, I could make out only the faint outline of two people in the moonlight, but I recognized James's voice instantly.

"If you can't guarantee the shipment, then I'll find someone else."

"How am I supposed to do that with those blasted U-boats firing on everything in sight? I can't afford to lose another ship." That was Arthur, Catherine's new beau. What on earth did he and James have to talk about in secret like this?

I crept closer.

"I've already told you the ship will be fine as long as you continue to deliver on your promises. The Germans won't attack an ally."

My stomach dropped, disbelief coursing through me.

"I'm not their damn ally. And I'm risking a hell of a lot here."

"You took the money," James said with a sharpness I hadn't thought him capable of. "It's too late to change your mind."

"You bloody bastard."

"Don't let me down. That information needs to get to Berlin one way or another."

No. This couldn't be true. Nausea churned in my stomach so forcefully, I could taste bile on my tongue. James was a traitor.

I had married a traitor.

A low, droning siren wailed in the distance, breaking my fugue. I spun on my heel and ran as fast as I could. I didn't know where I was going. I didn't even care. I just had to get away before James knew I was there.

My heel caught an uneven section of pavement. I stumbled, nearly crashing to the ground, twisting my ankle in the process. The pain seared through the joint, forcing me to stop and catch my breath. I looked around for any clue as to my location. I had no money, no friends of my own, and nowhere to go.

How could I have been such an idiot? My father had warned me about James, but I'd refused to listen. I had to tell somebody. The police or the military. But would they believe me? I had no evidence, and James's money and connections had already helped him escape prosecution once before. A fresh wave of nausea hit me, this time causing me to double over and retch. I wiped my mouth with the back of my hand, blinking away the tears burning my eyes.

The sound of heavy footsteps behind me made my heart slam against my ribs.

Had James heard me?

I started to run, but a sharp, searing pain jolted through my ankle. A pair of arms locked around my body in a viselike grip, yanking me off my feet. I tried to scream, but a hand slammed over my mouth as my assailant dragged me backward.

"You're coming with me," the man whispered in my ear.

Not James.

Roger.

Chapter Eighteen

IRENE

September 7, 1940

"Calm down, you fool," Roger hissed in my ear as I thrashed and fought against him. He dug his fingers into my flesh until I nearly crumpled in pain. "I'm not trying to hurt you."

"Let me go," I begged. We were tucked inside an alley, covered by the utter darkness of the blackout, with no one to hear me. The wail of the air raid sirens drowned out the sound of screams.

The release of his hands was so sudden and unexpected, I didn't think to run. I froze in terror like a cornered rabbit, pressed against the brick wall.

Roger towered over me, broad shoulders like a cage. "You need to come with me. I would prefer if I didn't have to force you to be quiet about it."

The threat wasn't lost on me. He would hurt me without a second's hesitation. But I refused to cower. "Why should I do anything you want?"

He didn't say anything, but the pistol he pulled out of his pocket spoke loudly enough. He nudged me forward to a parked car with the butt of his weapon. With the pistol still firmly pointed in my direction, he opened the passenger door. "Get in."

The fear that invaded my senses was unlike anything I'd felt before. It chilled my blood and turned the air in my lungs to ice. I knew that nothing good would happen if I listened to him, but I was too afraid to find out what would happen if I didn't.

The windows of the car were darkened. Roger got into the driver's seat, then sped off with no caution despite the darkness. A bright flash of orange crested over the sky before the sound of an explosion rang out.

"They're bombing London," I said, my voice shaking with horror.

"It was only a matter of time," Roger replied, his tone disturbingly flat.

It wasn't just one bomb. Dozens fell in the distance, lighting up the sky with terrifying flashes. How many lives were being torn apart in that moment? How many homes obliterated? The questions crowded my mind, more paralyzing than my own fear. As Roger drove, the shock of it dulled my awareness of time or direction. I only knew that we'd arrived somewhere unfamiliar, a part of town I didn't recognize. He parked on a narrow, unremarkable street and turned the ignition off.

"Out," he instructed.

I tried to retain my composure as we entered a small apartment building, fighting the urge to limp from my sore ankle. Surely if Roger were going to kill me, it would be somewhere far from London, not somewhere like this. Somewhere with regular people sleeping next door who would wake up to the sound of a fight or notice a body being dragged off. At least, that was what I told myself as we bypassed the elevator for the stairwell.

My body shook from exhaustion as we climbed the flight of stairs before he finally led me to a door. Inside was a tiny flat with only a ratty brown sofa and a single dining chair in the room. No art. No personal effects. No signs of anyone actually living here.

"Sit," Roger ordered, angling his head toward the sofa.

My legs were too shaky to argue. I collapsed onto the sofa. Roger pulled a yellow ribbon from his pocket and tossed it onto my lap—the same one I had bought for Margaret weeks ago.

"You were the one following me that day."

He shrugged. "I've been following you from the day you set foot in London."

The gravity of my situation finally overwhelmed me. Tears trickled down my cheeks.

Roger sat across from me on the chair, one ankle draped casually over his knee, smoking a cigarette as he watched me. "I didn't take you for a crier."

"I didn't take you for a kidnapper," I shot back.

"Yes, you did. You've been wary of me from the moment we met."

"My instinct for bullies is never wrong."

"In this case, it was." He stubbed out his cigarette and leaned forward, resting his forearms on his thighs. "I'm not your enemy. In fact, I'm the only thing standing between you and a prison cell at the moment."

I tried to swallow my reaction, but my throat was as dry as tinder. "What do you mean?"

He blew out a puff of cigarette smoke. "I know you told James about your father's work with the Committee for the Scientific Study of Air Defence."

I froze, my breath folding in on itself. "I don't . . . I don't know what you're talking about."

He raised his eyebrows and smirked like I'd amused him. "When James was arrested, he was found to be in possession of a number of classified documents."

"Maps," I said. "He told me they were maps of Britain. He was trying to predict where the next attacks would be."

"I've no doubt he's arrogant enough to believe he could manage that better than the entirety of Britain's military intelligence. But he had far more than just maps in his possession."

Bile rose in my throat. "If that's true, why was he released without charges?"

"Money and influence have always had a way of determining innocence. MI5 has been watching James for almost five years. His sympathies for the fascist movement have been known since he was a student at university."

"You're MI5."

He nodded.

I exhaled slowly, the pieces of this awful puzzle finally clicking together. "All this time you've been watching him, while claiming to be his friend."

"If you expect me to offer any remorse for that, you'll be sorely disappointed. Having a personal connection to James has made it easier to uncover some of his activities."

"I don't understand what any of this has to do with me."

He leaned forward, resting his forearms on his knees, cigarette ash falling to the floor. "Among the documents we found in James's possession were details of a technology that has the potential to render the German air force impotent. A device that would allow our planes to be equipped with radar technology. But in the hands of the enemy, it would give them an unprecedented advantage. Do you know what it was called?"

A chill fell over me.

"The cavity magnetron." He stared down at me for an uncomfortable moment. "I see you do recognize it. That would put you in the company of only a handful of individuals in this country."

"My father invented it."

"Indeed, he did. But that doesn't mean it belongs to him. It belongs to Britain. To the Committee for the Scientific Study of Air Defence. So why would a man like your father betray his country to give that information to James Atherton?"

"He didn't!" I shouted before I could stop myself. The expression on his face was enough to make me realize the trap I had just walked into.

"Did your father make a habit of entrusting you with his scientific discoveries?"

I closed my eyes, cursing myself for being so stupid. "No. He wouldn't do something like that. He's meticulously careful to maintain secrecy." But that wasn't the whole truth. My father had been sloppy of late. The pressures and worry of his work, of Margaret's health, and all the other responsibilities on his shoulders meant I had seen information I shouldn't have. And despite all his warnings, I'd told James about the invention, too.

"You may be surprised to hear I agree with you."

I frowned, confused by his admission. "You do?"

"Your father has spent over a decade working on behalf of the country, with not a single leak of information until James came into the picture. The only person who could be responsible for James's knowledge of the technology is you." He finally sat down once more, resting his forearms against his thighs so I had no choice but to meet his hardened gaze. "You have a chance to make this right, Irene. A chance not only to help your father, but your country as well."

"What are you talking about?"

Somewhere outside in the distance, a car horn blared. Roger ran his thick fingers through his hair, mussing it into an untidy mess. "For all his faults, James is not a stupid man. He's aware he's being watched. We know he's been gathering information about your father's work, but we don't know to what end or who he is working for. As close as I am to him, you are even closer."

"You want me to spy on James?" The notion was so absurd I could barely wrap my head around it.

He smiled for the first time all evening. "Exactly."

"But I'm not trained to be a spy. I have no idea what I'm doing. Surely you must have agents you could call on instead."

"The fact you aren't trained is the reason you're perfect for the role. He's been smart enough to realize he's being watched since his arrest. He'll be suspicious of anyone new that enters his orbit. You will gather information on his comings and goings. The names of anyone he meets. Books he's reading. Packages he delivers. Strange patterns to his behavior. And every second Thursday at three p.m., you will meet me at a location of my choosing to deliver that information."

"But what if James realizes what I'm doing? How will I hide it from him?"

"You're a smart girl, Irene. I'm sure you'll figure it out."

His answer left me with a chill. What Roger was asking me to do was an impossible task. James was too cunning not to discover my betrayal, and too cruel not to lash out when he did. He'd been so charming when we first met, but tonight, beneath that composed exterior, I'd seen a side of him that terrified me.

I gathered my breath for one last question. "If I agree, what do I get out of this?"

Roger stubbed out his cigarette in a glass ashtray. "The chance to avoid spending the next twenty years in Holloway."

Having seen James's true nature, I wasn't convinced of which was the better option. But I didn't have a choice.

Chapter Nineteen

Julia

Present Day

I went to check on Sam and Margaret a little before lunch. Margaret's nurse was just finishing testing her blood pressure when I walked into the orangery. Sam lay on the ground next to them, coloring on a blank piece of paper.

"Looking good today, Margaret," the nurse said jovially as she packed the cuff back into her bag. She was somewhere in her forties, with long black hair pulled into a sensible braid and vivid purple scrubs that had monarch butterflies printed all over the top.

"Humph," Margaret responded. "You say that every time, and yet you still insist I'm not allowed any sweets."

"I'm only looking out for you," the nurse said with a practiced mix of humor and rebuke. "I'll be back tomorrow. Try to get some exercise today if you can. A short walk would do you good."

"So would a chocolate biscuit now and again. It keeps the body young."

The nurse laughed. "Make sure she doesn't sit around all day," she said to me as she walked out.

I put my hands up in defense when Margaret narrowed her eyes at me. "I won't make you do anything you don't want. Promise."

Margaret lifted her chin. "I knew there was a reason I hired you."

"Speaking of that, are you up for looking at more garden plans?"

She waved her hand. "Yes, yes. But first Sam and I need to finish our game."

I looked at Sam. I had thought he was coloring, but despite all his scribbles, there was nothing on the white paper in front of him. In fact, the pen in his hand wasn't actually a pen but rather some kind of long broach with a sparkly gemstone at the end. "What game is this?"

"You'll have to wait and see," Margaret said, sharing a sly glance with Sam.

I pressed my lips together, wondering whether I ought to say something about the safety of the pointy instrument in Sam's fist, but he set it down a second later and lifted his paper triumphantly. "I'm done!"

"Pass me that book over there, will you?" Margaret said to me, gesturing to the large hardcover sitting on a small side table just out of her reach.

I picked up the book—a seventh edition of *Experimental Physics*—and handed it to her. She set it on her lap and placed Sam's blank page over top. Then, with the edge of a sharpened pencil, she began shading over the page with a surprisingly precise hand. As she worked, a delighted smile overtook her.

"Wonderful, Sam. Just wonderful."

Slowly, the graphite shadow was broken up by faint white lines where the pencil's lead hadn't reached. Margaret held up the paper to reveal what Sam had done. Using the brooch, he had made an indentation in the paper in the shape of a truck. Below it, he had carved his name in big, uneven letters, all of it hidden until Margaret had traced over the edge with the pencil.

"It's a secret message," Sam said, eager for my approval.

"That's incredible," I said. "Well done."

"One of the evacuees taught me to do this. Charlie and I used to pass notes to each other when we were meant to be studying. It used to drive Irene mad . . ." Margaret's voice trailed off, lost to a distant memory.

It was all I could do not to gasp at her mention of her half sister. She had said it so casually that I wondered whether she even realized it, but then a look of pain passed over her dark eyes. I pushed aside my disappointment. I wanted so desperately to ask her more about Irene. What she was like and how she'd become so fascinated by the language of flowers. Why did she leave? But the question that bothered me the most was how the florilegium ended up back at Havenworth.

Margaret cleared her throat, disrupting the charged silence. "It's been ages since I've been able to teach anyone my tricks. I'm grateful Sam is such a keen pupil."

The mention of secret messages made it impossible to tamp down the question that had been gnawing at me all week. "Margaret, have you ever heard of the language of flowers?"

"I'm ninety-two years old. There are few things in this world I haven't heard of."

"Did you ever use it? Or communicate that way?"

Her expression softened. "A long time ago. It was never something I had much interest in. Why do you ask such a thing?"

I wanted to tell her what I'd found in the florilegium, but my better judgment reined me in. This was something I needed to discuss with Andrew first. "Curiosity. That's all. Can I show you some of the designs I've been working on?"

She didn't believe my excuse. I could sense it in her narrowed eyes. "I suppose we can't keep putting that off. Show me what you have."

I knelt next to her and opened my laptop. "This is the parterre. The outer quadrants were carefully planted with distinct color schemes, but the inner circle that connected them was filled with white heritage roses. Parterres are typically very formal, but from what I can tell, the ones at Havenworth were done in a more free-flowing, meadow-like style. What do you think?"

Margaret nodded along, but there was no excitement or joy radiating from her, as I'd hoped.

"It should be straightforward enough to replace the laburnum tunnel that leads to the walled gardens in the back," I continued, hoping something would spark in her. "The moon garden was the smallest one over here. Followed by the cottage garden, and the kitchen garden over here. I don't have much information on the latter. Do you remember what vegetables your mother might have planted there?"

"I spent much of my childhood avoiding the mere mention of vegetables. I certainly wasn't involved in planting them."

Sam snickered.

I shook my head in mock disappointment. "We can leave the kitchen garden to another time. That won't require the same kind of planning as the rest of it. There's one last thing we need to discuss, though."

Margaret looked at me shrewdly, no doubt sensing the hesitancy in my voice. "And what is that?"

"Most of the hardscaping in the garden is in relatively good shape. The garden walls will only need a small amount of repair, but there is the back wall exit to the woodlands that's been bricked over. We could have that reopened if you like, but the folly—"

She uttered a soft, startled sound and pressed her hand to her lips. The sharpness faded from her brown eyes as she once again fell into the distant past. "I haven't thought about the folly in so long. Charlie and I used to play inside it, even though it was terribly unsafe. We called it our fortress. The place that would keep us safe when the Germans came. Can you repair it?"

An ache entwined my heart. "No. That's what I needed to tell you. I don't think I can. The cost alone would be prohibitive, but finding an expert who can build that kind of thing would take a lot of time."

She took in a sharp breath.

Instinctively, I inched closer to her. "Margaret, are you okay?"

She nodded slowly, a sad smile forming on her lips, and held out her hand. I took it in mine. She squeezed my hand with a tight grip. "I know you are doing everything you can. I'm not worried about the cost, or the time, even if I don't have much of it left. Some things are more important than that. Do you know what I mean?"

I swallowed hard and willed myself to nod even though I wasn't sure I understood at all.

◆ ◆ ◆

"What are you doing? Put those scissors down right now!"

The screeching tone in Helen's voice nearly made me accidentally slice off a chunk of my hair I hadn't intended. With my nerves on edge, I set the scissors on the edge of the bathroom sink. "What are you doing here?"

"Looking for you. Were you really about to cut your hair with kitchen shears?"

"They were all I could find," I admitted.

She crossed her arms in utter disgust. I probably should have felt a little bit of shame, but I had never cared too much about my looks. "Practical" was the most charitable word to describe my clothing, and my fingernails were perpetually lined with mud. I had neither the skill nor the patience to wear makeup regularly. The only time I made any real effort was when I needed to impress new clients.

"Wait here," she instructed. "I'll be right back."

She disappeared down the hall as quickly as she first appeared, still not telling me why she had come looking for me in the first place. I was tempted to finish the job with the kitchen scissors while I waited for her return, but I was certain Helen would give me the kind of lecture that would make me regret it. Instead, I peered across the hallway at Sam. He was sitting on the bed, practicing the secret-message technique Margaret had taught him, utterly mesmerized by his new trick.

Helen reappeared a minute later with a small pair of scissors in hand and instructed me to sit on the edge of the claw-foot tub.

"What did you do to yourself?" she asked as she tucked a small hand towel around my neck.

"Tree sap," I replied. "Peanut butter or rubbing alcohol can get it out, but it's easier to hack it off."

"You are utterly ridiculous. When's the last time you had it cut properly at a salon?"

I shrugged. "Probably a couple years."

"Stay still," she admonished. "You have lovely hair. If you took better care of it, you might realize that."

I did my best not to move or fidget while she snipped at my hair. Tufts of blond fell like snowflakes onto the tile below. I wondered, briefly, whether I ought to be nervous about letting her have free rein with my hair, but there was no hair disaster that couldn't be solved with an elastic and a few bobby pins. "You never did tell me what you were doing up here."

"Oh, I wanted to apologize for being late," she said in a voice that lacked her usual buoyancy. "And to thank you for taking care of dinner."

"It wasn't a big deal. Margaret didn't even complain about my cooking this time."

She stretched out a length of my hair with a comb and snipped off another chunk. The amount of my hair covering the floor had reached a terrifying level now. "You won't tell Andrew, will you?"

I looked up to study her, but she immediately tilted my head back to a neutral position. "I would feel better keeping a secret from your brother if I knew the reason." Tonight wasn't the first time Helen hadn't shown up when she promised she would. When we first met, I had pegged her as a little flighty. Well meaning but perpetually disorganized. But that didn't sit right now that I'd gotten to know her better. She was the kind of person who looked you directly in the eye when asking how you were doing. I had never seen her be anything but conscientious of others, especially with Margaret. The only thing flighty about her was her tendency to be late.

She sighed. "I started taking classes after work, and it's been difficult getting home on time to help with Margaret and all the things I promised to do."

"Is that it? I was expecting something a little more scandalous. Why would Andrew have a problem with that? He seems like the kind of person who supports education."

She pulled two strands of hair from either side of my face toward her, comparing their length before slicing off another inch. "Not this kind of education."

I twisted to look at her, wondering whether she was actually hiding something scandalous. She threw her hands up in frustration at my sudden movement. "Helen. You can tell me. I promise I won't say anything."

She guided my head back in line with my spine. "I'm studying to be a hairstylist."

I laughed, more with relief than anything. "I kind of wish you had mentioned that before I let you have a go at my hair. But I still don't get why you're worried about Andrew finding out."

"He won't be happy about it. It's something I've always wanted to do, but Andrew insisted I go to uni instead. He said we're incredibly fortunate to have Margaret looking out for us, and it would be a dishonor to her if we didn't pursue a proper career."

I winced on her behalf, imagining too easily Andrew delivering that lecture. My parents had been the same way, refusing to help me with college unless I enrolled in a practical degree that promised a lucrative future. When I landed my job with Hartwell & Sons, I was so proud that I had proved them wrong. My debts and successes were entirely my own.

But I couldn't help but hear the thread of truth in their warnings. Big dreams came with even bigger risks. I had lost my job, my reputation, and my life savings. I had no other skills to fall back on. "It's hard being an older sibling. I'm sure he just wants to protect you as best he can."

"Spoken like an eldest."

My smile was tight. "We can't help it. It's in our nature to be absolute know-it-alls. But even I know no one can tell you how to find happiness. You have to make your own choices because you're the one that has to live with them."

She sighed. "Of course you had to be sensible. Couldn't you have said something outrageously out of touch that would solidify my belief that no one understands me?"

"I wouldn't dare say anything like that when you're holding my hair hostage."

"Wise woman. The thing is, I know Andrew's right. Most children don't have a fairy godmother like Margaret. It would be wrong to waste that kind of opportunity. I ended up in accounting because I was always good at maths and numbers. I tried so hard to convince myself this was the right path for me, but no matter how hard I try, I wake up every day dreading it."

"Margaret doesn't seem like the kind of person who would be mad at you for following your heart."

Helen set the scissors down and sat beside me on the edge of the tub. "She's only ever wanted our happiness. But I don't think I could deal with Andrew's disappointment."

"Why don't you talk to him? If you told him how you really feel, he might surprise you."

She shook her head. "He won't understand. Duty is everything to him. Anyway, I've been talking too much about myself. You're all done. Tell me what you think."

I stood up and inspected myself in the mirror. The change was more drastic than I had anticipated. My once-long hair now sat just below my shoulders, with gentle layers framing my face.

"Please say you don't hate it."

It was different and different had always been bad. I hated change. And yet I couldn't find a single thing to dislike. The shorter length made me look younger, and the layers brought attention to my cheekbones. "You did great. Thank you. I can see why you want to be a stylist."

"You won't tell Andrew, will you? I don't think I'm ready for that conversation yet."

The idea of keeping another secret from him didn't sit well, but I was smart enough not to wade into a sibling disagreement. "I won't bring it up. But you are going to have to talk to him at some point."

"I know," she said with a resigned sigh. "Just not yet."

My phone, which I'd left on the edge of the sink, buzzed with an incoming text. I reached for it, but not before Helen caught sight of the message preview that flashed over the screen.

Please call me. I know you're upset but it's important.

"Who's Ryan?"

"No one."

"That didn't look like no one."

For the briefest moment, I wondered what it would be like to share my secrets with Helen the way she had with me. How would it feel to confess all the terrible mistakes I'd made? Trusting Rebecca. Believing I knew best how to help. Putting my entire career and reputation on the line to help her, when the only thing I did was lose her forever.

I deleted the message without reading the rest. "It's nothing."

Chapter Twenty

IRENE

September 8, 1940

It was nearly dawn when Roger dropped me off outside of James's flat. The Luftwaffe had ceased their terrifying attack, but my hands still shook as I fumbled for the key to let myself in. James must have noticed my disappearance last night. He would have questions. I wouldn't have answers. My once-beautiful dress was in shambles, the delicate lace shredded at the seams. I hadn't had the chance to look in a mirror, but I had no doubt my hair and face were just as tattered.

I'd tried to come up with a plausible explanation for where I'd been, but there was no good reason for me to go anywhere without him when I'd been entirely dependent from the minute I'd set foot in this city. Especially not when the bombs fell.

I hesitated with my hand on the doorknob. What if I didn't go in? What if I just ran away? What if I returned to the safety and security of Havenworth and begged forgiveness?

No. There would be no forgiveness if I didn't make things right. I had jeopardized my father's lifework. Possibly even the fate of this war. Roger had offered me a way out of the mess I had created. I had to do this. I twisted the doorknob and walked inside.

James wasn't in the living room or kitchen. For a moment I thought maybe he hadn't yet come home and I wouldn't have to explain where I'd been.

"Irene?" I heard him call out from the bedroom. "Is that you?"

I opened the bedroom door to find him sitting up, dressed in nothing but his drawers. At one time, the sight of his bare torso would have made me lose my breath, but now the only feeling I had was confusion.

I didn't want to believe all the awful things Roger had said about James. Roger was a creep and a liar. But the James I'd seen last night was not the man I thought I knew. How would I live with myself if James was working for the Nazis and I did nothing about it?

"Where did you go last night? I looked everywhere for you." His words were slurred from last night's indulgences, but the hurt sounded real.

"For a short walk," I answered quickly. "I had a burst of inspiration and wanted to draw the creeping jasmine under the moonlight. But then I heard the sirens. I tried to look for you, but I couldn't find you anywhere. A kind stranger directed me to a safe refuge in the tube station nearby."

"Quite a memorable way to end a party, wasn't it? I'm sure Leslie will be disappointed he was upstaged by the Luftwaffe. Not to worry, though. Only the East End was affected. The Germans wouldn't be so crass as to attack Buckingham Palace or anywhere close to it. We're safe here."

A chill slid over my skin. Could he really be so callous about what happened last night? "That's very reassuring. I was so worried about you."

He yawned and scrubbed his hand over his face. "I had some business to take care of. By the time I returned to Leslie's, everyone had scattered. I hope you didn't worry too much."

"It was hard not to worry when I heard the explosions."

"You don't ever need to worry about me." He flipped back the covers, urging me to slide in next to him. I hesitated a fraction of a moment, all the awful things Roger had told me replaying in my mind.

I wanted to run away as far and as fast as I could. But I had no choice but to obey. "I know how to take care of myself. Whatever happens, I'll be just fine."

It was spoken like a promise, but I couldn't help but wonder if it was a threat.

◆ ◆ ◆

James didn't leave me alone for the next three days. He insisted we needed time together to cheer my mood. I couldn't tell him my mood had everything to do with my fear and anger and confusion at the impossible situation I was in.

He took me to Kew Gardens and Hyde Park. All the places I had wanted to visit. But I took no joy or inspiration from the outings. Every time he held my hand or kissed my cheek, I wondered whether he knew what Roger had asked of me. Whether he knew of my betrayal the same way I knew of his.

I didn't want to believe he was capable of the things Roger had accused him of. It would mean I'd been as foolish and obstinate as Father believed. I'd been the one to give away his secrets and jeopardized everything he worked for. All because I'd allowed myself to fall for James's lies.

But even now, while my stomach lurched from his touch, my heart fought against the truth of it. I still desperately wanted to believe James was the man I'd fallen in love with. The man I had trusted with my heart and my body. The man I had pledged to love and honor for the rest of my life. But how could I trust anything to be real anymore?

There had been nothing unusual or suspicious in James's activities since the night of Leslie's party. No strange documents in the mail or secret meetings in dark alleys. I had no idea what I was supposed to be looking for. I doubted James would be stupid enough to leave out something obvious for me to stumble upon, even if he didn't know I was spying on him. With every day that ticked closer to my next meeting with Roger, I grew increasingly worried that I would have nothing for him.

"Are you not feeling well?" James asked one morning over breakfast.

"I'm fine," I replied, busying myself with the kettle.

"Something's clearly bothering you. You've barely eaten in days. Every time you think I'm not watching, you rub your temples like you're suffering a headache. Please tell me what it is."

I sucked in a breath, terrified I'd raised his suspicions with my distant attitude. I needed to be more careful. But how was I supposed to pretend to be a loving wife when every second spent with him felt like torture?

"You're not keeping anything from me, are you? I'd hate to think there are secrets between us."

My heart pounded so fast, I thought it would leap straight out of my chest.

"It's just . . . there was a man on the street the other day handing out pamphlets that claimed that Britain only entered the war because of a Jewish conspiracy to erode our national sovereignty and turn us into communists. Do you think that's true?" It was the first thing that came to my mind, but even as I said it, I felt unbearably vile. I was well aware of the growing antisemitism in this country. Blaming innocent people for the actions of a government was abhorrent and deeply unjust. But if James truly held fascist sympathies, these were the very kinds of views he might embrace.

He tilted his head with a half smile that would have made me weak with desire only a week ago. Now, all I could see was condescension. "I didn't realize you've taken an interest in politics."

"After everything you told me about your time with the RAF and with Michael . . ." I didn't need to fake the way my voice caught in my throat.

"There are a lot of people who believe Bolshevism is the biggest threat to Britain, and that fascism is the only defense we have."

"Is that what you believe?"

He rose from the table and retrieved the cup on the top shelf I had been struggling to reach. "I believe it does us no good to talk about things that upset you."

It wasn't an answer. He was too smart for that.

"Where will we go today?" I asked, deciding to change tactics. Every conversation felt like a game, each of us trying to ensnare the other into revealing our tightly held secrets.

"My uncle has called me back into the office, unfortunately. The bombings have caused quite the chaos in Parliament."

I smiled contritely, hoping he wouldn't sense the relief that had just washed over me. "I understand. You have important things to do."

He kissed my cheek. "I'll make it up to you soon, I promise."

I turned my back to him on the pretense of preparing my tea. It was all I could do not to shudder at his touch. Unfortunately, that didn't deter him. He cupped my shoulders with his hands. "You're upset."

"Of course not. I already told you I understand you have to work. How else would we have any food on the table?"

"Lonely, then?"

My sharp intake of breath gave me away.

"I'm certain Catherine or Leslie would be happy to keep you company. They both adore you. Or you could visit your family."

I dropped the teaspoon I was holding, scattering granules of sugar along the countertop. "What?"

"I know it's been hard for you to be away from your family. Especially your sister." He rubbed his hands along my arms, as though that would somehow undo the stabbing pain of his words. "A visit might do you some good. Especially until the Luftwaffe relents with their attacks."

"You're sending me away?" I was grateful he couldn't see my panicked expression.

He spun me around, forcing me to look at him. "Have you forgotten I know what it's like to lose one's family? I would give anything to have my parents back. I don't want you to deny yourself the chance to see your father or your sister."

"You're speaking as though you expect something terrible to happen."

As much as I wanted to avert my gaze, I forced myself to look at him and search for any hints or clues of something sinister beneath those smiling eyes, but I didn't see any. "Not at all, but there is a war on. No one can predict what will happen. But if not a visit, at least call them. I'm sure they're worried about you."

I sighed. "I'll think about it."

"Good."

He plucked the toast and raced out the door, leaving me standing alone in the kitchen, more uncertain than ever.

After James left for work, I counted to fifteen. And then I followed him.

He headed toward the tube station, striding purposefully through the crowds. I stayed a full block behind him so that I wouldn't be spotted, but that level of precaution wasn't necessary. He never once turned around.

Keeping up with him as he boarded the tube proved trickier. I rode a car down from his, nearly missing my chance to get off the train when I realized he'd exited. We were in the East End, near the docks. It was a part of town I hadn't been to yet, and it seemed like I had stumbled into an entirely different universe.

This area had been decimated by the attacks over the last few nights. Entire buildings reduced to piles of rubble while smoke plumed in giant tufts from the still-burning fires. The acrid smell was overpowering. And yet, while some people were sorting through the mess, most were simply out and about, carrying on with their lives as if nothing had happened.

With his tailored suit jacket, James stood out among the coverall-clad men working on the docks. He had no business of his own here. At least not any legitimate business.

Unfortunately, neither did I. It was one thing to blend in on the street, but entirely different navigating the maze of the docks. My shoes struggled to find traction on the slick, water-soaked stone walkways. As my heel caught, I stumbled forward, arms flailing. I managed to catch hold of the railing before I fell to the ground.

One of the dockworkers rushed over. "You all right, miss?"

I nodded, barely catching sight of James as he disappeared into a large brick warehouse. "Yes, thank you. I'm just clumsy."

"You don't look clumsy," he said. "You look like you've wandered into a place where you don't belong."

My shoulders stiffened. "I'm just here to bring my husband lunch."

His thick eyebrows furrowed as he took in the distinct lack of a lunch kit in my hands. "Why don't you tell me his name and I'll bring it to him."

"I'd rather bring it to him myself."

"Visitors aren't allowed on the docks. Especially not today."

I swallowed hard, realizing how terribly I'd caught myself in my own web of lies. "That's right. My husband did mention that, but I'd forgotten. I'd best go before he gets upset with me."

I walked away quickly, keeping my head down the entire time. But instead of leaving, I wound my way around the back of the rows of warehouses to see whether there was another way in. To my luck, I found a door propped open with a cinder block.

I peered in but couldn't see anyone inside. The warehouse was dark and filled with crates. The clatter of my heels against the concrete reverberated too loudly inside the large space. Nerves prickled my skin. How would I explain my presence to James if he caught sight of me?

Roger's warning played back in my head. My only other choice was a prison cell in Holloway, if I was lucky. It would be easy for him to prove that I had given James the information about the magnetron. I slipped off my shoes, cursing the damned rationing of stockings, and continued forward through the maze of crates. Each one of them was stamped with a large, six-pointed star and the words "Continental Shipping" beneath.

"It's just over here, as promised," a male voice said, startling me so much that I stumbled back into the crate behind me. I held my breath to see if anyone had heard.

"It better be good this time."

James.

I gathered my wits enough to sneak around the side of the crate as their footsteps echoed closer. A loud creak, followed by the sound of the crate door banging open.

"Bottles of Riesling. Straight from Rhineland."

"Impressive," James said. "I'll give you fifty quid for the lot."

"Twice that and I won't smack you for the insult."

"Eighty," James repeated. "Do I need to remind you who you work for?"

I tiptoed to the edge of the crate to catch a glimpse of them. I didn't recognize the other man, who wore a cap that obscured my view of his face. He and James were facing each other, oblivious to my presence. The threat of violence permeated the silence between them. Finally, the other man grumbled an acceptance while James laughed as though they'd just played a friendly game of chess.

"I trust you'll make sure this gets to our friends in Valencia." James handed him a small envelope that the man tucked inside his pocket.

"I'll make sure of it."

I waited until both men left before tracing my steps back the way I'd come. Too many thoughts and questions raced through my mind. Was this what Roger cared about? German wine? No, there had to be something else he wanted. Something more important than the wealthy indulging themselves.

The sun was blindingly bright as I sneaked out the door at the back of the warehouse. I bent down to put my shoes on, but something—someone—grabbed me and flung me against the wall. My back throbbed from the pain. I blinked away tears to see the dockworker who'd spoken to me earlier staring down at me. "I told you to get out of here."

I swallowed hard. "I'm just leaving now."

He leaned closer, the smell of sweat burning my nose. "Seems to me like you're looking for trouble."

"No. Please. Just let me go."

"We don't tolerate thieves around here." His fingers dug in tighter to my arms until I struggled not to cry out. "You rich types think you're above the law. Think you're so special the rules don't apply to you when the rest of us are working to the bone to keep you clothed and fed. Maybe I ought to hand you over to the police and see what they think."

"I don't . . ." I said quickly. "I don't think I'm special. I thought my husband was having an affair, so I followed him here."

The man laughed viciously and let me go. I rubbed my arms with relief. "Get out of here and don't come back. But if I ever see you again, I'll toss you into the Thames myself." He pointed a finger at me, leaving no doubt he was serious.

I retrieved my shoes and slipped them on, then took off as fast as I could, not stopping until the docks were as distant as a memory.

Chapter Twenty-One

IRENE

September 12, 1940

My heart still raced by the time I returned to the flat. I'd been too careless at the docks. What if that awful man knew James? What if he told him I'd been there? If James suspected I was spying on him for Roger, he would be furious.

I didn't know which man I ought to be more afraid of.

It took ages before my hands stopped shaking and even longer for my breathing to return to normal. I splashed cold water on my face, and then I waited.

Finally, I heard the lock of the door click open. I rose to greet him like I had every other day, not wanting anything to seem out of the ordinary. Except there was nothing ordinary about any of this. My husband wasn't returning from a long day at the office. And I wasn't the dutiful wife awaiting his return. Our entire lives were a charade.

"Hello, my love," he said, leaning in to kiss me on the cheek. The physical affection rattled my composure, my spine stiffening ever so slightly. It didn't escape his notice. He leaned back and regarded me with confusion. "Is everything all right?"

"Of course," I said with false cheeriness. "It's just that you said you wanted to go to dinner tonight, and I forgot to make a reservation like you asked. Please don't be cross with me."

He smirked. "What could have possibly kept you so busy that you forgot such a simple thing?"

"I was lost in a drawing," I answered quickly.

"It must be quite the drawing if it distracted you so. I'd love to see it."

My throat went dry. "It's not finished yet. I hate showing my work before it's done."

He squeezed my shoulders with his hands. "Then I'll just have to wait patiently until it's ready. As it is, I'm not upset about dinner either. In fact, I think it will be nice to stay in tonight. I brought you something."

"What is it?"

"Why don't you change into something a little nicer first?"

"Of course," I said with a strained smile. My skirt and blouse were pretty, but I had chosen them to blend in today, not stand out. James preferred when I wore my fanciest outfits.

I disappeared into the bedroom and selected a dress made from rich green satin, silently scolding myself for my carelessness earlier. But surely if James had any suspicions about me, he would have already acted upon them.

"Is this satisfactory?" I asked when I emerged from the bedroom, adding a twirl so that the skirt of my dress flared out. But there was nothing carefree about my actions. "Now what is this surprise you have planned?"

He took my hand and led me into the living room. I held my breath, terrified of what awaited me.

"What do you think?"

Perched on top of the coffee table were a bottle of wine and two glasses. My throat went dry. "What's this for?"

"Do I need a reason to spend a romantic evening with my wife?" He uncorked the bottle and poured two glasses of the straw-colored liquid. "I hope you like it. It's a Riesling. Very difficult to acquire these days, but I wanted the best for you."

He handed me a glass before raising his. "To the unbreakable bond of our marriage. May we always be as happy as we are today."

"To us," I said, forcing a smile to my lips as I tapped the edge of my glass against his.

James gave no indication of suspicion in the week following that first near-disastrous day at the docks. But even if he had, I had no choice but to continue following him. There was a pattern to his days that became almost predictable after a few weeks. Most days, he did go to work for his uncle. But on Wednesday mornings, he headed to the docks. I never dared follow him inside again, but it was simple enough to figure out what he was acquiring. He enjoyed his luxuries too much not to bring some home.

In the afternoons, he visited gentlemen's clubs and other less-reputable establishments, presumably to sell his goods. I memorized the locations of each place he visited, reciting them in my mind each night as I lay in bed, listening for the air raid sirens, praying the Luftwaffe wouldn't set their sights on this part of town.

I counted down the days with dread until I was meant to meet with Roger again. Knowing he worked for MI5 didn't improve my opinion of him at all. He was still a liar. I didn't trust him. Roger was the reason I was forced to remain here with James, pretending to be infatuated with him when he repulsed me right to my very soul.

We were set to meet in Hyde Park. The location had been his choice, but it was a good one. I wouldn't have to lie if James asked where I'd gone. The cloak-and-dagger routine didn't come naturally to me. If

James wasn't already suspicious, it was only a matter of time before my awkward smiles and hesitant conversations gave me away.

I lingered next to a redbud tree as I waited for Roger.

I didn't hear anyone approach, and yet I felt a presence behind me. My spine straightened instinctively. I didn't turn around.

"That's a beautiful tree."

"It's a redbud," I responded. "It symbolizes treachery and distrust."

"I hope that doesn't mean you intend to betray me."

I clenched my hands into fists at my sides. "That would be impossible, considering I owe you nothing. You are the one forcing me into this arrangement against my will. My only intention is to give you what you want so that you leave me and my family alone."

"Well then, let's hear what you have for me."

"I followed him to the docks last week. He's getting shipments of luxury goods. The first time was wine, but there's also been fruit and clothing and even perfume."

"We're aware your husband has been distributing rationed and contraband goods on the black market. No one is going to convict him for that, especially when a sizable number of his customers have the means and influence to keep him in business. What I need is evidence of treason. Irrefutable proof he's conspiring with the Germans."

I felt like a scolded child. "There was an envelope. He gave it to one of the dock workers. There may have been more."

"What was inside of it?"

"I have no idea. He didn't open it in front of me."

He let out a frustrated breath. "That doesn't help me."

"It's the best I could do."

"Try harder."

"How?" Exasperation grated the edge of my voice.

He shrugged. "Search James's papers. Listen in on his phone calls. Use your feminine advantage to make him reveal his secrets."

"What are you implying?"

"James has been known to spout his mouth off around the beautiful women he beds. I don't see why it would be different with you."

My cheeks heated with a mixture of embarrassment and rage. A group of women approached us on the path, chatting animatedly as they walked. Their presence was the only thing that stopped me from slapping Roger across the face.

My pulse thundered in my ears as I waited for the women to disappear. I turned to Roger, forcing him to meet my hard gaze. "You are vile."

"I'm also the only friend you have in this city." He adjusted the brim of his hat to cover his dark eyes. "You'd do well not to forget that."

"How can I when you remind me at every occasion?"

Chapter Twenty-Two

JULIA

Present Day

The crew arrived a week after Andrew finally signed off on the budget, unloading giant piles of soil and fertilizer from their trucks. The scent of fresh, healthy dirt buoyed my steps as I walked down the gravel path to greet them early that morning before the sun had risen to its full height. It was the scent of possibility.

Much of my work was solitary. Hunting through archives and old design plans, performing alchemy to render them into something real. It was a talent I'd honed for years. The physical part of the work—shoveling dirt and digging up old weeds—took collaboration. Some of it required specializations outside my wheelhouse, including expert masons to reconstruct elaborate features like the garden folly. I had no problems admitting I couldn't do it alone, but that didn't mean I wasn't still in control. Everything being done at Havenworth was under my name. It had to be perfect.

Andrew was up early and had offered to feed Sam breakfast while I met with the crew to go over today's plans. I hadn't worked with this team before, but I knew them to be good by reputation. The primary goal today was to remove the invasive weeds and ivy, and to uproot the dead boxwoods from the hedge maze. I had estimated at least a week for that work to be completed. After that, we would lay down the soil and amendments, and then the new plants would arrive.

"It's vital not to disturb any shrubs or trees that are still healthy," I told the crew leader. "Leave the camellias and rhododendrons unscathed. No chemical weed killers. This all has to be done by hand."

He was an older man with a short graying beard and weatherworn skin. "I'll make sure they're careful. They're the best in the country, and they'll treat every inch of this place like a newborn baby."

I thanked him for his reassurance, grateful that he understood the importance of a job well done over one done quickly. Still, I spent the better part of an hour walking around, making sure everything was going exactly according to plan. The crew leader was right, though. His team was impeccable, and there was no reason I couldn't sneak away for a quick breakfast.

Andrew and Sam were in the kitchen when I arrived, acting rather curiously. Sam was perched on the counter, cheeks bunched tight from a mischievous smile. Andrew was more stone-faced, but there was something odd about the way he stood with his hands clasped tightly behind his back.

"What's going on?" I glanced from one to the other, searching for a clue in their expressions.

"There's been a change of plans this morning," Andrew said.

Before I could ask what kind of change, Sam blurted out, "He got you a robot!"

"Well, not exactly a robot." Andrew stepped to the side, revealing a sleek metal espresso maker. "But it's proving to be as complicated as one."

My jaw refused to close as I stared at the gleaming appliance, which looked completely out of place on the butcher-block countertop. "But you don't even like coffee."

The slightest hint of pink tinged his ears as he ran a hand along the back of his neck. "It's rather repugnant, but I'm aware you enjoy it."

The idea of real coffee—not the horrid instant stuff Andrew had been providing for the last month, but actual espresso—was so exciting I couldn't help myself from throwing my arms around him. "Thank you!"

He stiffened, and I immediately regretted my impulsive action. Somewhere over the last few weeks, the animosity between us had given way to something verging on friendship, but we hadn't yet crossed the threshold of physical affection. And yet, before I could pull away and stammer an apology, his arms encircled me. "I'm glad you approve."

We broke apart, each of us as wooden as the branches of the wych elm near Havenworth's front gate. Rather than interrogate the moment, I busied myself grinding the beans.

Andrew hadn't skimped on good coffee either. The aroma was rich and earthy, enveloping me with a comfort I hadn't realized I'd been missing for too long. I took a sip and let out an uninhibited sigh of delight.

"I finally have a few days off from work," he said, with a self-congratulatory grin. "I was hoping you could give me a closer look at the work you're doing in the gardens."

My heart gave a tiny jolt. It wasn't unusual for clients to want a deeper look at the work, but Andrew had been putting a purposeful distance between himself and the gardens. "Yeah, of course. The crews are mainly on cleanup duty today. Once we've cleared out the weeds, I'll be able to get a better look at the stonework and assess what kinds of repairs are necessary. But you might find it interesting to see what's happening."

I wasn't nervous about Andrew's sudden interest in the gardens. I was confident enough in my work to show it off. But I couldn't keep putting off telling him what I'd found in the florilegium. I couldn't shake the feeling that nothing in the garden would feel complete if I didn't uncover the truth hidden in those pages.

We strolled the entirety of the grounds that morning, starting with the front, where workers were dismantling the vestiges of the hedge maze. The giant mounds of new soil made him do a double take, but he didn't complain. I explained exactly what would happen in each part of the garden. The plants. The color schemes. The feelings that each section of the garden should invoke.

"I admit, I don't have the same vision for this kind of thing that you do, but I'm impressed with how much you've accomplished in such a short time," he said when we finished walking through the back gardens. "My grandfather didn't talk much about his time here, but I know he adored the gardens. I'm excited to see how they would have looked when he and Margaret were young."

I glanced at Sam, who was entertaining himself with a snail he'd found crawling along the pathway. "Helen told me your grandfather was a child evacuee."

Andrew nodded. "He came here as part of Operation Pied Piper during the first year of the war. Over a dozen children from London were sent to Havenworth, but all of them save for my grandfather returned to the city after a few months. He was here for almost six years and became part of the family."

"Did he ever return to his real family?"

"Not until the war was over. It must have been a difficult choice to keep him here, but my great-grandmother was adamant he would be safer outside of London. And she was right."

"How so?"

"Their home was destroyed by an incendiary bomb in 1941. My great-grandmother survived, but one of his older sisters was killed."

I pressed my hand to my mouth. "That's awful."

"His father and two brothers all lost their lives on the battlefields of France. It was a tremendous hardship for my great-grandmother, but Margaret's parents made sure to send them money every month. Even after my grandfather returned home, Margaret's parents treated him like family. That's a funny thing about Havenworth. It seems like everyone who sets foot on these grounds never truly leaves. It takes hold of you."

"I can understand why."

We didn't say much after that. It was as though we had both said more than we meant to. It was dangerous to let myself get caught up in the fantasy of staying at Havenworth. Of thinking of it as a home where Sam and I could rebuild our lives. For us, Havenworth was only a job. One that would be over soon.

◆ ◆ ◆

Helen was late again for dinner that evening, but this time, when she came into the kitchen, she brought with her a stack of books from the library and an excess of excitement.

She set the books on the counter while I was drying the last of the dishes in the rack. "I know what Irene did!"

Her announcement was so unexpected, I nearly dropped the plate. "What do you mean?"

"Nobody in their right mind would escape to Nazi Germany during the middle of a war just because someone heard they'd done something wrong. I figured there had to be some kind of evidence against her that would make her do that. And that's exactly what I found."

I dried my hands on the tea towel and examined the titles along the spines of the old books. "The answer is in old science textbooks?"

She rolled her eyes. "History-of-science textbooks. And yes. It's all here. I swear."

I crossed my arms and leaned my back against the counter. "Okay. Let's hear it."

"I couldn't find any information about Irene Clarke when I searched either. But it did get me interested in the rest of Margaret's family. Andrew's always going on about how important it is to know our history. He made sure to tell me stories about our parents and grandparents growing up, but I've never really learned anything about Margaret's family, which is strange, seeing as they're kind of family by extension. So, I looked them up."

"And?"

She grinned. "There's lots of information about Margaret's mother, who descended from a baron. But it's her father who was really fascinating. Did you know he was the chair of the Committee for the Scientific Study of Air Defence during the war?"

"I didn't even know there was such a committee," I said.

"They were tasked by the military to develop antiaircraft technology. Their work was terribly important but not well known. There are loads of references to John Clarke's role on the committee on the internet, but not much beyond that. But I did find some information in these old library books." She flipped open one of the textbooks to a page she had marked with a torn piece of paper. "Read this."

Perhaps the most important advancement by the Committee for the Scientific Study of Air Defence was the cavity magnetron—a small vacuum tube capable of generating radar microwaves that changed the outcome of the war. Prior to its development, the British air force had few advantages over the German Luftwaffe, who terrorized the country in a relentless series of attacks known as the Blitz. The invention of the cavity magnetron allowed for even more powerful radar technology light enough to be installed on aircraft. It was a vitally important scientific discovery, but one that would have little benefit if it could not be produced efficiently and in great enough numbers for use by the RAF. The problem, however, was that Britain's factories did not have the capacity to mass-produce this very precise device, and were already overwhelmed by the construction of artillery and other war infrastructure.

Dr. John Clarke, the chair of the CSSAD, proposed a radical solution to this problem: Hand the technology over to the Americans. Clarke believed sharing the technology was the only way to ensure the mass scale-up of production. It was a risky proposal, considering the Americans had adopted a policy of isolationism and not yet entered the war. Many of his fellow committee members were opposed to the idea, but Clarke persisted.

On October 17, Clarke began Operation Josephine, carrying a prototype of the cavity magnetron and many of the country's other most valuable secrets inside of a metal briefcase. The covert journey, however, was not an easy one. The morning Clarke was meant to board the train to Liverpool, where he would then take a steamship to New York, the briefcase was stolen . . .

I pressed my hand to my lips, taking in the heavy information. "Do you think Irene was the one who stole it?"

"Who else? Don't you remember what Margaret said? How her sister betrayed the family? This must be what she meant. I've read everything I can about the mission, and they never found the stolen prototype. Look at the date."

October 15, 1940. That was the day after the last entry in the florilegium. The entry where she asked for forgiveness. "But how would she have known about the prototype in the first place?"

"It's possible her father would have let something slip about the nature of his work," she said, clearly stringing the facts and assumptions together in her head with the thinnest of threads. "Selling secrets of national importance to the Germans was one of the crimes she was accused of. What other kind of secrets would an eighteen-year-old girl know?"

I had no good answer for that. But something about it didn't sit right in my gut. Maybe it was because I had spent too much time getting to know Irene through her drawings. I didn't want to believe she was capable of doing something so unforgivable.

Footsteps echoed from the hallway. I looked over to see Andrew standing in the doorway. "What has the two of you so morose?"

"Nothing," I said quickly. "Why aren't you at work?"

"I was only due to cover a half shift today. Now what's this about Margaret?"

Helen and I exchanged a guilty glance.

"I think I know what happened to her half sister, Irene," Helen confessed. She relayed the same theory she had told me just a few moments earlier.

I expected Andrew's reaction to be just as reticent as mine. Instead, he nodded along as though it all made perfect sense.

"We can't be certain. Everything is just speculation. All we know is that she disappeared," I said.

Helen and Andrew didn't share many common features, but with their scrunched brows and slightly cocked heads, their expressions of pity were near identical.

"What other explanation could there possibly be?" Andrew asked gently. "The simplest answer is almost always the real one."

I turned my head and stared at the spot on the wall where an old water leak had discolored the paint. Pity was the worst kind of judgment.

"I know you're right. But . . ." I searched for the right words. "I don't like what it means for Margaret. I think the entire reason she wants to renovate the gardens is to find forgiveness for Irene and find some peace. But how can you possibly forgive that?"

Helen sighed. "I don't think you can."

Chapter Twenty-Three

Irene

September 26, 1940

Espionage did not turn out to be as exciting or dramatic as I had imagined. I spent most of my days tailing my husband across town and scouring our flat for any evidence against him that would satisfy Roger. On others, Catherine would insist on meeting for lunch, where she would regale me with the latest escapades in her love life. Sometimes we would shop along Oxford Street or Knightsbridge. It was jarring to indulge so ostentatiously when so many others were suffering, but any protest on my part would have aroused too much suspicion. Each day, London was fading into a shadowed version of the vibrant city I had come to know over the summer. Blackout curtains hung in every window. People walked with their heads down at clipped paces, a veil of fear hanging over them.

In the days since our meeting at the park, Roger had grown increasingly frustrated with my lack of progress. I had nothing to offer him. James never left a shred of incriminating evidence. If I hadn't overheard him the night of Leslie's party, I might not have believed Roger's accusations against him.

One late-September afternoon, James arrived home with a small package he asked me to deliver to Leslie the following day. It was light and wrapped in paper, bearing no markings. James told me it was supplies for his photography.

I hadn't been to Leslie's flat since the night of his party. Less than a month had passed, but it felt like a lifetime.

I took my time walking to his place, taking in all the changes the Blitz had wrought in the neighborhood over the last few weeks. Fortunately, Leslie's building had been spared from the bombings.

Leslie answered my knock with a wide grin. "Irene, darling. I was beginning to think you had forgotten about me."

I greeted him with a kiss on the cheek. "I could never."

He led me to the living room and poured himself a drink. He offered me one, but I shook my head. It was too easy to lose myself in the oblivion of alcohol. "To what do I owe the visit?"

I handed him the package. "James asked me to deliver this to you."

"How exciting." He sliced through the paper with a letter opener, revealing a dozen cylindrical canisters.

"What is it?"

"My sustenance. My raison d'être. My medium. Also known as film. It's impossible to find lately." He held up one of the canisters and inspected it. "Perhaps you would like to be my muse?"

"I'll have to pass."

"Then at least tell me you've brought some of your art to share."

I glanced instinctively at my purse, knowing my sketchbook was with me. The slight movement was enough for him to notice. He raised an eyebrow expectantly.

"All right. I can show you some of my sketches, but you must promise to be kind."

"I never make promises I can't keep. Show me anyway."

Leslie sat next to me and flipped open my sketchbook. "Mmm, very interesting," he said as he flipped through the pages, landing on one I'd done of the irises at Havenworth in full bloom. "The composition in this drawing is quite lovely."

Perhaps it was silly to care so much about something so trivial, but art had always been the thing that gave my life meaning and worth. Leslie's praise and insight were invaluable. He nodded approvingly at first, commenting on color choices and details. But as he made his way through the book, his enthusiasm gave way to subtle tilts of the head and frowns.

"You don't like it," I said.

"It's not that exactly. You're incredibly talented, and your attention to detail is remarkable. But these are illustrations. Real art is about urgency. Communicating something that only you can." He set the book down and took my hands. "My dear, there must be something burning deep inside of you that you desperately need to say."

I opened my mouth, but no words came out. Until now, my art had been nothing but an escape. A place to hide. But the weight of the secrets I carried had stolen my ability to draw. Could Leslie be right? Could art be the way to tell the world everything I could not say?

"Would you show me some of your work?"

Leslie rose to his feet with an exaggerated sigh. "I suppose fair is fair."

I followed him to his darkroom, where a dozen photographs hung on the drying line. The black-and-white images were an eclectic mix of scenery and objects and people, but each one was captivating in a different way.

"These are stunning," I said.

"The ability to develop film is as much an art as taking a good photograph. Everything about the darkroom is set up with exacting perfection. Would you like to learn?"

He explained the process from how to load the film in the development tank to the final bath. The science of it all was lost on me, but I did my best to memorize each step. It was utterly fascinating. I'd never realized light and dark could create such incredible beauty. He answered my questions patiently, no matter how silly. If anything, he seemed to appreciate the opportunity to provide more in-depth insight.

"Would you like to try?" he asked when the lesson was finished.

"Really? You would let me do that?"

"Of course. It's the only way to learn. I have some old negatives you can use."

He handed me a loupe to explore an old set of negatives and choose one of the images to develop. I landed on one of a young man alone in a field wearing a soldier's uniform. Something about the loneliness of the soldier spoke to me in a way I couldn't explain.

I was about to pick up the paper with the tongs when Leslie placed his hand on mine. "You need to use the ones over here; otherwise you will contaminate the liquid. The liquids must stay separate. That is the only way to maintain the integrity of the chemicals."

"Right," I said, chastising myself for the near error.

Leslie guided me the rest of the way. The result wasn't perfect. The bottom right corner of the image was blurry, but it was nevertheless a photograph that I had developed. Pride surged inside of me. Despite the poor quality, there was something familiar about the person. "That's you," I said with a gasp.

"In my younger years."

"Did you fight in the Great War?"

"I was a medic in the army. They sent me to treat the injured in Passchendaele."

It was so strange to think of Leslie on the front lines. He never spoke much about the current war. Like everyone else in James's circle, Leslie acted as though it weren't even happening. "Does it ever bother you that so many people you know have used their wealth and connections to live like kings while others are sent to fight?"

He was silent for so long, I feared I had upset him. When he did finally speak, he turned away from me. "There is no good that comes from war, though I have accepted it is at times a necessary evil. I cannot judge a man for wanting to avoid the horrors that I was forced to bear. Without men like your husband, I would not be able to do things that make life worth living."

"And what is that?"

One elegant shoulder rose. "Art. Liquor. Sex."

I let out a small laugh.

"I never said I was a sophisticated man. Deep down, I have the same wanton desires as anyone else. We all like to believe there are lines we will not cross, but there are always ways for those lines to bend."

I took my time returning to the flat. Leslie's guidance had filled me with an urge to pay attention to everything about the city I had missed these last few months. The Blitz had caused so much destruction, but there was something else rising out of it. The long grocery queues and blackout curtains and young women driving ambulances through the street. I used to perceive it all as sacrifice and burden. Now, I saw the courage in all those tiny actions. The small acts of defiance against the German effort to break the country's spirit.

It made me think of my father, too. I had resented his dedication to his work for so long. But he had known the war was coming. He had predicted the destruction the German air force would wreak and had devoted himself to finding a way to stop it. I didn't know if I would ever truly forgive the way he neglected me after Mother's death, but at least I now understood why he had.

Perhaps, if I found a way to appease Roger, my father would find a way to understand me, too.

The fact I had not produced any evidence in nearly a month of watching and spying on James weighed on me. My husband had stopped sharing even the smallest details of his days with me. But if he was suspicious, why did he keep me around? I was no longer naive enough to believe he truly loved me. He had only ever pursued me to gain access to my father's work, which I had handed over like a fool. So what use was I to him now?

There was something I wasn't seeing. Something that kept my nerves on permanent alert.

To my relief, James wasn't home. I pulled out my sketchbook, hoping the meditative act of drawing would allow my brain the freedom to find the missing thread that would pull everything together.

I didn't know where to start. I had never sketched from memory before. All my drawings were representations of what I saw in front of me. But I recalled Leslie's advice to me earlier in the day. What was it that I desperately needed to say?

The answer came to me in a rush.

I filled the page with elegant begonias, lush lavender shrubs, and a tall spire of foxglove. It was a combination of flowers I had never seen in any gardens, but the meanings behind them were the reason for it all.

Warning. Distrust. Secrecy.

This was what I needed to express. The message I needed my family to hear.

The tip of my dark-green pencil had worn down to a nub as I filled in the foxglove's broad leaves. As I searched my purse for the sharpener I kept with me, my fingers grazed something unexpected. A small envelope, bent and crinkled from too much time spent at the bottom of my purse. It was the note Catherine had given me weeks ago to pass on to James when we'd gone shopping during my first week in London. I'd forgotten all about it.

I tore it open.

In Xanadu did Kubla Khan
A stately pleasure-dome decree.
Where Alph, the sacred river, ran
Through caverns measureless to a man
Down to a sunless sea.

My excitement gave way to utter confusion. I recognized the poem from my school days. Why on earth would Catherine need to give such a thing to James? I had folded the paper back out to inspect the envelope when I did notice something strange. It was such a subtle thing that I thought my eyes were playing tricks on me. The dot above the first "i" had indeed fallen clean off the paper. It was caught in the crease of the page. The dot, unlike the rest of the letter, hadn't been made from the nib of a pen.

I stared intently at the dot, trying to make sense of it. Ink didn't simply fall off the page. The dot had to have been glued to the paper to look like a regular marking. But why?

Taking great care not to jostle the paper lest I lose the tiny dot, I set it down on the table and retrieved from my purse the loupe Leslie had given me as a parting gift this afternoon. I held the glass device to my eye as I leaned over the small dot.

I gasped in disbelief. This wasn't ink. It was a photograph of another message shrunk down to a microscopic size. Even with the loupe, I could barely make it out.

It was a series of coordinates, I realized. Each one carefully inscribed in black ink.

Chapter Twenty-Four

Irene

October 10, 1940

Roger was waiting for me at the bookstore in Mayfair, engrossed in a copy of *Crime and Punishment*. If he heard me approach, he gave no sign. He'd suggested we change meeting locations each time to avoid suspicion, and this particular shop was his choice. Judging by how naturally he blended into its dark ambiance—among the dusty shelves and dim lighting—I suspected he was a frequent visitor. The shop itself was quiet, with not a patron in sight. The lone shopkeeper, an elderly woman with reading glasses perched low on her nose, sat at the counter near the front. Even the jangle of the bell as I entered failed to draw her gaze from the book in her hands.

"This is how he's doing it," I said, handing Roger the strange letter I'd discovered.

He glanced away from the book long enough to inspect the page. "A poem?"

"Do you see how the dot above the 'i' is missing?"

He nodded.

"That's because it's here. See?" I carefully extracted the tiny dot from the envelope and balanced it on my fingertip.

Roger's eyebrows shot up, and he gave me his full attention now. "What do you mean?"

"It wasn't made of ink. Look at it through this." I retrieved the loupe from my pocket.

Roger hesitated before setting the book back on the shelf and taking the loupe from me and drawing my hand close.

I studied him as closely as he did the image. Stubble had formed along his chin. Dark brown with a hint of red. The shadows under his eyes were more pronounced than ever. I didn't know what he did for MI5 in the days between our meetings, but the stress of it was weighing on him.

"Microdots," he whispered, as he let go of my hand. The note of awe in his voice caught me by surprise. "It's a simple but ingenious technique developed by the Germans to conceal top-secret information in film negatives by reducing it to an unremarkable size. How did you get this?"

I hesitated for a moment, the thought of betraying my friend a sharp ache in my heart. Catherine had only ever been kind to me. She was the person who had shown me around London and made me feel like I belonged in this world. The one who didn't judge me because of my accent or my upbringing. "Catherine gave it to me a few weeks ago. I was meant to pass it to James, but I forgot. I only just found it."

"You think she's involved?"

"You know her better than I do," I said pointedly.

The slight furrow of his brow was his only reaction to my insinuation. "I've never known her to hold fascist views, but she's easily susceptible to influence. Her new beau, Arthur Douglas, is the owner of the shipping company James has been using to acquire his contraband goods."

Oh, Catherine. How could you? "I think it's coordinates. But it's difficult to see, even with the loupe."

"I'll need to take this for processing in one of our labs, but I'd hazard a guess these are from somewhere in England."

"Is that proof enough that James is a traitor? Can you have him arrested for that?"

He shook his head. "The technology is widespread across all intelligence agencies, and there's no proof he's passed anything on to the Abwehr. But it's a start."

"How much more can you possibly need?"

"I need evidence, not hunches."

I swallowed my frustration. "How am I supposed to do that?"

"You were clever enough to discover this much. I'm sure you'll figure it out."

James and I had plans to meet Catherine and her father for dinner only a few days later. It was my first time meeting James's uncle—the man who had secured James's swift release from Holloway and ensured he would never return to active duty. After everything I had learned from Roger, I couldn't help but suspect George Atherton was somehow involved in James's treachery. He was a powerful man within the government with far-reaching connections. He was also a sharply intelligent man, by James's account. My nerves were a frazzled mess all day. I needed to keep my wits about me tonight. There was no doubt he would be sizing me up, just as I would be doing to him.

James was on edge the entire afternoon leading up to the dinner, too. He criticized my clothing choices, insisting I trade the elegant black dress I had on for something more subdued. On the walk to the restaurant, he didn't say a word.

George Atherton was nothing like I'd imagined. In fact, if Catherine hadn't called out to us with an excited wave of her hand, I might have walked past their table without so much as a second glance. He was a wiry man with round spectacles too large for his face, and a dour expression entirely out of place in the glitz of the Savoy.

George rose to greet James with a formal handshake.

"Uncle, I would like you to meet my wife, Irene."

"It's a pleasure to meet you," I said, holding out my hand.

He shook it, offering the slightest hint of a smile. "The pleasure is mine. Catherine has told me many wonderful things about you."

There was nothing particularly strange about the evening. Catherine gabbed endlessly about herself. I feigned interest in her stories while keeping my attention firmly on the stilted conversation between James and his uncle, who spoke only of inconsequential things. The weather. The price of goods. Nothing that suggested a shared appreciation for the fascist movement.

"Irene, are you listening to me?" Catherine asked impatiently as the waiter refilled her glass of wine. "I just told you I'm thinking of breaking up with Arthur Douglas."

"Oh, yes. I'm sorry."

"No need to be. Daddy doesn't approve of him," she said, casting a sideways glance at her father, who showed no interest in engaging with this particular topic of conversation. "He thinks he's a fascist sympathizer."

"Arthur? I had no idea," I said, pretending to be shocked.

"He was a close friend of Sir Archibald Ramsay before his arrest," George said sternly. "It's unwise to associate with known traitors."

This was not the response I was anticipating. If George was the one behind the information James was passing to the Abwehr, surely he wouldn't look so negatively upon other fascist sympathizers. Testing him, I said, "Believing Britain ought to have stayed out of the war does not make one a traitor."

George's eyes narrowed on me. "I can assure you it is more than an isolationist attitude that landed Ramsay in prison."

"That's not what the newspapers said. I read that Churchill personally disliked him and arrested him for not toeing the party line."

"Ramsay is a bigot," George countered.

"Because he admired Hitler? Germany has toppled every country they've gone up against. It's only a matter of time before Britain is next. Perhaps it's wise to try to earn Hitler's favor before he invades our soil."

"Irene," James said firmly. "That's enough."

The entire table fell silent. The vile taste of my words lingered like ash on my tongue.

"You'll have to excuse me," Catherine said abruptly, pushing her chair back with a screech.

I excused myself as well and followed her to the bathroom. The room was dark with its maroon-and-gold wallpaper, but the row of vanities along the back wall were brightly lit. I found her sitting at the farthest one from the door, applying pressed powder to her nose. Her eyes made contact with mine through the mirror, and she snapped the compact shut.

"You're upset with me," I said carefully.

She lifted her narrow chin a fraction. "Because you were acting like an absolute ass in front of my father."

"James told me he appreciates people who can engage in political conversation. I wanted to make a good impression."

She let out a scornful laugh. "You believe the garbage you were spewing back there is simple political conversation?"

I winced. My plan had been to bait Catherine and her father with my comments. I hadn't expected her to react this way. "I thought you and your father held the same views."

"You thought terribly wrong. And clearly I did, too, in believing we were friends."

"I don't understand."

She rose to her feet and faced me properly. "Then I'll make it simple. My father has been fighting against the scourge of fascism for the better part of a decade. It is the ideology of the depraved. Anyone that believes Hitler's actions have been anything but a travesty is either evil or a fool. I never took you for a fool."

A fool indeed. I cursed myself for misjudging my friend so drastically. I'd been so quick to assume she held the same views as so many of the rich and privileged people in our circle. But she'd always been kind and thoughtful, despite her penchant for a good time.

She stalked off toward the exit.

Shame heated my cheeks. "Wait!"

She didn't stop. I caught up to her, tugging at her elbow. "What?"

"I don't believe any of that," I admitted. "I only said it because I wanted to know if you did, too. I was trying to trick you. I'm sorry."

Her eyes narrowed to steel slits. "Why on earth would you want to do that?"

I sucked in a breath. There was so much I wasn't supposed to tell her. But I was tired of playing by Roger's rules. I had to know for certain what Catherine's role in all of this was. "Because of the letters you've been passing to James," I finally said in a hushed whisper even though there was no one else in the bathroom with us.

"The letters? You mean those silly poems?"

I nodded. "They contained a secret code. One that revealed classified information about Britain's military secrets. I know it's difficult to believe, but it's true."

"You're lying."

"I'm not. I swear. MI5 approached me last month. They've been watching James for some time, but they don't know who he's working with." The words left my mouth so fast, I didn't have time to stop myself from confessing the truth. It was an overwhelming relief to finally unburden myself of these awful secrets. But as soon as I finished speaking, a wave of panic coiled around my lungs. If I was wrong to trust Catherine, it wasn't just my secrets in danger. It was my life.

Her face blanched, and the tension in her shoulders deflated like an emptied balloon. "You think I'm capable of that?"

"All I know is that the letters you've passed on could get you in a lot of trouble if you aren't careful. But if you tell me who gave them to you, I could help."

"No." The word was so quiet, I wasn't sure I heard her right.

"Catherine—"

"No," she repeated louder. "You might be capable of betraying your husband, but I can't do that. Not to James."

She walked away once more. This time, I didn't try to stop her.

Chapter Twenty-Five

IRENE

October 12, 1940

"That was quite the evening," James said as we left the restaurant.

I wrapped my arms around my waist even though the mid-October air was still warm, and kept my gaze fixed to the pavement. Dusk was coming earlier with each passing day, making even the simplest journey a treacherous affair. "Your uncle is a nice man."

"He's a churlish grump, but I owe him a debt for keeping me gainfully employed. And he seemed to like you."

"Did he?" After Catherine and I returned from the bathroom, I'd attempted to make up for my misstep, avoiding any talk of politics. In fact, I had barely talked at all the rest of the evening.

"As well as he likes anyone. Which isn't to say very much. But you're my wife now and forever, so his opinion is largely irrelevant."

Now and forever. The words sent my pulse racing again. Even when this was all over and I found the evidence Roger needed, I still had no way to free myself from James. "I hope I made a good impression. I wouldn't want to reflect poorly on you."

"I thought you were rather insightful and measured. I hadn't known you held such sophisticated views."

I smiled, even as the nausea churned in my stomach. "I've been reading the newspapers and listening to the wireless. I think it's important to stay up to speed on current affairs." How long could I keep up this charade? Every day, it grew harder to pretend I was still a naive, lovestruck girl, when every word out of my mouth felt like barbed wire being yanked from my throat. One of these days I was going to slip up, and he would find out I'd betrayed him.

If he didn't already know.

"Catherine seemed rather upset at the end of the evening. Did something happen between you two?"

My heel struck an uneven section of pavement, and I stumbled forward. James caught me by the elbow. My encounter with Catherine had left my nerves rattled. Had I made a mistake in trusting her? Or had my desire to spare my friend from suspicion clouded my judgment?

"A little too much wine with dinner," I said.

The air raid sirens wailed, drowning out whatever he meant to say next. It wasn't panic that took hold of everyone on the street so much as dread. The constant alarms, the sleepless nights, the endless fear that slithered into our dreams. The attacks had been happening for weeks now. I didn't know how much more of this I could handle.

"I think we should go to a shelter tonight," I said, noticing an air raid warden across the street, directing people toward a nearby church.

"There's no need. We'll be fine at the flat." He took my hand in his, sliding his long, powerful fingers between mine in a viselike grip.

"Please, James. The planes sound closer this time. I'm scared."

"Don't be ridiculous," he scolded. "We're not sleeping on a dirty, hard floor like peasants. I've told you already, the bombs won't drop in Mayfair."

An explosion rang out in the distance, vibrating the ground beneath us.

"You can't possibly know that," I said stupidly when the ringing in my ears ceased enough to speak.

His hand squeezed mine even tighter. "I know more things than you realize. There's no reason to be afraid."

He yanked me forward, giving me no choice but to follow, even though he was wrong. I had every reason to be afraid. His facade had been slipping lately, revealing terrifying hints of the man he truly was. Eventually, one of us was going to crack.

When we arrived home, he was still in a sour mood. He slammed the door shut, doffing his coat without offering to help with mine like he normally did. My moment of defiance had irritated him. I needed to be more careful, but the bombings had taken a toll on my patience.

"Please don't be cross with me," I pleaded. "I know you're right, but it's hard not to be frightened."

He angled his head as he smiled at me, pleased that I was once again his meek young wife. "We'll go to Café de Paris tonight. It's underground and much more pleasant than a church basement."

We hadn't been out to any nightclubs in the weeks since the bombings started. The idea of it now was too exhausting to contemplate. "I'm so tired. I just want to sleep." I yawned for effect, but it quickly turned into a real one.

His jaw tensed, a sign his annoyance had returned. "Have it your way. But I'm going. Leslie's been insistent on a night out."

"Of course. You should have fun with your friends."

Once he left, I contemplated heading for a shelter, but he would be even more suspicious if he came home to find me gone. Instead, I lay in bed awake for most of the night, listening for the attacks, even after the all-clear sirens had rung. It had all been for nothing, though. James never did come home that night.

I slept in late the next morning, only to be startled awake by an urgent banging. I rose with a groan and slipped on my robe. Trepidation weighed heavy in my legs as I approached the source of the noise. Who could possibly be visiting at this hour?

I unlocked the bolt and opened the door. "Catherine? What are you doing here?"

Her face was unusually bare of makeup, and her hair pulled into a neat chignon. If it weren't for her exceptional height, she would've been nearly unrecognizable. "I came to give you these."

She handed me a plain navy metal tin, roughly the size of two hatboxes, with a small white envelope resting on top. On the side of the tin was a small white six-pointed star, just as I'd seen on the cargo boxes the day I first followed James to the shipyards.

"I found them this morning," she said. "The box was dropped off a few days ago by a courier. This isn't the first time a package like this has arrived for James, but I've never bothered to open them. I assumed he was using my address out of convenience while he was with the RAF. Now I wonder if it wasn't just so he wouldn't draw suspicion to himself."

The tin was heavier than I anticipated, and cumbersome to hold. "Thank you."

"I hope you know what you're doing," she said darkly.

She walked off without another word. I didn't bother to chase after her, knowing it pained her greatly to betray James.

The tin was sealed tight. I eventually managed to pry it open with a butter knife. Of all the things that might have been inside, I did not expect to find a dozen children's dolls. Each one was exactly alike, with blond hair and a green dress. They looked like the kind of dolls Margaret liked to play with—the ones where you could manipulate the skinny plastic limbs into the silliest of positions.

I retrieved my loupe and opened the envelope next. Like the other letters, there was no return address, but the post office stamp indicated it had been sent from London.

Season of mists and mellow fruitfulness,
Close bosom-friend of the maturing sun

Another poem, written in black ink. The lines were familiar, but I couldn't remember the title or the author.

With the loupe pressed close to my left eye, I scanned the page carefully. The hidden message was above the "i" in "soft-dying day."

EUSLIV Oct 15, 2:30. We no longer need the girl. Get rid of her.

I leaned back against the sofa, a terrible dread swirling in my stomach. "EUSLIV" was the train code for Euston to Liverpool. The train my father was supposed to be on.

◆ ◆ ◆

I called Roger, despite his earlier warning never to do so unless it was an emergency.

"We need to meet," I said. "It's urgent."

"Saint James's Park. Near the canal."

I arrived there fifteen minutes later, but Roger wasn't in sight. After weeks of clandestine meetings, I'd learned he never liked to show himself first. He was always watching. Waiting.

I paced next to an iron park bench, causing the dry dirt to cast a slight stain on my shoes.

"That's a hell of a way to draw attention to yourself."

I stopped abruptly, turning to see Roger standing behind me, with an expression that was somehow amused and annoyed at the same time. There was a bruise around his eye that had faded to a putrid yellow, and it appeared he hadn't seen a razor in days.

I waited for a group of women to stroll past before I opened my purse and removed the tiny doll I'd wrapped in a pillowcase. "He's not just receiving hidden messages. I think he's using the microdots to send information to Germany, too. It took me a while to find, but there's a microdot on the inside of a skirt with a photograph of a map. The doll was inside of a box that had the same symbol that was on the cargo boxes when I followed James to the shipyards last month."

Roger was turning the small package over in his hands, wise enough not to unwrap it. "That's very clever of you."

"I am clever," I shot back. "Despite what you think of me."

For the first time since we'd met, he appeared genuinely surprised. His forehead wrinkled with a frown. "I have never not believed you were clever," he said in a voice so quiet, it was nearly a whisper.

"You did. You thought I was a fool for marrying James. And maybe I was." My throat was inexplicably tight, tears biting at the corners of my eyes. His nostrils flared with a sharp intake of breath, but he didn't say anything. "But I'm the one who's found every piece of evidence you have on James. Not you. I'm the one risking my safety. So don't you dare act like I'm a little dog trained to do your bidding, earning a pat on the head for fetching you a stick."

I fought back the urge to cry. He didn't deserve to see how his condescension upset me.

"I'm sorry," he said in a low whisper. "I was an ass."

I sucked in a breath. "You're always an ass."

"Perhaps, but I have never once thought of you as anything other than brave and cunning and honorable. I hate that I've had to involve you in the way I did, but I had no other choice. James has used his money and connections to elude MI5 at every turn. He's a danger to this country and everyone around him. Including you. Whatever mistakes you made are well in the past. You've managed to outwit him in ways no one else can."

We were standing close—too close. I smelled the faint trace of cigarettes on his breath. My pulse quickened, though not with fear. With something else I wasn't ready yet to admit. My heart was too easily led by praise and attention. I wasn't going to be a fool again. "I'm glad you're happy with the results. Hopefully this is enough to satisfy MI5 that I am not a threat to anyone."

He cleared his throat, taking a step back to put some space between us once more. "You might not be a threat, but we still don't know who's behind all this."

"We know it's not George Atherton."

His thick eyebrows shot up. "What makes you believe that?"

"In all the time I've been watching James, he's barely spent any time working for his uncle. I think he only gave him the job title to keep him out of trouble, but he doesn't trust him. We had dinner with his uncle last night. I pretended like I was a Nazi sympathizer. He looked at me like I was a rat sneaking across the floor to steal his crumbs."

"He could have been keeping up appearances in a public space."

I shook my head. "No. It was genuine. Catherine was there, too." I bit my lip, unsure whether to say anything else. I'd dragged her into this more than was fair already, but what choice did I have? "Apparently James has been using her as the go-between for his communications. When she realized that, she gave these to me."

"She's always been a bit of a bleeding heart. That doesn't mean her father holds the same views."

"Would you please listen for once?" I growled. "There's someone else behind this. There was a letter, too."

"What did it say?"

"It said E-U-S-L-I-V. October 15, 2:30 p.m. It's a train code. My father's supposed to be on that very train."

A grim expression came over him. "They must be planning something. Was there anything else?"

I bit my lip. Repeating the words aloud felt too close to an omen, as though I would be speaking them into existence. But Roger would find out soon enough. "Whoever James is working for knows about me. The message said I'm no longer useful and should be disposed of."

Roger cursed with a violence I was prepared for. "I'm pulling you out. It's too dangerous."

"What?"

"Your life is in danger now. You can't go back to James."

"But what about MI5 and all the threats you made about sending me to prison?"

His mouth hardened.

"What aren't you telling me?"

239

An expression I'd never seen in him before darkened his features. Shame. "That night I grabbed you at Leslie's party, I didn't tell you the entire truth."

My breath hitched. Every instinct in my body teetered on the edge of fight or flight. "What do you mean?"

He ran a hand through his dark hair, causing the ends to stick up in all directions. "MI5 isn't involved in this. After James was released from Holloway, my director told me to drop the case even though we had evidence he was attempting to pass information about your father's work to the Germans. The top brass thought it was a waste of time and resources to follow someone who wouldn't be convicted without absolute incontrovertible evidence. They redirected me to work on a different case, but I couldn't leave it alone. Not when I knew James was guilty."

My heart thundered in protest, disbelieving Roger's terrible confession. "You went rogue?"

He nodded. "People like James get away with everything. It's not right. When I saw you with him that first night, I knew you were the only way I could prove he was guilty and figure out who he was working for."

I swallowed hard, despite the painful ache in my throat. "MI5 has no idea I've been working for you, do they?"

He turned away, too ashamed to meet my gaze. "I know. That's enough."

My head spun. How could I have been so foolish? All this time I'd believed the danger I was putting myself in was worth it because I was helping Father. But Roger had no intention of helping anyone but himself. I'd gone from trusting one liar to another.

"Irene—"

I slapped him. "Don't you dare speak my name ever again."

With my hand stinging, I stormed off, leaving him too shocked to stop me.

240

My mind raced as I hurried down the path, too distracted to notice anyone or anything around me. How could I be so stupid? All this time I'd let Roger push me around and manipulate me with fear. I was so tired of being afraid and powerless.

Hot tears burned my eyes. I wiped them with the heel of my palm, too distracted to realize someone had crept up behind me until my purse was yanked from my shoulder. I gripped the strap before my assailant could steal it, my rage fueling me with an extra dose of adrenaline. The thief was young—barely my age—with a desperate viciousness in his eyes. We tussled with the purse for another moment before he let go. But he didn't give up.

He grabbed me by the arms and dragged me off the path, slamming me against a tree. His sweaty hand slapped against my mouth, cutting off my cry. He shoved his other arm against my throat, crushing my windpipe. I clawed at his arm and kicked wildly, but he was too strong. My lungs screamed for air. He wasn't just trying to steal my purse. He was going to kill me.

The dark spots bursting in my eyes grew until the entire world was black.

I fell to the ground. My knee slammed into a hard knot in the tree root, but I could breathe.

"Get off her!"

Roger was here. He'd shoved my assailant off me. But Roger didn't chase him down as he ran off. He let him go, instead turning all his attention to me. "Are you okay?"

Roger helped me to my feet, examining me with a look of unabashed worry.

"I told you . . . not . . . to follow me." My throat was raw, the words barely coming out in a ragged whisper.

"I always follow you," he admitted, inspecting me for more signs of distress while I clung to his arm to keep my knees from buckling.

"Always?"

He nodded. "I know I've put you in danger. It's my responsibility to keep you safe."

"You should have told me." I wanted to scream, but my swollen throat wouldn't allow it. I was so tired of everyone thinking they knew what was best for me. "You should have given me a choice."

"I know." He pulled me in close, wrapping his burly arms around me. I was too surprised to push him away. Or maybe, in truth, I needed the embrace more than I wanted to admit. I melted into him, letting him hold me until the violent tremble in my body finally receded. He released me, giving me a moment to regain my dignity. I hitched my purse higher on my shoulder and dragged myself away from Roger.

He chased after me. "Wait. Where are you going?"

"Back to James's flat."

"Didn't you hear me? I just told you it's over. You don't have to do this anymore."

"It's not over! If MI5 isn't going to stop James, then I have to."

"A man just tried to kill you."

"And that's exactly why I need to go back. Whatever was in that message is a threat against my father. He's supposed to be on that train next week. I have to find out what James is planning. I have to stop him. Because no one else will."

Chapter Twenty-Six

JULIA

Present Day

Andrew found me in the parlor later that evening. There was something about the room that drew me back each day—a quiet sense of history lingering in the patterned wallpaper and mismatched furniture. With no formal office, it was a convenient space to work after Sam was asleep.

"What's all this?"

I would have tried to hide the sheets of paper laid out on the carpet in front of me, but there was no way to do it quickly without rousing his suspicion. "Just playing around with the designs."

He stood over me as I sat cross-legged on the floor and peered at the papers. Each of the sheets held a rough, hand-drawn sketch of a section of the grounds. I had nowhere near the talent of Irene, but the purpose of these quick sketches wasn't aesthetic.

"You pierce my heart," he read from the paper in front of me.

I sighed, realizing I wouldn't be able to put off this conversation any longer. "Gladiolus. I'm trying to map out the designs with the meanings in the florilegium. I thought there might be some kind of pattern in here."

He lowered himself to the floor next to me and inspected the papers. "Have you found anything?"

"Not yet."

His knee brushed against mine as he angled forward and rested his chin in his hand. I swallowed back the hitch in my breath, annoyed at my body's ridiculous reaction. But the longer he studied the drawings, the harder it was for me to keep my heart from tumbling in my chest like a cement truck.

"I thought she might have taken inspiration for the meanings from the gardens, but there's not much rhyme or reason to it from what I've mapped out. From what I can tell of the drawings, the garden designs follow a more traditional pattern in keeping with the style of the times. But I know she used the meanings to communicate. Margaret said as much."

"What do you mean?"

"A few weeks ago, I showed her an image of Astrantia. She told me it meant courage. I didn't understand what she meant at the time." I opened the florilegium to the drawing of the delicate, starburst-like flower. "That's the meaning Irene gave it."

"Margaret has never once said anything about this."

"I don't think she remembered much about it until the restoration. But I can't shake the feeling Irene tried to use the florilegium to leave messages for Margaret."

His eyebrows shot up. "What kind of messages?"

"I don't know," I admitted. "But there's something unusual about the last entries. I know Irene was accused of some awful things, but what if she didn't do it? What if it was all a misunderstanding?"

I showed him the strange final drawings in the florilegium, explaining my theory about the daisy and the messages. Andrew took it all in in his quiet way, occasionally nodding along but giving no signs or clues he believed me.

"That's a lot to extrapolate from some eighty-five-year-old drawings."

"If I show Margaret the florilegium, it might trigger some memories. Or, at the very least, it might bring her some closure."

I braced myself for his admonishments and warnings that it wouldn't work. He had been clear from the start that protecting Margaret was the only rule at Havenworth.

"I'm not sure this would be enough for Margaret either. The people who love the most fiercely are often the ones who feel betrayal the deepest."

"Shouldn't she have the right to decide that for herself?"

He rose to his feet, not giving me an answer.

I stifled the urge to apologize. I hadn't meant to upset him, but it wasn't right to keep things from her. She was old and sick, not fragile. "Andrew, wait—"

"No, it's okay," he said calmly, holding out his hand for me. "I'm not upset. Or at least not with you. I just think I could handle this conversation better with a drink."

I slipped my hand into his, letting him pull me to my feet. Something electric and urgent prickled over the skin of my palm. He held on to my hand a second longer than necessary, and I wondered if he felt it too.

"Do you like whiskey? Margaret's always been partial to it, and I'm afraid we don't keep much else in the house."

"That sounds like exactly what I need right now."

He led me to a large wood cabinet along the far wall that housed a few bottles of good whiskey and some other liqueurs that looked like they hadn't been touched in ages. He poured the amber liquid into two tumblers.

I held the glass to my nose, letting it adjust to the intense aroma before taking the first sip. The whiskey was rich and earthy, the flavor redolent of walking through a damp forest. The alcohol gave me the courage to try again to get through to him. "I know it's not easy to see the people we love in pain. But if there's anything I know, it's that you can't protect them from the world either."

He stared at his untouched glass. "I don't understand how dredging up old wounds will bring closure. We'll likely never find out what happened to Irene."

"Maybe not. But maybe that's not what Margaret needs. Maybe it's forgiveness. Irene was remorseful about what she was doing. I think the sketch was her way of apologizing to Margaret."

"If she was truly remorseful, she would have turned herself in. Not run away."

"A person doesn't need to deserve forgiveness for you to give it."

He was quiet for a long time. The yellow light of the chandelier cast a shadow over his face that made it difficult to read his expression. Finally, he took a sip of the whiskey before asking, "If you had the chance to forgive your sister, would you?"

The question siphoned the air from my lungs. It was the question I had been running from for the better part of the year. The one I couldn't answer without dragging the darkest parts of my soul into the open. "I want to. But I've been too scared to let myself understand why I'm so angry."

"You could start by talking about it."

I laughed ruefully. "Is this your way of deflecting the conversation from Margaret?"

His arch smile disentangled my defenses like they were nothing more than pieces of string. "Perhaps a little. But I can sense the burden you're carrying. It's in your eyes, even when you try to hide it."

My throat was painfully dry. I finished the whiskey and set the tumbler on the marble top of the liquor cabinet. "I'm angry at Rebecca for dying. I'm angry at her for not trying harder for Sam's sake. I'm angry that I gave her every chance I could, and she threw it all back in my face."

He refilled my glass. "Addictions are complicated. Relapsing doesn't mean she wasn't trying or that she didn't care. Modern medicine can only do so much. There's often unspoken trauma behind these kinds of things that is hard to address."

I blinked back the tears stinging my eyes. "I think if I'm being honest, it's not her I'm mad at. It's myself. I'm so angry I couldn't save her. I nearly lost everything trying to, but it didn't work."

Emotions hiccuped in my throat. He pulled me close, enveloping me in his arms. I melted into the comfort he offered, knowing I would regret it in the morning. I hated showing weakness. What if he couldn't look me in the eye the next morning? How was I supposed to finish this job if my professionalism was in question? But he cupped the back of my head with a gentle touch, and every one of those worries faded like shadows in the night.

It would have been too easy to lose myself entirely in the firm muscles of his chest and the scent of his aftershave. I held on as long as it took for the hot tears to retreat. "I thought the whiskey was supposed to make these conversations easier," I said, rubbing my eyes with the heel of my hand.

His hands still rested on my shoulders, not quite letting me go. "Not easier. Just less inhibited."

He cocked his head to the side in an unexpected motion, frowning as he studied my face.

"What?" I swiped at my lower eyelids, even though I had no makeup on.

"Did you . . . cut your hair?"

The question surprised me enough I laughed earnestly. "Almost a week ago. Are you honestly telling me you just noticed now?"

A hint of pink colored his cheeks. "I'm not always the most perceptive with these kinds of things. You look lovely."

I didn't know if it was the compliment or the whiskey, but something changed in that moment. Like the magnet between us suddenly reversed poles, drawing us together with a force impossible to resist. His lips found mine, or maybe mine found his. I didn't care. The feel of his tongue sent shock waves throughout my body. There was no gentleness to the kiss. Only urgency. Our lips hungered for each other like it was the only way we could breathe.

His hand was on the small of my back, pressing me close. I threaded my fingers through his hair, but it wasn't close enough. My desire for him flamed an ember inside of me I thought had burned out long ago.

Just when it felt like we were about to lose all control, he broke the kiss. For the briefest moment, I worried he would confess his regret and push me away. But his hands stayed firmly around my waist, the tips of his fingers having found the bare skin beneath my shirt.

"That was unexpected," I said, breathlessly.

"Not for me," he admitted.

I looked up at him, too stunned for words.

He exhaled slowly, pulling together his well-hewn composure. "Good night, Julia."

My heart ached in a way I couldn't explain as I watched him walk out of the parlor.

There was no use trying to work any more that evening. My mind was too distracted by the lingering taste of his lips on mine. I gathered my papers and stuffed them into my laptop bag before making my way back to my room.

It was only when I laid my head on the pillow that I remembered Andrew never did answer my question about telling Margaret what I'd found in the florilegium.

I worried things between Andrew and me would be awkward after our kiss. But he dismissed that fear the next morning, when I found him waiting in the kitchen with a perfect cup of espresso already prepared for me. He pulled me behind the pantry door after breakfast and kissed me again. Soon we were stealing moments together whenever we could. But they were just moments. His work schedule kept him too busy for any kind of serious conversation about what exactly was happening between us.

I tried not to let my mind or my heart race too far ahead. I liked Andrew. Maybe more than I was willing to admit to myself. He was smart and funny and handsome. Most importantly, he was kind to Sam. But there was no future for us. Once this job was over, Sam and I would fly back to Chicago and rebuild our lives. The restoration needed to come first, for Margaret's sake and for mine.

On a sunny morning a week after our first kiss, Andrew came to find me while I was digging a hole for the white hydrangeas in the moon garden.

"Do you have a moment?"

My pulse quickened at the sight of him. He looked like a dashing hero from a Jane Austen novel as he leaned against the round stone gate. But there was a graveness in his voice that made me worry.

"Just as soon as I get this last one planted."

There was nothing elegant about removing a five-gallon plant from the plastic pot. Still, I managed to loosen the roots without damage and carefully set the shrub in the ground. I forced myself not to rush as I filled the hole. This was a living, breathing thing, and it needed to be treated with care from the start if it was to flourish.

"Okay, all done. What did you need to talk about?"

"Actually, it was something I wanted to show you."

I wiped the dirt from my knees and doffed my gloves before following him back to the house. He threaded his fingers through mine and led me to a room on the third floor in the far wing I hadn't yet explored. It was smaller than I expected, with a simple white desk in the middle and walls of bookshelves.

"I've been thinking about our conversation the other night," he said. "What you said about your sister. How she's still such a part of you, despite all that happened. It made me consider that Margaret's parents might not have truly erased Irene either. I've spent the last few days searching."

I sucked in my breath. "Did you find something?"

"Nothing of significance yet. This was Margaret's mother's office. I don't come in here often, but I did a thorough inventory a few years back when I began helping Margaret with the estate management. Most of it are her notes and lab journals from when she assisted her husband with his work, but she also kept much of her correspondence. I found this."

He handed me a letter written in deep navy ink on simple stationery. The paper itself was so old and crinkled, I worried it would break apart in my hands.

December 18, 1921

My dearest Mary,

Season's greetings from America. I hope you are keeping well. I apologize for the scarcity of letters these past few years. My professorship has kept me rather busy. I've been working on a device that will better harness the energy of radio waves. I believe you would find it fascinating. There are a great many brilliant minds here but none who challenge my ideas quite the way you do. I miss our late-night conversations and debates. I wish I could tell you more about my work, but one cannot risk giving away too much information in this business.

I can tell you that I have recently become a father. Irene Rosalie Clarke was born three weeks ago. She is a tiny thing with a cry like a siren. Fortunately, she is healthy and does not demand too much attention. She is quite content to lie in her crib and watch the mobile for most of her waking hours.

I think of you often.

Love,

John

It took me a long moment to process what I had just read. "Heck of a way to talk about your newborn child. He doesn't mention anything about his first wife either."

"It's odd. Margaret always said he was a wonderful father. But there's little sign of it here."

"Maybe he was different with her. There's a twelve-year age gap between the girls. That's a long time to grow and change, even for an adult."

"Or maybe he wasn't happy in his first marriage, and it reflected on his relationship with Irene."

I suspected each of our theories was correct. For the most part, my parents had been decent with me. Our relationship only soured when I was old enough to realize things were radically different for Rebecca. I was the golden child, praised for the simplest achievements, while I only ever heard my parents criticize my sister. "Do you think there's more information somewhere in here?"

He opened the top drawer, where dozens of letters were neatly wrapped with string. "If there is, it's likely to be in here. I've only read through a handful of these so far. I can get through them quicker if you help."

"What if we come across some things I'm not supposed to see?"

"I trust you're capable of discretion." He handed me a stack that was nearly six inches high. "Why don't you start with these and we'll see what we can find."

I offered a small smile, relieved that the awkwardness between us hadn't shaken his trust. Carefully, I worked at the knot binding the collection of envelopes, knowing patience was required, given their age. These letters were all from Margaret's father, the first sent from the battlefields of France during the Great War. He had served as a soldier in the British army. His tone was spare and direct, providing few details of the war, but it was clear Margaret's parents were deeply in love.

Andrew peered up from the letter he was reading. "Did you find something?"

"Not exactly. But I think Margaret's parents must have been in love, even when her father was married to someone else. He isn't the most effusive person, but you can sense the longing in his words."

I handed Andrew the letter. His jaw tightened as he read. "I doubt Margaret will have known that. She always talks about her parents like they were the epitome of propriety."

"People do strange things for love." I swallowed hard, knowing I was skirting the edge of a conversation I wasn't ready for.

"Yes," he said with no hint of discernible emotion. "I suppose they do."

For the next hour, we pored over the ancient envelopes, searching for more evidence of Irene's existence. The silent reading was easier than confronting the elephant in the room between us.

I was deep inside another of John's letters when Andrew tapped my shoulder. "I've found something."

June 18, 1940

Dear Mary,

In answer to your question, I do not know James Atherton well enough to comment on his character. I believe he is the nephew of George Atherton. James and Michael were schoolmates and developed a strong friendship that proved rather irksome. The pair were always in some kind of trouble with the headmaster. It would be uncharitable to place the blame entirely on James, but Michael was a model pupil outside of his influence. Nonetheless, the fact James enlisted so eagerly alongside Michael in the RAF is a notable sign of his character. While I would firmly discourage any kind of courtship with Deborah or Pamela, your step-daughter's peculiar ways of thinking and disregard for authority might indeed be a good match. At the very least, seeing her married off would be a relief.

Regards,

Your cousin Gwen

It was an awful way to speak about a young woman. Had Irene ever been welcomed at all into the family at Havenworth, or had she always been treated like an outsider? "This just suggests she was rebellious, not that she was capable of passing secrets to the enemy."

"It suggests she didn't conform to expectations. People like that are often vulnerable."

"And sometimes they're the people who have the most integrity and strength. They're not always bad. Sometimes they're just misunderstood." Each tiny slice of information about Irene Clarke magnified the cracks in the story Margaret had been told about her. "But even if she did pass secrets to the Germans, it doesn't mean she was evil. She might have been misled or confused. The only thing we do know is that she was remorseful before she disappeared."

He scrubbed a hand over his chin. "Have you considered that the reason you're so invested in proving Irene's innocence is because you haven't been able to do the same for your sister?"

Anger surged inside me, only to sputter out before I could utter any words in my defense.

"I'm sorry," he said quickly. "I shouldn't have said that."

I let out a long breath. "You're not wrong. No matter how much I wish you were. But I don't think I'm wrong about Irene either. I know we're going to find something if we keep looking. I can feel it in my gut."

"Okay. Let's keep searching."

We did find something. It took almost another hour of reading through the letters Margaret's mother had saved, but a letter from her husband in the winter of 1940 gave us all the answers we were looking for. Just not the ones I expected to find.

November 25, 1940,

My dearest Mary,

There is little I can share with you other than to say I have arrived safely in Boston, despite the setbacks. I still can scarcely believe my daughter capable of such duplicity and violence, but there is no room for doubt after the attack on the train outside of Euston station. I can only be grateful that you and the children were not on that train, and that we were spared our lives only by sheer luck. I'm afraid Irene's actions are even worse than feared. She is considered a suspect in the murder of an MI5 agent. I cannot impress upon you enough that if you hear or know anything about Irene, you must report it to the authorities.

These are dark times, but I have faith my work will be successful, and we will soon see an end to this war.

Love,

John

I handed the letter to Andrew.

"Margaret can never know about this," he whispered.

"But—"

"No." His voice was firm now. "It was one thing to believe Irene passed on classified information during the war, but this is an accusation of murder. She tried to kill her own family. This will devastate Margaret. Promise me you won't say anything to her about this."

I swallowed back my protest, even though my gut was screaming that he was wrong. Margaret wanted closure. She wanted forgiveness. She couldn't do that without the truth. But it wasn't my place to interfere. "I won't say anything."

Chapter Twenty-Seven

IRENE

October 13, 1940

Despite what I'd told Roger, I was terrified to return to James's flat. Crime had been on the rise in London ever since rationing rules tightened, but I didn't believe for one second that my attacker had been just a common thief. The real question was whether James had sent him after me—or if it was someone James worked for.

Still, I had to trust James wouldn't harm me in his own home. He'd been too careful to distance himself from any suspicion.

Before heading back, I detoured to Harrods, where I purchased a new scarf to conceal the bruises that had formed around my neck, and to give myself time to think. I'd known since the day I left Havenworth that Father was scheduled to travel to Liverpool this week, where he would board a steamer for America. He was planning to deliver Britain's most important technological development to the Americans. If James knew that, it would be all too easy to arrange an ambush, intercept Father, and hand the technology over to the Germans instead. I had to find out what James was planning. I had to stop him.

My husband was home when I finally returned. He sat at the kitchen table with a bottle of wine and two glasses. He was waiting for me.

"What's all this?" I asked, hiding my fear.

"An apology. I felt terrible about how I treated you last night. You were afraid and I was selfish."

His answer startled me. "There's no need to apologize. You were right. The bombs weren't anywhere near Mayfair. I was just being silly."

"I'm your husband. I will always protect you," he said. "Even if that means sleeping in a ridiculous shelter. Now come share a drink with me so we can put that ridiculous fight behind us."

My heart pounded as I sat down.

He won't hurt you. Not here, I reminded myself. And yet, I didn't trust the bottle of wine before us. James poured us each a glass. The deep-red liquid clung like blood to the edges of the crystal. I waited for him to take the first sip before appeasing him with one of my own.

"Did you get the package Catherine delivered for you? The blue tin? She said it had been delivered to her flat by mistake." I had left it in the living room with a note after carefully rearranging the dolls so that it would not appear anything was missing.

He nodded, swirling the wineglass along the table. "It wasn't mine. Catherine was confused when she brought it here, but we've sorted it out."

"She can be a bit absent-minded. I'm glad it got to the right place in the end."

He smiled, but there was something off about it. "Is that a new scarf?"

My fingers instinctively flitted to the silk around my neck. "I hope you don't mind. I saw it in Harrods and had to have it."

"It's beautiful. You should wear it tomorrow. My uncle's given me the day off. There's someplace special I'd like to take you."

My breath hitched. "Where is that?"

He grinned like a cat circling an injured bird. "A surprise."

He knew.

"That would be wonderful. It's been too long since we've spent a day together." My smile was tight, fighting to mask the fear in my eyes.

That night, I lay awake in bed, too afraid to sleep. If James weren't a light sleeper, I would have tried to sneak out. But where would I go?

I was on my own.

The telephone rang in the early hours of the morning, when it was still pitch-black outside. I kept my body as still as stone, even as James shifted on the mattress.

A moment later I listened to him pad toward the front hallway to answer the phone.

"I told you never to call me here." James's low whisper echoed through the flat.

In all our time together, I had never actually seen James angry, but there was a fury in his voice that resonated throughout the flat.

"I don't care what excuses you have. I told you it was going to cost more. If you can't pay it, there are plenty of people who will." After a long pause, he added, "Today. Or else."

The sound of the telephone's handset slamming against the base rang out. I kept my body utterly still as he walked back into the bedroom. The mattress dipped from his weight. Even with my eyes clenched shut, I felt his gaze on me, inspecting me for any sign of alertness. I kept my lips parted and my breath light and steady, just as if I were asleep.

His fingers brushed my shoulders, so soft and delicate, it took everything in me not to shudder. I felt him watching me. Studying me. But I refused to give him any sign of deceit. Finally, he lay back down and went to sleep.

James woke in a foul mood the next morning. He dressed quickly without much care for the fact I was still in bed, banging the cabinet drawers and stomping heavily. I rose up on my elbow and rubbed my eyes. The subtle movement was enough to draw his attention.

He set his hands on his hips, regarding me like a problem he'd have rather forgotten. "I have to run some errands today. I'll be back later. We'll have our date then."

"I'll be waiting," I said.

He hurried out the door without another word. I allowed myself only the briefest exhalation of relief before throwing on some clothes and chasing after him. Whoever had placed that phone call last night had given me a reprieve, even if they hadn't realized it, and I was determined not to let it go to waste.

I'd gotten so used to following James these last few weeks that it had become second nature to slip unnoticed down alleyways and blend into the flow of pedestrians as I walked half a block behind him. I knew to keep my head down, my clothes simple and unremarkable.

By now, I wasn't surprised to see him spending his days trading illicit and rationed goods for secrets among the London elite—people with no allegiance to their country. But the sight of it still sickened me. It weighed on my conscience, knowing I played a part in his grift and treachery. That I had once been so easily swayed by his charm and empty promises. I'd been so naive then, but the people James met in exclusive restaurants and gentlemen's clubs couldn't say the same. They knew what was at stake for this nation. Even as London burned from the incessant bombs every night, they traded with James not in spite of the damage it might do to the war effort but rather because of it.

I would never absolve myself of the shame of having once believed the war was some distant, phony thing. The scale of tragedy over the last month had been unimaginable. Thousands of people were dead—many of them women and children. Homes and churches and businesses destroyed. I couldn't change my past, but I had no excuses anymore. My determination to uncover James's every secret burned hotter as I followed him to Regent's Park. My pulse quickened each time he glanced over his shoulder. The park teemed with walkers, making it easy to stay hidden. I stayed off the main paths, darting behind the trees and shrubs to keep out of view.

He eventually made his way to Winter Garden in the northwest corner of the park. He didn't spot me hidden several yards away behind a large horse-chestnut tree with low-hanging branches covered in yellowed leaves. For the first time since I'd known him, James seemed truly nervous.

He stiffened as someone stepped in front of him, blocked from my view. "Do you have the money?"

"Yes, yes. Of course I have it."

That voice. There was something so familiar about it. I inched forward for a better view, but I still couldn't see past James's broad frame.

"Then hand it over."

"How do I know you aren't going to go back on our deal again?"

"You've asked me to blow up a bloody train. It's going to cost what it will cost."

I gasped, disbelieving my own ears. James was a criminal and a traitor, but surely not capable of that kind of violence.

"I don't want innocent people hurt."

"Just your friend," James added with a brutal taunt.

"A necessary sacrifice for the good of our country," he said, almost pleadingly. "Have you gotten rid of the girl yet?"

"Soon."

"I told you she would be nothing but a liability. Her father isn't stupid enough to share anything important with her. If I hadn't uncovered Clarke's itinerary, you wouldn't have a target for your friends in the Luftwaffe."

That voice. I knew it from somewhere.

"She's proven useful enough," James said. "You wouldn't even know what precious technologies you're so desperate to steal if I hadn't seduced the information out of her."

"After it's done, I never want to hear from you again." The man handed James a thickly stuffed envelope. As he did, I caught sight of the familiar gray beard and ruddy cheeks.

The air heaved from my lungs.

Edward Howell, Lady Montgomery's cousin-in-law, was plotting to kill my father.

Chapter Twenty-Eight

IRENE

October 14, 1940

I ran until I found a telephone box a safe enough distance away. My mind raced with too many thoughts while my hands fumbled to find a coin for the call.

"Number, please," the operator's crisp voice rang out, shaking me back to the present.

I gave the number for Havenworth.

"Havenworth residence," a quiet female voice said in a rush.

"Annie? Is that you?"

"Miss Clarke?"

"Yes, it's me." The sweet familiarity of her voice reminded me there was still hope. "I need to talk to my father. It's urgent."

"I'm sorry, miss. He's not here."

"Lady Montgomery, then."

"She's not here either."

"Margaret?"

"No. They've all left."

"What do you mean they've all left? When will they be back?"

I could hear her hesitation. "I'm not supposed to tell anyone where they are."

"They don't have to know it was you who told me. I won't say anything."

She sighed deeply. "I suppose they didn't mean you when they told me not to tell anyone."

My stomach clenched. I had no doubt those instructions were explicitly meant for me.

"They're in London."

"What? No! That makes no sense. Why on earth would they be in London?"

She hesitated again. "Well, you see . . . it's Margaret. Since you left, her cough has been getting much worse. Lady Montgomery has been beside herself with worry. They're visiting a specialist in the city."

My family was in London. The last place they would ever be safe from James. "Please, Annie. You must tell me where they're staying. It's a matter of life or death."

"Is everything all right, miss?" Annie asked cautiously.

Things were so far from all right that I nearly laughed at the sheer absurdity of it. "No, Annie. It's not. But if you can tell me where they are, I might be able to help them."

"They didn't tell me that. I'm sorry."

I muttered a curse. "Is there anything you can tell me that would give me some kind of a clue how to find them?"

I squeezed the handset tightly in the seconds of silence that followed. Finally, she said, "Lady Montgomery wrote down the name of the specialist. Dr. Houghton. I'm not sure when the appointment is, though."

"That's okay, Annie. You've helped more than you know."

The operator was able to give me the number for Dr. Houghton's clinic. I called, pretending to be my stepmother. The receptionist confirmed the address and the time of Margaret's appointment, which was only an hour from when I placed the call.

They must have already gone inside by the time I arrived. I sat down on a park bench across the street and waited.

Time passed agonizingly slowly. An early-autumn chill had settled over the city today, bringing with it a drizzle of rain. I had no umbrella. Not even a proper coat. Just a long-sleeved jumper that had become too damp for warmth.

Finally, after almost an hour of waiting, the clinic's door opened. Lady Montgomery stepped out first. Margaret and Charlie came next, huddled close together. Hope swelled inside me at the sight of her dark curls and bright-red raincoat. It had been almost two months since I'd seen my sister. When I left Havenworth, I feared I would never see her again. Now, I feared she wouldn't want to see me at all. But I had to try. I had to warn them before Father got on that train.

I leaped to my feet and hurried across the street to catch up with them. "Margaret!"

She turned around, staring at me blankly as though I were a stranger. I put my hand to my mouth to stifle a gasp. She was so thin. The soft roundness of her face had vanished, leaving hollowed cheeks and a purple cast beneath her eyes. What had happened to her since I'd left? She'd been unwell before, but not like this.

It was my stepmother who spoke first. "Irene?" She wrapped an arm around each of the children.

"Thank god I found you," I said, still breathless from the effort. I reached for my sister, desperate to hug her after such a long absence, but she reared back, tucking herself farther into her mother's protective grasp.

"What are you doing here?" Lady Montgomery asked.

"I need to speak to Father about something vitally important."

"He couldn't come. He had to—" Lady Montgomery's mouth snapped shut, as though she'd already said too much.

"I know he's going to Liverpool tomorrow, and I know why. But I can't let him do that," I said. "It's not safe for him."

"Is that a threat?"

"No!" I looked to Margaret, then Charlie. Surely they couldn't believe I was capable of that. Except the fear on each of their faces told me otherwise. "I can explain."

"I hope you do," Lady Montgomery said with a graveness I had never heard from her before.

I drew in a breath. "James knows about the cavity magnetron. He'll do whatever it takes to stop Father from taking it to America."

My stepmother's face hardened. "You told him about your father's work? How could you betray your father like that? How could you put him in that kind of danger?"

"I . . ." The words died in my throat. I *had* told James about the cavity magnetron. I deserved every bit of my stepmother's anger.

"I don't know what you're hoping to achieve with this stunt, but I won't hear another word of it. You've done enough damage to our family already." She tugged at the children's shoulders, urging them to leave.

"Please, Margaret," I said to my sister. "You cannot let him get on that train. You know I wouldn't lie to you. Not about something like this."

"I don't believe you," she shouted. "You're lying. Just like you lied when you said you would never leave me!"

The hurt in her voice was so terrible, I could barely breathe. "I'm so sorry, Margaret. I should never have left Havenworth. I made a terrible choice to run off with James. He never loved me. This whole time he was using me to target Father." My voice choked off. The shame of my foolishness was unbearable, but it was the only way to make them understand. "But I'm not lying now. You have to believe me—I'm trying to keep Father safe. To keep you all safe."

I dropped to my knees against the cold concrete, silently pleading with my sister to see the truth. She was the one person who had always believed the best in me. If Margaret didn't listen to me, no one would.

Her chin quivered, uncertainty warring in her sweet face. I reached for her, desperately wanting to wash away all her fears and doubts.

She batted my hand away with a viciousness I didn't expect.

"I hate you," she hissed. "And I never want to see you again. Ever."

The force of her words knocked me backward. There was so much anger in her voice. So much rage. She meant every word. She would never forgive me. And I couldn't save her.

My grief overtook me as she spun on her patent leather shoes and ran off, Lady Montgomery and Charlie tailing after her. My chest heaved, my body convulsing with anguish. I hadn't been there for Margaret when she needed me. I hadn't believed my fierce, beautiful sister was capable of succumbing to illness. The guilt of it was too much.

Something brushed my arm, so faint I almost didn't believe it at first. When I looked up, it wasn't Margaret standing in front of me, but Charlie.

He stared at me with those big, endless eyes, full of pity. I wiped the tears from my cheeks and pulled him into the tightest embrace. He was still so painfully skinny, but he hugged me back firmly.

"I believe you," he whispered in my ear so quietly, there was no chance of anyone else hearing.

"Thank you," I said, running my hand along the soft hair on the back of his head. "I'll find a way to fix things. I promise. Just don't let anyone get on that train."

It was too much responsibility to put on a boy his age. But what other choice did I have?

I followed Charlie, Margaret, and Lady Montgomery into the tube station. I had gotten all too capable at trailing people undetected over the last month. They were staying at a small inn a few stops over from the church in a quiet part of East London—far enough from where the bombs had fallen every night for the last few weeks that they should be safe, but I couldn't help myself from worrying anyway.

I lingered outside the inn, peering into storefronts in an effort not to draw attention to myself. I didn't have a plan. Not a real one, at least. I just knew I couldn't let Father on that train tomorrow.

A woman dressed in coveralls and an air raid warden's helmet with a white "W" on the front ran down the street, gesturing animatedly at the pedestrians before finally approaching me.

"Best be getting inside soon, miss. Jerry's sure to make another appearance tonight." She was young—no older than me—and pretty, with thick curls tucked into her helmet, but the frown lines between her eyes were etched deep.

"It's not even dusk," I said.

"Word is, Jerry's coming early today. They've been raiding the rest of the coast since the morning."

"I'll be on my way soon," I said, despite the anxiety coursing through me.

She stepped past me to approach someone else.

"Wait," I called after her. "Can you tell me where the closest shelter is? In case I don't make it home in time."

"The underground station just down the street over there." She pointed to the station I had emerged from a short while ago. "You'll want to hurry over. It gets mighty crowded, with lines all the way up to the street some nights. There's no other shelter for at least a mile."

I shuddered, trying to imagine so many people crammed into such a dank, uncomfortable space for the night. No beds, no toilets. People lined up next to each other like sardines in a tin. But the alternative was far worse: risking the collapse of your own home above you, the deafening wail of bombs shredding the streets, or the piercing cry of a neighbor trapped under rubble. At least here, as grim as it was, there was safety in numbers and the faint hope that the shelter's walls might hold. "Thank you."

She hurried off but was still distantly in sight when the sirens blared. Within seconds, people began streaming out of their homes toward the underground station. Most of them mothers and children, all of them knowing better than to hope for a false alarm.

Within minutes, the sirens wailed, followed by the ominous drone of the Messerschmitts. They were close. Too close.

It was only moments later that I saw my father emerge from the inn's doors, carrying Charlie in one arm and Margaret in the other while my stepmother hurried after them. The enemy planes zoomed above with deafening speed, lighting waves of fear and panic. Margaret and Charlie weren't supposed to be here in London in the middle of it all. They were supposed to be far away. Safe.

They'll be okay, I reminded myself. *They will survive a night in the shelter.* It was up to me to ensure they survived the rest of the week.

As long as I survived the night as well.

Clutching my purse tightly, I began to run toward them, hoping a captive night together would give me the chance to convince them of the danger they were still in.

The boom of an explosion jolted me to a halt. The antiaircraft guns were out in force. But even with the lingering daylight, they were no match for the onslaught. The whistle of a bomb falling chilled my blood. The sky lit up in a horrible orange glow as another piece of London was destroyed.

Margaret was crying as Father ran toward the station, Charlie stoic. I wanted to chase after them, but I couldn't. The only thing that mattered right now was their safety.

A different plan popped into my head in that moment. A stupid, reckless one.

Instead of running to safety as the planes surged above me, I ran back to the inn. The door was unlocked, the front counter empty. I knew there had to be a key cabinet somewhere. I found it on the back wall, left unlocked in the chaos. Four spare keys were tucked inside. I grabbed all of them and raced up the stairs to the guest rooms. A dim overhead bulb provided just enough light to see.

I didn't know which room belonged to my family, so I started with the first door. A horrible crash ripped through the air just as I inserted the key. The floor and walls shook violently, sending terror coursing through me. The bombs were too close. I needed to work faster, but my hands refused to steady.

After a few moments of fumbling, the lock finally clicked open. Inside, a single suitcase lay open on the bed, clothes strewn everywhere. This wasn't the right room. I ran to the next door.

Another bomb detonated nearby, the shock wave knocking me off my feet. The keys flew from my hands, skittering across the floor. I scrambled to pick them up and jammed the key into the lock. My chest squeezed tight when I saw my sister's cherished teddy bear forgotten on the bed.

I tore through the room, yanking open drawers and tossing aside bedcovers. I didn't know exactly what I was looking for, only that it had to be here. I dropped to my knees and felt beneath the bed. In desperation, I yanked the bed frame away from the wall. The faint light glinted off a small metal briefcase. It was less than two feet in length, but surprisingly heavy for its size.

This was the precious cargo Father was transporting—the only reason for him to get on that train tomorrow morning. But he had left it behind for the sake of his children. He must have believed it would be safer here than in a crowded underground station with hundreds of other people—too many of whom had sticky fingers. After all, no one was supposed to know what he was carrying.

But I did. And so did James.

Father would never forgive me for stealing it, but it was the only way to keep him from getting on that train tomorrow.

Using a hatpin my stepmother had left behind, I quickly scrawled a message on the back page of my sketchbook and left it on the bed so there would be no doubt who had taken the briefcase if I didn't survive the night.

I wondered, briefly, what James would think of me as I absconded with stolen goods like the common criminals he employed for his black-market hustle. He probably wouldn't believe it even if he saw me. He had underestimated me from the start, using me like a disposable pawn, but I wasn't a fool. Not anymore.

Just as I exited the inn's door, a man stepped in front of me. I nearly crashed into him, stopping myself just short of where he stood. My breath caught in my throat when I recognized his dark hair and broad shoulders.

"Irene?" Father's eyes, wide with shock, gazed down at the metal briefcase in my hand.

I wanted to reach for him once more and feel his embrace. I wanted to tell him everything that had happened over the last few months, but there was no explanation that would ever earn his forgiveness.

"One day you'll understand," I said in a choked voice.

He was too stunned to chase after me as I disappeared into an alleyway.

Chapter Twenty-Nine

JULIA

Present Day

The restoration went smoothly over the next few weeks. But even though it was a success by every objective measure, I couldn't find any satisfaction in the work. Every day that I held on to the secrets from Margaret's past felt like a betrayal to the woman who had given me a second chance in my career.

Deep in my heart, I knew the restoration would be a failure if it didn't help her find closure. She deserved to know what had happened to her sister. Andrew didn't understand that. He hadn't experienced the anguish of losing someone when you were too angry to speak to them. He didn't know how words never said could haunt you forever.

It was close to three in the afternoon when Sam and I made our way to the orangery for his regular date with Margaret—something that had quickly become the highlight of his day.

"Are you here for our game of jacks?"

Sam let go of my hand and raced to his usual spot next to her.

"I wonder if you'll be ready for chess next. It's a complicated game, but I think you're clever enough to figure it out with a little help."

Sam nodded eagerly.

It was good to see Margaret so lively. She had been too tired to hold much of a conversation, much less play with Sam—though she was always happy to simply be in his company.

"The gardens are looking lovely," she said to me. "You've accomplished so much in such a short amount of time."

"The crews I've contracted to do the heavy work have been extremely efficient."

"Under your guidance. I've seen you out there with them. You're working just as hard, and I appreciate it."

"Thank you."

"Is everything all right?" Margaret asked, seeing through my false smile.

"Yes, sorry. Just working through some thoughts."

"I find it helps to share my stubborn thoughts when I can't work through them on my own."

"I think I would prefer to just put them out of my mind."

"In that case, one can't go wrong with a jujube." She reached into the pocket of her trousers and retrieved a small bag of candy.

I laughed. "I thought you weren't supposed to have sweets."

Her eyes twinkled with a mischievous glint. "Our little secret. Besides, what is the point in denying myself at this age? I've lived longer than most. If there's anything I've learned, it's that you must live the life you want, not the one you've been told to follow." She let Sam reach into the bag and come away with a small handful of the candies.

"Is that what you did?"

She popped a red jujube into her mouth and stared out the window. Her long silences used to unsettle me, but I'd spent enough time with her now to know she was simply taking the time she needed to sort through decades of wisdom before responding. "Not as much as I should have. There was one lesson I refused to learn for too long. I can only hope I have enough time to set my regrets right."

"What lesson was that?"

"It's almost impossible to explain what it was like during the war. I was barely older than Sam." She ruffled his hair, silently reassuring me she would be careful with her words. "Everything was about survival. We gave no thought to what would be meaningful for the future. But my sister was the opposite."

My pulse quickened. "Do you mean Irene?"

"She cared so much about the gardens. I used to think she was silly for caring about something like that. But sometimes I wonder if she was the only one who understood what would be truly meaningful. She saw the need to preserve and protect the beauty around us and keep it alive for future generations. She entrusted me to do that when I grew up." She turned her attention to Sam. "Of course, one mustn't grow up too fast and miss the fun either. Remind me whose turn it is."

Sam and Margaret returned to their jacks. I took out my phone to finally take care of some of the bills I had been putting off paying for far too long. I opened my bank app and checked the balance in my account. My breath caught in my throat when I saw the amount.

A deposit for ten grand had been made by my former employer.

I excused myself to the hallway and dialed his number.

"What the hell is going on?" I asked without preamble as soon as Ryan answered.

"Hey, Julia. It's good to hear from you. How are you?" He sounded shockingly cordial for a man who had fired me six months ago.

"What is all that money doing in my account?"

"I explained everything in the emails and voice messages," he said with a slight hint of exasperation. "I've been trying to tell you for weeks that there was a mistake. It turns out your sister never took all that money."

It felt like the floor gave way beneath me. "What?"

"After you left, more money kept going missing. We hired a forensic accountant, who traced it all back to Jack Nelson."

Jack Nelson was one of the accountants at Hartwell & Sons who managed most of the funds for our projects. My head spun.

Rebecca had stolen from the company—there had never been any doubt about that. She had confessed to it when I confronted her. But she insisted it hadn't been as much as Ryan had claimed. She said she had taken $200 from petty cash in a moment of weakness. The bookkeeping records showed over $10,000 had been slowly siphoned away in the months she'd been employed. I believed the records.

Ryan had given me the choice to pay off the debt myself or he would press charges against her. I used half of my savings to keep her out of jail and the other half to cover the costs of the rehabilitation center I'd forced her to attend. The place where she had managed to get hold of something deadly anyway.

But now Ryan was telling me it was a mistake.

"Look, I know this is a lot to hear. We made a mistake, and we want you to come back."

"A mistake? My sister is dead," I hissed.

"I know and I'm sorry. At least consider the offer. We've been contracted for the Seaton Garden in Newport, but they know your work and they're insisting on you leading the project. We're offering a fifty percent pay increase."

I stood there in shock for a long time, barely able to breathe.

"Julia? Are you still there?"

"I . . . I'll think about it." I hung up and pressed the heels of my palms into my eyes.

I hated myself for even considering the offer, but that kind of money and stability would be life-changing for Sam and me. I could pay off my debts and maybe even buy a house for us to live in. We wouldn't be facing a future of uncertainty, never knowing when the next contract would come.

"Are you okay?"

I opened my eyes to see Andrew in front of me, looking at me with concern. "Yeah. Fine."

"That didn't sound fine."

How much had he overheard? "It's nothing that needs to be worried about right now."

He nodded, suspicion still darkening his eyes. "I was just about to check on Margaret."

"She's in the orangery with Sam."

I followed Andrew to the orangery, more uncertain about my future than ever. But Sam wasn't at his usual spot next to Margaret. He was lying in front of the chair where I had been working just moments ago. My satchel was open on the floor, the contents spilled out. My phone, ChapStick, a handful of pencils.

And the florilegium.

Sam had it opened in front of him, a graphite pencil in hand.

"Sam, no!"

I snatched the pencil from his hand, but it was too late. He had colored all over the back page of the book.

He looked up, eyes wide with confusion. "I was just coloring."

"Not on this, Sam," I said with aching distress. "Never on this."

"Show me that book," Margaret insisted with a force that left no doubt she recognized it.

"Margaret," Andrew said gently. "I don't think that's wise."

"That's not for you to decide," she snapped. "Hand it over now."

I nodded at Sam to bring it to her, despite sensing the tension in Andrew next to me. Neither of us dared approach Margaret, and she opened the soft blue cover.

She let out a small gasp as she examined Irene's drawings. "Where did you find this?"

"It was hidden beneath the mattress in the room with all the old photo albums," I said.

"Charlie . . . he must have retrieved it when my father threw it away."

"Why?" Andrew asked. "Why would he want to keep something from her?"

After so much secrecy, his question surprised me. But maybe it shouldn't have. This was his family's history, too.

"Your grandfather was so scared when he first arrived here with all the other child evacuees at the start of the war. Barely spoke at all. He was the smallest of the bunch. I didn't take to him at first. I wanted to be with all the other children who were excited to be at Havenworth. But Irene was kind to him. She checked on him every night and made sure he was eating and sleeping properly. She urged me to be his friend, which I only did after all the other children returned to London. Once it was just him and me, we were inseparable."

"How did he get a hold of the florilegium when Irene left for London?" I asked. "Some of her drawings were from that time, so she must have had it with her."

Margaret ran her fingers over a drawing of delicate blue forget-me-nots. "We had to leave Havenworth that autumn. Father and Mother feared the proximity of the air force base would endanger Havenworth when the Luftwaffe came. We spent the rest of the war at a country home in Shropshire that belonged to one of Mother's distant relatives. But we had to pass through London on the way so I could visit the doctor. I'm not sure how Irene found us, but she did. It was the last time I ever saw her."

My pulse quickened with the awareness we were on the verge of unraveling another piece of the mystery. "What do you mean she found you? What did she say?"

Margaret clutched her hand to her heart and shook her head. "I can't recall. Only that I was so angry at her for leaving us the way she did. There was a terrible raid over the city that night, and we were forced to shelter in the underground. She followed us to the inn and stole Father's briefcase. Inside of it was the prototype for his cavity magnetron, though I didn't know that at the time. I just thought it was funny that he had such a strange metal case and carried the key on a chain around his neck like a piece of hidden jewelry. When Irene stole the briefcase, she left the florilegium behind. I never knew why. Perhaps she wanted him to know it was her who had done it."

Sam tugged at her shirtsleeve.

"What is it, boy?"

"She left a message for you," he said. "I found it."

I looked to Andrew, who was just as confused as I was. Had Sam overheard Andrew and me talking about my theory?

"Her last few drawings weren't sketches of things she saw. I think they were messages using the language of flowers." I walked over and carefully opened the final page of the florilegium, where Irene had left a drawing of asphodel, columbine, and hyacinth. "I think she was expressing her remorse for what she had done."

"No, not that page," Sam insisted. "Another one."

"Show me," Margaret said with steely resolve.

I clenched my hands into fists as I watched Sam turn the page over to the once-blank side he had ruined with a pencil. "Here."

I saw it. The tiny white lines that appeared inside the gray shading. A concealed message. Just like Margaret had taught him to do weeks ago.

Dear Marg—

The rest of the message hadn't yet been revealed.

"Get a pencil," Margaret ordered. Sam dutifully raced back to my bag to find one. Margaret handed him the florilegium. "Careful. Just like I taught you."

My stomach squeezed so tightly, I was almost nauseous as I watched Sam slowly reveal the message inside.

Dear Margaret,
I have done terrible things, but I am no traitor. James and your uncle Edward have been conspiring against Father, and I've been working in secret with MI5 to stop them. Though we may never see each other again, I cannot bear the thought of you believing I would ever hurt you or betray our family. I took Father's briefcase to keep him from boarding that train—it

was the only way to save his life. If this letter finds you someday, I hope you'll understand. And forgive me.

Love,

Irene

The air was so still, it felt like time had frozen. A string of tears fell down Margaret's cheeks, her eyes filled with a pain so raw that I couldn't bear to look.

"I was supposed to be on that train," she whispered.

"What do you mean?" Andrew asked gently.

"Father was supposed to take the train to Liverpool the next morning. We were to accompany him as far as Birmingham. But we never got on the train. Father needed to find a replacement for the prototype. He said he would meet us in Birmingham, but Charlie absolutely refused to board without him, so we delayed the trip by another day. We found out later the train we were meant to be on was targeted by a German Stuka just as it pulled out of the station. Most of the passengers were killed."

I pressed my hand to my lips.

"All this time I believed the worst about her. My own sister." Margaret let out a sob. She clutched her heart again, but this time it was different. Her skin was too pale. Her breath shallow and rapid.

"Andrew!" I shouted, but he was already racing toward her.

He took her hand. "Margaret, look at me."

It was too late. Her eyes rolled back in her head, and she slumped, lifeless, in her seat.

Chapter Thirty

IRENE

October 14, 1940

The German attack didn't stop. More and more planes covered the skies until it seemed like the entire city was blanketed. It was impossible to tell how many of them were RAF, fighting to protect us. Bombs fell in a cacophonous storm, filling the air with the acrid scent of death and destruction. People scrambled for underground shelters, only to be turned away when they were full. There was nowhere safe. Nowhere to go.

Smoke and dust filled my lungs as I ran through the dimming streets. Dusk was settling like a shroud. How long would this go on? How much suffering could we possibly face?

All I knew was I had to get the briefcase to Roger. He was the only one who would know what to do with it. I couldn't let it fall into the wrong hands.

His flat in Marylebone was a last resort—he had given me the address for emergencies only. Under normal circumstances, it would have been a brief journey. But tonight, with so many roads reduced to rubble, it took me nearly an hour to reach it.

By some miracle, I arrived at the building unscathed. I could only hope he was still there. I had no other plan.

As soon as I entered the building's foyer, I saw him. He wore a hat that shadowed his face and dark clothes that blended into the dim surroundings, but I instantly recognized him from the broad set of his shoulders. For the first time all day, the knot in my stomach loosened.

I had barely taken a step inside of the shadows when I heard his voice. "What are you doing here?"

I froze. He wasn't speaking to me. Someone else was here.

"I should be asking you the same thing," came a familiar voice.

James. The air rushed from my lungs.

"What a strange question to ask someone in their own home," Roger said calmly, lighting a cigarette, seemingly unaffected by the tension crackling around him.

"Lying doesn't suit you. Nor does your disloyalty," James shot back, his voice sharp and cutting.

Roger took a slow drag on his cigarette, seemingly unfazed by James's accusation. "You forget I was never loyal to you. I've always been loyal to the Crown."

"All this time, I thought you were nothing more than a sniveling twat desperately clinging to my coattails. I only allowed you into our circle because I pitied you. And occasionally because I enjoyed taking the piss out of you."

"I've known what kind of man you are from the beginning. It was no surprise to any of us that you would betray your country so callously."

"Enough. Where's Irene?"

How did James know I would come here? Had he known all along I was working for Roger?

Roger tossed his cigarette to the ground, stubbing it out with his foot. "Have you lost track of your new toy so quickly?"

I knew Roger was baiting him, but the comment pierced my heart nonetheless. I *had* been nothing but a toy to James. A doll for him to manipulate and play with. But I had managed to play him in return. I had the undeniable evidence of James's involvement in a conspiracy too.

Roger straightened abruptly, jolted by something I couldn't see. I took another step forward, angling for a better view. My heart crashed in my chest. In James's hand was a pistol.

"Tell me where she is," James repeated.

"She's long gone. The evidence she had has already been given to the bureau. This time not even your uncle will be able to get you out of Holloway."

Roger was buying me time to get away, I realized with a jolt. I needed to run, but my legs had rooted to the ground like tree stumps, too heavy with fear to move.

"You're lying," James hissed.

Run, you fool. Run before he sees you.

"Your arrogance was always going to be your downfall," Roger said, impossibly calm with the barrel of a gun pointed at his heart. "It's not too late to do the right thing."

"You're the one who's out of time."

The pistol went off with a brutal crack. I let out a scream as the bullet pierced Roger's chest, blood bursting out in a horrible splatter. He staggered backward, his desperate gaze catching mine with a final plea before he fell to the ground.

I threw myself at the door, pushing it open with all my force. Another shot rent the air, the glass shattering into a million pieces.

I ran into the darkness, my feet pounding against the pathway with a speed I hadn't known myself capable of. James fired again and again. A searing pain ripped through my shoulder. I fell to my knees, clutching the briefcase against my chest.

"It's too late," James called out.

I had seen so many sides of this man. He was cunning, charming, and exceptionally cruel. But this was a darkness I had never imagined. The void in his eyes held no trace of humanity. He would kill me without a second's remorse. Just like he had killed Roger. The weight of that realization stole my breath, but fear was a luxury I couldn't afford. My arm burned as I staggered to my feet and forced myself forward, each stride fueled by sheer will and the promise that I wouldn't let him win. Not this time.

The haze of smoke from burning buildings made it nearly impossible to see anything as I ran. I didn't stop until my knees threatened to buckle under me. I didn't know where I was. The few buildings left standing were unrecognizable. But there was no sign of James.

Only then did the gravity of my situation hit me.

Roger was dead. The only person on earth who could prove I wasn't a traitor was dead.

Panic crowded my lungs, leaving no room for air. Where was I supposed to go now? Who would believe me?

My ears still rang with the sound of the gunshots, so loud I didn't notice the strange whistling sound above me until it was too close to ignore.

"Run!" someone screamed.

I couldn't run. I couldn't move. I could only look up to see a buzz bomb spinning toward me.

"We have to move!" A pair of strong arms grabbed my waist and pulled me back. Everything passed in a blur. I remember only clutching for the briefcase.

"We need to hide," the man repeated. An air raid warden.

"Where?" I looked around frantically, but there was nowhere to go.

The warden pressed me against the brick wall of the building and shielded me with his body. There was no time to run. Nowhere to go. I cried out in desperate panic and braced myself for the end. A sickening clang rang out as the bomb collided with the concrete right where I had been standing.

Time slowed down to an impossible stillness. I thought how I would finally see my mother again. Of my father, and how he would never know how hard I'd tried to redeem myself. Of Margaret. Of how there would be no one to watch out for her.

"Open your eyes, dear," the warden said. "You're all right."

His words washed over me like a spell. I blinked my eyes open. I wasn't dead. I squeezed my hands and feet in disbelief. I wasn't even hurt. The man who had saved me was much older than I expected, with hair so white it nearly glowed beneath the moonlight.

"What . . . what happened?"

"A miracle is what. The bomb didn't explode on impact."

My knees caved in with relief. He caught me by the arms with surprising strength for a man his age. "Don't go having a fainting spell. The bomb could still go off, and there's plenty more planes still out there. We need to get to the shelter. There's still space in the church nearby."

We hurried the last few blocks, stepping over broken glass and debris from crumbled buildings.

"Almost there."

We reached the church a few minutes later. There was nothing to signal it as a shelter. But when the warden opened the door, a woman in a matching helmet was there to greet us.

"Still catching strays, Harry?" she asked the man.

"I'm hoping this is the last one." He turned to me and urged me forward. "Go on. They'll take good care of you down there."

In spite of all we had just been through, I hesitated. There was no light to guide my way down the stairs, and that familiar, insidious fear of the darkness spooled down my spine. "Aren't you coming?"

He shook his head. "Not while there are still people looking for a place to go."

"Harry, please. It's not safe," I pleaded. After what we had just been through, I couldn't bear the thought of watching him walking back out to the streets.

"I survived the Germans the first time they tried to kill me thirty years ago. I'll be fine. I promise."

He turned around, helmet askew but head high, and marched back out with more bravery than I could have ever conjured.

The woman gave a gentle tug to my arm. "Come along. We need to get everyone safely belowground before it's too la—"

A deafening explosion drowned out the rest of her words. A rush of air so violent it threw me off my feet. The sensation of falling overwhelmed me until my head slammed against the ground. The briefcase flying from my hand was the last thing I remembered before blackness took hold of my consciousness.

Chapter Thirty-One

Irene

October 15, 1940

The first thing I remembered was a hum. Not the lacerating rumble of the Luftwaffe that overwhelmed my senses, but a gentle one. Soft and delicate on my skin. A song.

I forced my eyelids open, only to be blinded by a rush of light. I winced and my head screamed in protest.

"Careful now, you've had quite the knock." A woman was kneeling next to me, one hand pressed firmly against my forehead, the other holding a rag against my bleeding shoulder. This was the same woman who'd tried to get me into the shelter. Her graying hair was matted with the same dust and blood that streaked her skin and clothes. In another life she might have been a kind, matronly woman, but she wasn't smiling now.

"What . . . what happened?" My clothes were torn and stained unrecognizably, my skin covered in angry purple bruises and cuts.

Pain laced her kind eyes. "A bomb. It knocked you down the stairs. I wasn't sure you were going to wake up at all."

The memory ricocheted through me. The deafening screech of the blast that threw me backward before the world went black.

I pushed up onto my elbows despite the searing ache in my head. "Harry. The air raid warden who was with me. Is he okay?"

"No," she said in a heavy whisper. "Some of the other men in the shelter went to look for him after the all-clear went up. They found him buried beneath the rubble. It was too late to help him."

My lungs were too raw for breath. He wasn't supposed to get hurt. He'd been trying to save me. To save everyone. That wasn't how this was supposed to be.

"Try to breathe. We all need to stay calm and brave. It's what Harry would want," she said, wiping a tear from her cheek with the back of her hand.

I sucked in a ragged breath, clinging to her words. Calm and brave. How could anyone feel that way after the hell inflicted upon us? But what other choice did I have?

"Grace, we need your help with this boy," another voice called out.

"Rest as much as you can," Grace said. "I'll come check on you again in a bit. I've stitched up your shoulder, but it's your head I'm worried about."

I looked around, the blur in my vision finally receding enough for me to make out my surroundings. All around me, people lay on the ground, blood-soaked rags wrapped around hands and torsos and heads. People old and young. A girl no older than Margaret with hair matted black from soot wept against the still body of an older child just a few feet over from me. This wasn't the shelter. This was some sort of makeshift hospital, only with no supplies or doctors or even running water to clean the wounds.

"Wait," I called after Grace. "Do you know what happened to my briefcase? It was small and metal."

Her eyes widened in surprise. "I'm not certain, but my son, Fred, would know. He was one of the rescuers who brought you in. He's just over there by the supply table."

I climbed to my feet, a sharp pain stabbing in my left ribs.

"You shouldn't get up so soon," Grace protested. "Nothing is more important than your health."

She was wrong. If I'd lost that briefcase, I'd lost everything.

I limped toward the teenage boy she had gestured to seconds before. "Excuse me, were you the one who brought me here?"

He tilted his head with a bashful expression that revealed just how young he was. He couldn't have been more than fourteen or fifteen. "You were in quite a state."

"Thank you," I said. "For everything. But I need to know if you saw a briefcase. It was made from metal. It's very important."

I bit my lip and poured every last shred of hope and desperation into my silent prayer. It was impossible enough that I had survived the wreckage. How could I expect the briefcase to do the same?

Fred rubbed his whiskerless chin. "The one with the lock?"

My heart leaped in my chest. "Yes!"

He reached under a long table covered with bandages and other supplies and pulled out the briefcase. "I found it when I carried you out. Seemed too special to leave in the rubble, so I grabbed it. Didn't realize it was yours."

I nearly crumpled with relief. It was dented and covered in dust, but it was unopened. "Thank you! Do you know if the trains are still running?"

He straightened his back in a gesture of pride. "Yes, ma'am. London isn't going to stop running just because of a few bombs."

Without the survival of the briefcase, I would not have had the will to continue. It was the hope I needed in the face of the devastation that surrounded me when I emerged from the church. The destruction from last night's attack was even worse in the daylight. Where buildings once stood remained only their crumbled remnants. Gaping holes marred the streets. Buses and trams were overturned. And everywhere smoke billowed in dark spires in the spaces where buildings should have been. Death hung in the air like a fog.

But in spite of it all, the people of London were not broken. They boarded up their broken windows and picked through the rubble with a determination and courage I couldn't fathom. They had been through absolute hell for weeks, and still their spirit did not die.

I was not the one who could stop any of the Luftwaffe's destruction, but my father could. I had to make sure the device inside this briefcase didn't fall into the wrong hands. I clutched it to my chest like a piece of armor as I made my way to the train station.

The chances of James finding me among the chaos were low, but I scanned my surroundings obsessively for signs of him as I walked nonetheless. He was obsessive in his pursuit. If he was alive, he wouldn't stop looking for me.

If he was still alive.

I knew it was evil to hope he hadn't survived, but I couldn't stop the thought from racing through my brain with every step. But as much as I hated him for all the horror he'd wrought, I had only myself to blame for my part in it. I'd been so naive to fall for his charm and believe that we deserved more than everyone else. I'd justified the gifts and extravagances simply because I'd wanted them. I had never thought to question their true cost.

I used the last of the money I had to purchase the train fare, leaving me without so much as a shilling for a sandwich, though my stomach ached with hunger. I couldn't remember when I'd last eaten. Thankfully, the elderly woman seated next to me on the train took notice of my state and offered me some of her biscuits, which I accepted with gratitude.

"Is Cambridge home for you?" she asked as I bit into the stale biscuit.

Home. For the last eight years, I'd wanted nothing more than to escape Havenworth. Now, I would do anything to be welcomed back into the safety of those stone walls. "It's where my family's from."

She patted my knee. "It's good of you to visit them. They must be very worried about you all the way in London. Especially at such a tender age. My granddaughter lives in a village just outside Peterborough and has asked me to stay with her. She said it would be a favor to have me around to help with the little ones, but I suspect it's more about helping me than anything else. I don't think I could tolerate many more nights like last night. My back can't handle sleeping on the hard floors of the underground. I do appreciate the pretense, though. It helps an old woman like me feel a little more useful."

"I'm sure it will be a relief to have you there," I said.

She nodded. "In times like these, family is what truly matters. All the buildings and houses can be rebuilt. Everything physical can be replaced eventually. It's only love that's irreplaceable."

Tears bit at the corners of my eyes.

Had I done enough to protect my family? Would they understand why I had to do what I did?

"It's okay," she said, patting my knee. "Your family will be all right. You'll see."

"Would you tell me about your family?"

The stories of her great-grandchildren were a welcome distraction from my thoughts for the rest of the ride. It made me feel like there was still goodness in the world. There was still hope. Even for someone like me.

I had no money left for a taxi when I arrived in Cambridge. My legs ached and protested, but I managed the long walk to Havenworth without collapsing. The journey was made easier knowing each step brought me closer to the end.

Roger was dead. I was finally free to tell my family the truth. I couldn't feel any anger for what he had put me through. If he hadn't, I would never have discovered the true depth of James's treachery.

Twilight had darkened the sky to a hazy indigo by the time I reached the long gravel lane leading to Havenworth. It was so quiet, I could hear the gentle rustle of the foxes and badgers in the fens. I stopped at the front gate and inhaled deeply, taking in the fresh, familiar scents.

Home. This was where I belonged.

There were no lights visible through the windows, but that was to be expected. Lady Montgomery had always insisted on being careful about that. I understood now that it wasn't silliness or paranoia. She had lived through the worst of humanity once before and knew it was inevitable that we would walk down that dark path once more. But even in the darkness, I knew something was different. I walked up the front steps and banged on the knocker. When no one answered, I jerked on the handle. The door was locked. I knocked again. Surely someone was here. Annie or Albert or any of the half dozen Land Army girls who had been here all summer.

I followed the winding path along the side of the home to try the back entrance at the orangery. That was when I realized what was so wrong.

There were no plants left in the orangery. The room was empty, without so much as a single plant remaining. The doors at the back were locked, too, with no sign of life anywhere.

The truth hit me like a blast from the sky. Everyone was gone. Margaret wasn't in London solely for a visit with the doctor. She was leaving Havenworth. My stepmother had always been concerned about Havenworth's proximity to the RAF base. The Blitz must have been the final push for her to leave.

A plan formed in my mind. I could stay here as long as the home remained empty. No one needed to know. There would likely be enough food in the cellar to get me through the first few weeks, at least. Enough time to come up with a better idea.

But there was still a chance James would come looking for me here. I had to hide the briefcase.

There was only one place where it would be safe. Where no one would look for it, but I could be certain Margaret would find it.

Clutching the briefcase tightly, I followed the familiar path to the parterre. The roses had been ripped out, I realized with a pang of sadness. The Land Army must have used the space for a vegetable garden, but there were no signs of broccoli stalks or lettuce that ought to have sprouted by now. All the beauty and life that once grew here was gone, with nothing to show for it.

I passed through the laburnum walk to the cottage gardens that had become strangled with weeds. Even my beautiful moon garden was in shambles. My eyes strained in the dark as I navigated my way through the wild forest to the abandoned folly. This was the only part of the gardens I didn't know by heart, and I had no doubt my sister had left behind a series of traps. My steps were slow and careful, but I finally reached the crumbling entrance of the folly.

My breathing turned shallow. I did not want to go inside, especially not in the dark.

You can do this. You must do this.

I dropped down to my knees, setting the briefcase in front of me. The sunken opening was so small and narrow, my shoulders barely fit through, and I had to duck my head to avoid banging it on the rough brick.

I nudged the briefcase with trembling hands, forcing my knees forward. My injured arm screamed in pain from the awkward movement.

Just keep going.

The musty smell of sodden dirt was oppressively thick, sticking to my esophagus. My claustrophobia raged more powerfully with every inch, flooding my brain with images of my mother. Finally, I reached the inside of the folly. The squeezing sensation abated. I could breathe.

It was pitch-black inside the folly—too dark to see the hidden world Margaret and Charlie had created. I set the briefcase against the wall close to the entrance, too afraid to venture farther into the structure in case I lost track of how to escape. The folly terrified me with its crumbling walls and endless darkness.

I took a deep breath to steel myself for the tight crawl out of the folly. Just a few seconds and it would be over. I braced my hands against the dirt. The faintest sound in the distance made me pause. The drone of a plane passing overhead. It was a sound I had become all too familiar with these last few weeks. But there had been no sirens. No alarms.

An RAF plane, most likely.

But the strange whistling that followed sent a chill down my spine. I scrambled for the exit as the sound grew louder, banging my head against bricks. The pain was so fierce, my stomach heaved with the urge to vomit. The whistling grew to a deafening screech.

The bomb was right overhead.

I had to get out of here.

I had to get out of here . . .

Chapter Thirty-Two

JULIA

Present Day

I had already packed my and Sam's things by the time Andrew returned from the hospital nearly twenty-four hours later. Margaret's weakened heart had had a minor attack, but she was in stable condition thanks to Andrew's quick action. For now, she was okay. But Sam and I weren't.

It was time for us to leave.

Sam was too young to really understand what had happened, thankfully, but I could sense a flicker of doubt when I told him she would be fine. Maybe because I hadn't been sure at the time either.

I'd already texted Ryan that I was accepting his offer. The final designs for Havenworth were complete. I'd done the most important part of the job. Any decent gardener could take over from this point—if Andrew decided to finish.

When Sam awoke the next morning and saw our suitcases packed by the bedroom door, he had a meltdown. I was barely able to drag him out of the room for breakfast amid the tears and refusals. He was too young to understand I was doing this for him. That leaving was inevitable.

I had finally coaxed him to the kitchen with the promise of Ovaltine for breakfast when Andrew returned. His eyes were bloodshot and skin dulled from the lack of sleep. He had already texted me to let me know Margaret was stable, but he still looked destroyed.

"Are you all right?" I asked, unsure of the ground we were standing on. He had every right to be furious with me for what had happened last night. He'd warned me countless times that talking about Irene would hurt Margaret, but I'd refused to listen.

His head tilted with only the suggestion of a nod. "Somehow, having a medical degree doesn't make this any easier."

"How long will she be at the hospital?"

"A few days. Possibly a week. We were lucky she didn't need any surgical intervention, but she's still going to be weak when she returns. Helen's with her right now."

"I'm glad she's recovering," I said, wishing I knew the right words to say. The last twenty-four hours hung like invisible chains around my shoulders, holding me from reaching out to comfort him.

He let out a long exhalation, gathering himself. "I saw your suitcases by the front door."

An ache bloomed in my stomach. "It's for the best."

"It's not!" Sam whined.

"We should talk somewhere else," I said to Andrew.

I reassured Sam I would be back in a few minutes, leaving him to finish his drink while Andrew and I talked in the hall.

"You don't need to leave," he said. "The contract runs through for two more months."

The contract. That was what truly mattered to him. That was why I had to leave. "My old firm has offered me my job back with a pay increase I can't ignore. I have to take it. For Sam's sake. He needs the stability of a permanent home. I've made arrangements with the crews to complete the work. The design plans are finalized. Any decent landscape architect can finish the work from here."

His shoulders sagged. "I don't want to hire just anyone."

"I'm not the right person for the job anymore. I got too invested in Margaret and Irene. In . . ." *In you.* "You were right when you said digging into the past would only cause more problems. I should have listened to you." I turned and started walking back to the kitchen, refusing to let Andrew see the anguish in my eyes.

"Julia, wait. It's not your fault." He caught my wrist, turning me to face him once more. "I was an ass. I've been so absorbed with trying to protect everyone that I forgot to listen to them."

His thumb grazed slowly over my wrist with an aching gentleness that set fire to my skin. I sucked in a breath, my pulse quickening beneath his touch. His eyes darkened with an intensity I hadn't seen in him before.

"Please," he said. "Don't go."

He cupped my cheek and brushed his lips against mine in a whisper of a kiss. I pressed my hand to his chest to push him away but found myself pulling him closer instead. It would have been so easy to lose myself in him. To allow the faint outline of the fantasy to become bright and real and full of color. Instead, I poured every ounce of regret and disappointment into the kiss, telling him everything I didn't have the words to say. And then I pulled away.

"I have to," I said between heavy breaths, dropping my forehead to his chest. "We both know it."

I went back to the kitchen to check on Sam. His plate was on the table, toast only half eaten, but there was no other sign of him. I called his name, only to be greeted by silence. I stepped deeper into the room, knowing there were a million spots a boy of his size could be hiding. But he wasn't inside the cabinets or hiding under the table.

Andrew stepped into the kitchen. "What's wrong?"

"I can't find Sam."

"Outside," he said, pointing to the back door off the kitchen, open just enough for a sliver of sunlight to slip through.

I cursed under my breath. "Sam was upset when I told him we were leaving. He must have run off."

It was one thing to lose Sam inside the house, but the gardens were an endless source of hiding spots. And danger. I knew these grounds like the back of my hand, but I had no idea where to begin.

"I'll start in the front. You look here and then we'll work our way toward the back," Andrew said.

Whatever awkwardness festered between us was put aside for Sam's sake. I searched the parterre, the greenhouse, even the old gardener's cottage. But Sam wasn't anywhere. Not in the back gardens, either, where the trees and shrubs were denser. I called for him relentlessly. If he was here, he didn't want to be found.

Because he didn't want to leave.

My heart split like glass on the verge of shattering. Everything I had done these last six months had been for him, and yet I'd still failed him. He was happy here. He didn't want to leave. I was the one who had made it impossible for us to stay.

Desperation grew into panic when an hour passed with no sign of him. I'd already sent away the taxi meant to take us to the airport. At this point, we likely wouldn't even make the flight. But that was the least of my worries now.

"Where is he?" I shouted in frustration.

Andrew, who'd managed to keep a more level head, set his hand on my shoulder. "We'll find him."

"We've searched everywhere. What if he's run off or been kidnapped or—"

"Breathe. We just need to think."

I didn't want to breathe. I wanted to scream.

He scrubbed his chin, looking around the gardens that we'd inspected three times over. "I just wish Margaret were here. She told me she used to get into all sorts of trouble hiding around here when she was Sam's age."

His words crashed through the fog in my brain like a streak of lightning. "I know where he is! The folly!"

Andrew didn't hesitate. He raced ahead toward the front entrance, easily outpacing me with his long legs.

"He's inside," he said after I breached the slight clearing in the thick forest where the folly was hidden. "I can hear him crying."

"Sam?" I called into the dark entrance. "Can you hear me?"

The crying stopped.

"He must have gone inside and not known how to escape," Andrew said.

"It's okay, Sam. I'm coming to help." I dropped to my knees at the entrance and peered inside. A dank smell of mildew and something else I couldn't name hit my nose, making it hard to breathe.

"Be careful," Andrew said. "I don't know how secure the structure is."

I tried not to think about that as I stepped over the patch of cowslips. The entrance was so dark and tight, my only option was to army crawl on my stomach. My bare arms and shoulders scraped against the rough bricks with each inch forward. I held my breath, terrified I would bring the entire thing crashing down on me or Sam.

Using my phone as a light, I quickly caught sight of his shoe. "I'm almost there, Sam. You'll be okay."

His sobbing had turned into a whimper. There wasn't a single source of light other than the beam from my phone. He must have been petrified all alone in here.

It felt like hours before I reached him on the inside of the folly. I managed to get myself upright and pulled Sam to me. "It's okay. You're safe. We'll get you out now."

He clung to me with his tiny, viselike fingers, tears spilling out anew. With the light from my phone, I checked him over for any sign of injury. He was covered in mud and shivering, but not hurt, thank goodness.

"Come on, time to climb out. I'll shine my light, and all you have to do is be brave."

Andrew shone his phone from the other side of the entrance, reaching his long arm out to take Sam's hand. He hauled Sam free and clear of the folly.

I exhaled in relief.

Even though my instincts screamed at me to get out of here as fast as possible, I couldn't help but look around inside the place Margaret had spent so much of her childhood. The folly might have once been grand—at least ten feet in width, but it had been sinking into the soft ground for decades before the bomb further decimated half the structure.

Margaret's initials were carved into one of the bricks. There were small rocks collected in one corner and the decaying plastic of what was once a child's doll deeply embedded in the mud. As I angled my body to explore the rest of it, my foot struck something heavy. Something that moved.

"Are you coming out?" Andrew asked.

"I think I found something." I cast the beam of light onto the object.

My heart stuttered.

A metal briefcase.

Every inch of my skin tingled with excitement at the realization of what I had just found. I lugged it toward me, shocked at its heft. What if this was the briefcase Margaret had spoken about? The one Irene stole? It would mean she hadn't sold it to the Germans or betrayed her family, and everything she wrote in that secret message would be true.

Millions of questions raced through my mind. How did she get it here? And if she wasn't a traitor, why did she disappear? Why did she never come back and explain?

My light caught on something small and white near the crumbled bricks where I'd found the briefcase. Another doll?

I crawled closer to it. The air drained from my lungs. It wasn't a doll at all.

"Julia," Andrew called again. "You need to come out. It's not safe."

"I know what happened to Irene," I called back in a choked voice, staring at what could only be the bones of a woman's hand.

EPILOGUE

Julia

One Year Later

We laid Irene Clarke to rest beneath the magnolia tree in the moon garden on a sunny June morning.

Margaret wore a new cornflower-blue dress Helen had gotten her for the occasion. She insisted no one wear black. She didn't want this to be a funeral. It was a memorial. A chance to remember the young woman who had given her life to save the people she loved.

Margaret cleared her throat and motioned to Helen to help her stand. Since her heart attack last year, she'd grown too weak to walk on her own, relying on a wheelchair for mobility.

"My sister never cared for the war. She believed it was art and beauty that would save humanity from destruction, not guns and bombs. Some might call that fanciful thinking, but in the end, she wasn't wrong. We needed the unshakable bravery and sacrifices of the military, the incredible cunning of the codebreakers and scientists like my father, and the tactical leadership of politicians. But Britain needed the heart of our people just as much. We needed a reason to fight.

"Irene dreamed of running away to America and attending art school when she was young. I used to hate her for wanting to leave.

She was my big sister. I didn't understand how she could ever want to leave Havenworth. In the end, she sacrificed her life for mine and for my family's. I wish she could have had the adventures and grand life she deserved. Looking back, I think her spirit stayed with me long after we ceased to acknowledge her existence. She was the one who gave me the courage to live as fully and authentically as I have. To experience all the marvelous things there are in this world.

"My only regret is for how I doubted you. How quick I was to believe the worst about you. We will be reunited soon. I can only hope you forgive me."

Margaret turned her gaze toward me, tears clouding her dark eyes, and whispered, "Thank you."

Andrew slipped his palm against mine, intertwining our fingers. Even after a year, I still felt a little thrill in these quiet moments of affection.

"I think I'd like some time alone now," Margaret announced.

"Sam, would you like to join me back in the kitchen for some biscuits?" Helen said.

He nodded eagerly, going to her with an ease that filled me with gratitude. Havenworth was meant to be only a temporary stop in my and Sam's journey, but somehow we had found our family here. Our home.

"I'm glad it's finally over," Andrew said as we walked along the parterre, where the roses and lavender were in their full glory, giving Margaret her moment of peace.

The journey to this point had been a long one. The police had treated the grounds like a crime scene for weeks before accepting the DNA evidence indicating Irene's skeleton had been there for the better part of a century. Extricating the remains had been a tedious and exacting job, too. I'd stayed to oversee the careful deconstruction of the folly, just in case Margaret decided she wanted to rebuild it. But she still hadn't quite made up her mind about that.

That time had also allowed me to finish the restoration in its entirety. There was a new life to Havenworth, even as Margaret's inched closer to the end. She was much weaker now. It was a matter of days and weeks, not months or years. But the closure had brought her peace.

Andrew had changed, too. He was still painfully serious at times, but the pain he carried had lightened. He wasn't so afraid of crossing boundaries or deviating from plans. He'd even accepted Helen's decision to quit her job.

"I've been thinking," he said to me when we reached a secluded section of the gardens behind a large elderberry bush awash in fragrant white flowers. "With the restoration complete, we need to talk about your plans."

We had avoided this conversation for too long. At first, because there was too much distraction. After, because it was simply easier not to think about the future. "I've been offered a contract for another estate near London. That's only a short train ride away."

"Don't take it."

My throat went dry. "Why?"

"Havenworth is in need of a permanent gardener to maintain the grounds. It would be a terrible shame to let all this work go to waste. I know it would be a step down for you and terrible use of your skills and expertise, but we need you to stay." He clasped both my hands in his. "I need you to stay."

My head spun from the offer. Staying at Havenworth was a fantasy I'd indulged in for the past year, but I always knew it would come to an end.

But what if it didn't have to?

"You can still work on other projects," he said quickly, mistaking my shock for hesitation. "You can build your business however you need and hire whatever staff you want. But don't leave. I love you. And I love Sam. Havenworth is where you belong."

"Yes, of course I'll stay," I said with a smile wide enough to cause an ache in my cheeks.

As we walked back to Havenworth to share the news with Sam, my thoughts drifted to Irene. It had taken more than eighty years for her truth to come out. She'd held on to her courage to do what was right, even when the bombs fell and when everyone around her believed the worst in her. Everything she had done was driven by love. I made a promise to myself in that moment to honor Irene's memory by being brave enough to fight for the people I loved. For Sam and Andrew and Helen. For Margaret. And even for myself.

AUTHOR'S NOTE

The story and characters in this book are entirely fictional. However, the character of John Clarke and his role in bringing the cavity magnetron prototype to America was inspired by the real-life Henry Tizard, an English scientist who was instrumental in the development of radar technology during World War II. In the fall of 1940, Tizard led a top-secret mission to share British military research with his counterparts in the United States in exchange for the industrial resources to mass-produce the technologies. It was a risky venture. German U-boats were a significant danger for anyone crossing the Atlantic, and there were no guarantees the Americans would agree to the trade.

A particularly interesting real-life fact about the mission is that one of the team members—a young scientist by the name of Edward Bowen—nearly lost the metal box containing the top-secret prototypes and blueprints when it was tied to the top of a taxi. A porter at Euston station collected the box from the taxi while Bowen collected the rest of his luggage. Ultimately, Bowen did retrieve the box and the mission was successful, bringing about a new era of scientific collaboration between Great Britain and the United States.

It was all the possible what-ifs that inspired me to write this story: What if the cavity magnetron was actually lost? What if those who greatly opposed the idea of giving away Britain's most valuable secrets tried to sabotage the mission? What if Henry Tizard had a family who didn't understand the gravity of his work? In researching this fascinating piece of history, I found *The Tizard Mission: The Top-Secret Operation That Changed the Course of World War II* by Stephen Phelps and *Top Secret Exchange: The Tizard Mission and the Scientific War* by David Zimmerman to be quite helpful.

I have tried to keep most historical events referenced in the story accurate. There were, however, a few dates and events that I altered slightly to make the story work. Victory gardens were encouraged by the British government as early as 1939, but most historical accounts suggest they were not widespread until later in the war. The specific locations and timings of the Luftwaffe attacks in this story have also deviated from fact to suit the story, though the Blitz did begin on September 7, 1940, with October 14, 1940, being one of the most devastating nights due to the attack on Balham station.

The language of flowers is also a real concept that I drew upon for the story. There is no definitive guide or dictionary, and many resources provide contradictory meanings for various flowers. To maintain consistency, I relied upon *Floriography: An Illustrated Guide to the Victorian Language of Flowers* by Jessica Roux and *The Complete Language of Flowers: A Definitive and Illustrated History* by S. Theresa Dietz (both of which contain stunning botanical illustrations) to source most of the meanings referenced in the book. In a few cases, I simply invented meanings for the sake of the story.

ACKNOWLEDGMENTS

Writing can be a lonely and difficult endeavor, especially when the words do not flow easily. I'm so grateful to my phenomenal agent, Erin Niumata, for supporting me throughout this process and believing in me even when I was mired in self-doubt. I'm incredibly thankful for the team at Lake Union who brought this book to life, especially Chantelle Aimée Osman, for championing my writing, and Ronit Wagman, for her brilliant editing. Thank you to Carmen Johnson for all your support and for guiding this book through to the finish line. Thank you to the absolutely incredible copyeditors, sensitivity readers, proofreaders, cover designers, and everyone at Lake Union who worked on this book for their invaluable contributions. I am forever grateful to my family for being my biggest cheerleaders and always giving me the inspiration to create. Finally, I am eternally thankful for all my readers. So many of you have reached out to me with kind words and support when I needed them most.

ABOUT THE AUTHOR

Sara Blaydes is the author of *The Last Secret of Lily Adams*. She has been obsessed with books ever since she demanded her parents teach her to read at four years old so she could steal her older brother's comic books. It was only natural she start crafting stories where she, a perpetual daydreamer, could escape into worlds of her own creation. She currently lives in British Columbia with her handsome husband, two amazing children, and an overly anxious Boston terrier. She believes books are magic, summer is the best season, and parsley is never optional. For more information, visit www.sarablaydes.com.